"Do you suppos[...]
too often?" Pau[...]

"I'm not sure that's possible, like being too thin or too rich," Dane replied, nibbling at the seam of her lips.

"Sometimes I feel horribly guilty about keeping you out of circulation. You should be finding a younger woman, someone who can give you a family, and—"

"Now, you hush." He kissed her deeply. "I don't want a family. I just want you . . . only you. . . ."

He kissed her into senselessness, until he was Paula's only reality. He stroked her until she ached inside, and he told her how much he loved her, wanted her, needed her.

It was easy to believe they would be together forever when their bodies were fused like this. In a haze of passion, anything seemed possible. Only in the languid aftermath did Paula admit there could never be a future between them. . . .

ABOUT THE AUTHOR

Barbara Kaye is a Superromance mainstay, having written for the line since its inception. One of the first romance writers to explore relationships between "mature" protagonists, Barbara was the natural choice to write a miniseries about older men and women reevaluating their life-styles. Barbara lives in Oklahoma with her husband.

Books by Barbara Kaye

HARLEQUIN SUPERROMANCE

46–A HEART DIVIDED
124–COME SPRING
161–HOME AT LAST
206–SOUTHERN NIGHTS
219–JUST ONE LOOK
257–A SEASON FOR ROSES
270–BY SPECIAL REQUEST
316–THE RIGHT PLACE TO BE
332–TRADITIONS
379–RAMBLIN' MAN
411–CHOICE OF A LIFETIME (HAMILTON HOUSE: BOOK I)

HARLEQUIN AMERICAN ROMANCE

19–CALL OF EDEN

Challenge of a Lifetime

BARBARA KAYE

Harlequin Books

TORONTO • NEW YORK • LONDON
AMSTERDAM • PARIS • SYDNEY • HAMBURG
STOCKHOLM • ATHENS • TOKYO • MILAN

Originally published December 1990
Second edition January 1991

ISBN 0-373-70433-X

CHALLENGE OF A LIFETIME

CHAPTER ONE

THE SOUND of a man's singing wafted through the trees, disturbing the tranquility of the morning and bringing Paula Steele out of her private reverie.

At first she thought the song was part of her daydreams, but after she shook her head vigorously to clear her mind, the singing persisted. It was real, all right, and it seemed to be coming from near the river. She stood very still and as she listened, a tingle ran down her spine. The baritone voice was smooth, rich and mellow. That alone would have captured her attention, but the song the unknown troubadour was singing was "Tears I've Shed in Vain," one of Justin's classics. Intrigued, Paula followed the sound.

Although the calendar said summer was officially two weeks away, the season had arrived in earnest in central Alabama. Already the days were very warm, and the humidity level hovered around eighty percent. There had been a storm during the night, but now, at midmorning, the sun was out and the woods were redolent with the aroma of decaying leaves and damp earth. Above it all was the smell of the river. She carefully picked her way down a small rise until the water of the Coosa River came into view. That was when she spotted the man.

He was sitting on the ground under an enormous tree, his back propped against its trunk, his legs stretched out in front of him, ankles crossed. A straw hat sat low over his eyes, and in his hand he held a fishing rod. It was a scene straight out of *Huckleberry Finn*. After watching him a minute, Paula got the distinct impression that a biting fish would have been an unwelcome interruption. The man was the picture of lazy ease, lost in a world of his own.

His singing was strong and sure, right on key, and not once did he stumble over the lyrics. He sang with the confidence of someone who had done the song hundreds of times. Could he be a performer? Enthralled, almost mesmerized by what truly was a remarkable voice, she stood rooted in place and listened until the song ended. Then, automatically, she applauded.

The man turned with a start, pushing back his hat as he did so. When he saw her, he jumped to his feet.

"Please, don't get up," Paula said. "I don't want to interrupt your fishing."

"No problem. This isn't serious fishing."

His speaking voice was as low and as rich as his singing voice. His eyes, still registering surprise, scrutinized her from head to toe. When his bold inspection was finished, he reeled in his line and laid the rod on the ground at his feet.

That action gave Paula a moment to study him. He was about six feet tall, perhaps an inch shorter. His physique was lean and muscular but not musclebound; hale and hearty, he looked like a man who wasn't a stranger to physical labor. His hair beneath the tattered hat was very dark, almost black, but she couldn't make out any of his facial features until he straightened and moved toward her. Instinctively, she took a step backward, but he stopped some distance away and stood with one knee bent, his thumbs hooked into the pockets of his jeans. His stance was one of unconscious—or perhaps deliberate—masculine arrogance.

He had a pleasant face, Paula decided. One might even have gone so far as to call him boyishly handsome if it hadn't been for the coldness in his eyes. They were as dark as his hair and spoke of wariness and suspicion, not only of her but of the world in general. His lopsided half smile exuded a certain amount of roguish charm, but one could only look at his eyes and come to the conclusion that here was a man who had never been a boy.

After what seemed like minutes but could only have been seconds, he spoke again. "Don't recall ever seein' you before. You lost or something?"

"No. I was just out for a morning walk, and I heard you singing. You have a marvelous voice."

"Thanks."

She extended her hand. "My name's Paula. I'm visiting the Greggs."

The man glanced down at her outstretched hand. For a second Paula thought he might not take it. He did, finally, encasing it warmly. She had been right about his being no stranger to work; his hand was leathery and callused, its color a permanent bronze. "Dane Markham," he said simply. "I work for the Greggs."

An amused glint came to Paula's eyes, and her gaze pointedly fell to the fishing rod on the ground. "Tough job."

"Verna and Jim don't begrudge me a little fishing time. Are you kinfolks?"

"No. Friends."

Dane Markham's eyes made another blatant sweep of her, and he liked what he saw. She was a fine figure of a woman, just tall enough to be beyond the petite category, and she was built like a brick house. The khaki jump suit she was wearing showed off her splendid figure to perfection. Her tumble of brown hair had been twisted back in a careless knot, leaving a good part of it to fall free. Her complexion was smooth and her eyes a clear green. Dane decided she probably was one of those health nuts. What else would account for such natural, wholesome beauty? No smoking, no drinking, lots of spinach and carrots. For sure no late nights in smoke-filled bars. No fun, either, he thought wryly.

He tried guessing her age, but it was hard to tell with women these days, especially the health nuts. She wasn't a kid; there was nothing ingenuous about her. So he guessed thirty-five, and a damned fine thirty-five at that.

From force of habit he looked at her hands, searching for a ring. There was a stunning solitaire on the ring finger of her right hand but nothing on her left. He was fully aware that his assessment of her went far beyond normal curiosity, but he didn't care and certainly did nothing to disguise his interest. His vast experience with women had convinced him that they liked being appraised like so much horseflesh. Even the ones who pretended to be offended liked it. But, he admitted, he rarely had occasion to meet women like the one standing before him.

Paula shifted uncomfortably. It crossed her mind that Dane Markham's expression had something predatory in it, and they were a relatively long way from the house. "That song you were singing—it was one of Justin Steele's biggest."

"Yeah. Were you a fan of his?"

"Yes."

"I guess everyone who likes country music was a fan of ol' Justin's. The night he died, the little waterin' hole my friends and I go to played nothing but his records all night. All of us just cried in our beer."

How many variations on that theme had she heard? All those thousands of letters from unknown people all over the world. *I met my husband at one of his concerts.... I have every record he ever made.... I can't believe he's gone.... I just cried and cried....*

"You did the song very well," Paula said. "Have you ever sung professionally?"

Dane snorted a little laugh. "Yeah, every Saturday night at The General Store."

"The General Store?"

"It's a place out on the Birmingham highway."

"Do you have a band?"

"Nah, just whoever shows up and wants to play, plays. Sometimes it's only me sitting there, pickin' and singin' half the night."

"Then music must be a passion," Paula said.

"Passion?" He uttered that dry laugh again. "It's a way to kill some time."

Wrong, she thought. *No one sits in a joint half the night, singing and picking, just to kill time.* She'd known more musicians than she could count, and, thanks to Justin, she'd learned to smell the passion a mile away. Dane Markham might not realize he had it, but he did. She'd bet on it. "Well, I'd like to hear you sing at The General Store sometime."

"You? I figured you were more the Boston Pops type."

Paula laughed lightly. "Looks can be deceiving. If I'm still here Saturday night, I might ask Verna and Jim to take me to hear you."

"Don't waste your breath. Verna and Jim wouldn't be caught dead within a country mile of The General Store," Dane said. "Once you see the place, you wouldn't be, either. It's not exactly a high-class joint."

"Oh, I imagine I've been in places that were a lot worse than The General Store." She stepped back. "I really must go now. I didn't tell anyone I was taking a walk, so Verna will be looking all over for me. I meant it when I said I enjoyed hearing the song. You sing very well, Mr. Markham."

"Thanks. But it sounds funny hearing myself called Mr. Markham. It's Dane."

"All right, Dane. Perhaps I'll be seeing you again. Don't work too hard."

She turned to go, but his voice detained her. "Tell me your name again. I was so surprised to see you that I didn't catch it."

"Paula," she said. "Paula Steele."

"Paula," he repeated, then stopped and frowned. "Steele? Say, you weren't related to Justin Steele, were you?"

"You could say that, yes."

"Well, I'll be. No wonder the song got your attention." Once again he looked her up and down. "You his daughter?"

"No, I was his wife. Goodbye, Dane."

"VERNA!" PAULA CALLED as she entered the farmhouse.

"In here, Paula. The kitchen. I just made fresh coffee."

Verna Gregg, neé Simpson, had been Paula's best friend during school days in the nearby town of Sylacauga, and though Paula's marriage to Justin Steele had taken her far from the fold, the two women had managed to stay close through the years, thanks to the telephone and Paula's periodic trips back to Alabama. Verna was a tall, angular woman of sun-swept handsomeness, bursting with life and vitality, the kind of person one referred to as "the salt of the earth." In her younger years Verna had been considered the prettier of the inseparable duo, but time had altered that. Verna had matured early, while Paula's beauty had blossomed later in life. Few people who saw them for the first time guessed that the two women were the same age, which was forty-five. But even during their school days Verna had acted much older than Paula, and now Paula looked on her friend as a big sister figure.

They sat at the big kitchen table, as they had on countless previous occasions, sipping coffee and making small talk. After a few minutes had passed, however, Verna leaned forward and spoke earnestly. "You looked so tired when you got here last night that I didn't want to bombard you with questions, but you must know I'm dying of curiosity. How long since you were last here? A year or more? And then it was only for a few hours. I'm thrilled you want to stay several days, of course, but you can't blame me for wondering why."

Paula set her cup down. "I guess for the same reason I've always turned to you. For a lift. Reassurance."

Verna propped her elbows on the table, laced the fingers of her hands together and rested her chin on them. "How a woman who looks like you do can need reassurance is beyond me. Honestly, Paula, you seem to get prettier with each passing year. I should be so lucky. Every woman should be so lucky."

Paula made a scoffing sound. "How good can I look? I'm forty-five, for heaven's sake!"

"Is that what's bothering you? Age?"

"Oh . . . maybe a little. That and just missing Justin so much."

"Of course you miss him. You were together twenty years. And with Justin being the way he was—all that *energy*—you'd have to miss him."

Paula smiled. "There was always something going on when he was around, that's for sure. Now the house is so damned quiet."

"How are Mitch and Rona?"

"Fine, the same. They look after me the way they looked after Justin—constantly."

"Good. I don't worry about you with Mitch around. The man could hunt bears with a flyswatter."

"It's Rona who's been the lifesaver. You wouldn't believe the mail that's poured in since Justin's death, and it's still coming a year later. Somehow Rona and I stay on top of it—I couldn't do it alone."

"What about Lou?"

Paula chuckled. "Lou's still around, too. He suffers from the same malady that afflicts Mitch and Rona—total devotion to Justin Steele, which has now been transferred to his widow, mainly because they don't know what else to do with their lives."

"I'm the last one to knock friendship," Verna said. "I think it's wonderful when two people can remain close for so many years. And men tend to compete with each other so much that it makes friendship difficult. But I often thought Lou carried it a little far."

"I know. Lou's in love with anyone or anything Justin loved. It's sad how much he misses him. He'd turn that house into another Graceland if I'd let him. When I rearranged the furniture in the den and got rid of that ancient recliner of Justin's, Lou was ticked off at me for days."

A few minutes of silence fell over the table while Paula sipped her coffee. Finally, Verna got up for a refill and asked, "How many cups of coffee do you suppose we've had together, Paula?"

"About a million, I guess."

"We sure go back a long way. Funny we're still as close as we are, considering that our lives took such different paths. I married a farmer and stayed within a stone's throw of the place where I grew up, and you married a superstar and moved to Nashville. When I watched you two drive off after the wedding, I figured I'd never see you again."

"Aw, I couldn't do without you, you know that."

"That wedding is still the biggest thing that ever happened around here."

Paula smiled. If Justin hadn't thought to have a friend film it, she doubted she would remember a thing about her wedding. She had existed in a daze that entire day. An air of unreality had hung over the proceedings. In fact, even their courtship had had a fairy-tale quality to it.

When she'd met Justin she was a new Auburn graduate working for a Birmingham publishing firm whose chief claim to fame was a popular weekly television guide that was stuffed inside the Sunday paper. It was a tiny operation employing only a handful of people, and Paula was the editor's girl Friday and chief gofer. Justin was in town to do a televised benefit performance. In one of those fortunate coincidences that people later refer to as fate, the man who normally handled celebrity interviews was covering a popular rock group, so Paula was sent to interview Justin. She recalled being almost paralyzed with nervousness, chiefly because she expected to encounter a pompous ass. But the man she met in his hotel suite, in the company of several members of his entourage, had been a gentle, self-effacing music legend who enjoyed talking about almost everything but himself.

She learned he was widowed—he mentioned his late wife, Marjorie, several times—and he talked about his golf handicap. But when it had come to his spectacular success, Paula had had to drag out the details. Before the interview was over she had found herself answering his questions about her. When she told him she was attending the evening's performance, he'd asked her to have dinner with him afterward. For reasons she still didn't completely understand, she accepted without hesitation. Her instincts had told her she had nothing to fear from Justin Steele, and her instincts had been right. She had never met a more perfect gentleman nor spent a more perfect evening.

Still, when he telephoned her at the office the following week to ask her to join him in Atlanta for the weekend, she had flatly refused. Her sense of propriety had been offended by the invitation. Though she had tried to be polite, she had actually come across like someone who had been raised in a convent. When she'd hung up the phone, she had been certain she had seen and heard the last from Justin Steele.

Like many young women in the sixties, Paula had been an emerging feminist, a curious mixture of modern thinking and traditional values. A part of her had wanted to be career oriented, financially independent and liberated from the stultifying morality that had governed the previous generation. Yet, just as large a part of her believed in engagement, marriage and family, in that order. She wasn't a prude, but she was governed by principles. Under no circumstances would she have spent a weekend in Atlanta with a man she hardly knew.

Unaccustomed to being refused, Justin had been both amused and intrigued. Instead of forgetting her, during the next year, whenever he was within hailing distance of Birmingham, he'd made a special effort to see her. The rest was history.

Verna sat back down. "So, how's the business?"

"Hamilton House Incorporated, is humming along nicely, thanks. Fifty-two restaurants now." Paula's eyes twinkled merrily. "And I'm happy to say that the Southeastern Division is the fastest-growing one in the entire organization."

"Vanessa Hamilton must be getting along in years," Verna commented. She had never met the company's co-founder and C.E.O., but she had listened to Paula rave about the woman for years.

"Almost eighty, as hard as it is to believe. She was such a dynamo when I first went to work for Hamilton House. The years sure pass quickly."

Verna sighed. "Vice president, Paula. Lord, it makes me tingle just to think about it. I'm so proud of you, and you have to be proud of yourself."

"I guess I am. But more importantly, Justin was proud of me, too. When I was promoted to V.P., you would have thought he'd just won twelve Grammys." Paula's eyes clouded. "It was a lot of hard work for a lot of years. Now I wish there was more of the old grind. Thanks to Vanessa, Hamilton House is such a well-run organization. Sometimes I long for a few crises here and there to keep the adrenaline flowing."

"You need a project, my dear."

"I know. Justin always had so many projects going at one time it was hard to keep up with them. I guess I miss the kids most of all. There were always one or two around, studying at the master's feet, so to speak. Sometimes I think Justin and I were frustrated parents."

"How I wish you had had a couple of your own," Verna said. "There were times when I cheerfully would have sold both of mine for $2.98 plus tax, but now that they're away at school, I really miss them."

Paula smiled ruefully. "Well, if we'd had kids, they would be gone now, too, and I'd be in the same boat."

Verna looked at her with sympathy. "I know you, Paula. You'll find something to give your life a jolt. You've always been one for making things happen. Justin once told me the best thing about robbing the cradle for a wife was that he got you young and trained you the way he wanted you. That was a joke, of course. What he liked best about you was, one, you weren't a musician, and, two, you had youth and freshness."

"But a twenty-year age difference makes for a relatively young widow, and it's not a role I relish. I know everyone predicted the marriage would last maybe six months, but Justin and I were wonderful friends. Most people didn't understand why the wife of a star of Justin's magnitude wanted to work. Not just work but climb the corporate ladder. But he understood. Sometimes he seemed to understand me better than I understood myself." Paula pushed her cup toward the center of the table. "Enough of this. Tell me about you, about the farm."

"Oh, we're doing fine. Some years are better than others, but I guess Jim and I would stay here even if we were starving to death."

"You really love it, don't you?"

"When I came to this place as a young bride I thought I'd found paradise. A place of my own. A house I could run the way I wanted to, not the way my mother told me to." Verna laughed lustily. "Paradise it hasn't been, but, yes, I love it. This ought to be a good year. The weather's been near perfect. We're almost out of debt. I wish Jim didn't have to work so hard, but . . . I guess our biggest problem these days is the shortage of decent help."

Paula perked up. "That reminds me, I ran into one of the hired hands while I was out for a walk. Dane Markham."

Verna rolled her eyes. "Dane! Peck's Bad Boy of central Alabama."

"He was fishing."

"That sounds like him. The man has the ambition of a worm. I think Dane's been in trouble since the day he was born."

"Trouble? You mean with the law or something like that?"

"No, no. Just trouble. Always fighting. He has a real chip on his shoulder. I try not to judge him too harshly since he's had a miserable life. His mother ran off and left them when Dane was just a kid. His dad's the town drunk. They live in an old trailer south of town. Any money they have Dane has to make. He's just had a lousy life. Still and all, you'd think a man his age would want to do more than work somebody else's farm."

"How old is he?"

Verna gave it some thought. "He must be around thirty-five or six."

"How come I never knew of him?"

"You were off at school when Dane began to make a . . . er, name for himself around here."

"If he's such a problem, why do you keep him on?"

"Because he quite simply is the best worker we've ever had. He'll do anything we ask him to, and he can do anything. He keeps my car and Jim's truck running, fixes the washing machine, does carpentry. If he wants to take a few minutes off to go fishing, we look the other way. For all I know, he's catching his supper. It's probably one of the few pleasures he has in life."

"He sings," Paula said.

A startled look crossed Verna's face. "He does?"

"Uh-huh. I heard him, so I followed the sound, and that's how I met him. He has a beautiful voice."

"Well, I'll be damned. Somehow Dane and a beautiful voice don't seem to go together."

"He told me he sings at a place called The General Store every Saturday night. I'd love to go listen to him."

"Oh, Paula, you don't want to go to a place like that."

"What's wrong with it?"

"Well, let me put it this way. If you own a motor-cycle T-shirt, The General Store would be the perfect place to wear it." Verna rolled her eyes again. "Redneck heaven!"

Paula chuckled. "You have no idea how many redneck joints I followed Justin into just because he's heard of a new singer or piano player or guitar picker. That's how I developed this ear. I'm the most unmusical person alive." She sobered. "Once Justin retired from performing, the one driving force in his life was the sure knowledge that he was going to discover the next Willie or Waylon or Merle or whoever. And he came close, so close with Tommy Lord."

"That's the kid who got killed in the car wreck, right?"

Paula nodded. "He was drunk, or it wouldn't have happened. Unfortunately, Tommy usually was drunk. Try as he might, Justin just couldn't get him to leave the stuff alone for long. He even moved the kid into our house, where he could keep an eye on him, but that didn't work, either. Isn't that something—a twenty-five-year-old alcoholic. And he could have been a gigantic star. What a waste."

Verna glanced at her watch. "I've got some errands to run in town. Want to come along? How long since you've seen beautiful downtown Sylacauga?"

"Quite a while, but I'll pass it up today. If you don't mind, I think I'd just like to laze around. I brought some books I've never gotten around to reading. It's so peaceful out here. I'm going to rejuvenate my soul. It needs it. God, how it needs it!"

"Be my guest. I want you to do exactly what you want to do while you're here."

"Do you mean that?"

"Of course."

"Okay, then what I want to do is hear Dane Markham sing at The General Store on Saturday night."

"Oh, Paula, why?"

"I don't know. I just do. Call it instinct, call it habit."

"Just suppose for the sake of conversation that Dane turned out to be the greatest thing to come down the pike since George Strait. What would you do about it?"

"I'd point him in the direction of a bunch of folks who could do a lot about it. Chiefly, Lou."

Verna shook her head. "Go figure people in the music business. Okay, I'll ask Jim about Saturday night and let you know what he has to say. See you at lunch."

CHAPTER TWO

"SHE WANTS to do *what?*" Jim Gregg asked Verna in disbelief.

"She wants to go to The General Store on Saturday night to hear Dane Markham sing."

"Are you talking about the Dane Markham who works for us?"

Verna smiled. "How many people by that name do you know?"

"What makes Paula think he can sing?"

"She heard him. Oh, Jim, I know you don't want to go. I don't especially want to go, either. But Paula comes to see us so seldom, and if she'll get a kick out of it, what's the harm?"

Jim scowled. "I work my ass off all week, and all I ask is a peaceful Saturday night to do what I want to do. And The General Store is nothing but a crummy joint, Verna. You know that."

"Come to think of it, I don't know that from experience, only hearsay. Come on, Jim, be a good sport. I hate to tell Paula no. We won't stay long, I promise."

He growled and grumbled for another minute or two, but in the end he relented, as Verna had suspected he would.

So what Jim actually had to say about spending his precious Saturday night listening to some galoot sing at The General Store was not repeated to Paula. Verna merely told her that he had agreed to escort them because there was no way on God's earth he was going to let the women go alone.

As it turned out, the popular joint didn't live up to its reputation, and Paula saw plenty of unescorted females there—young ones dressed in skintight jeans and old ones in the same. True, the building was a bit seedy looking on the outside, but it wasn't too bad inside. Paula could think of at least two dozen establishments in Nashville she'd been in with Justin that were worse. There was a big dance floor, a stage, dozens of tables and a long bar at the rear that was obscured by the throng of people gathered at it. As Paula, Verna and Jim threaded their way through the maze of tables, every head in the place turned in their direction. Although the women had tried to dress down for the occasion, it was obvious they were not habitués of The General Store.

The stage was empty save for a microphone, some drums and a piano, but a dozen or so couples were dancing to jukebox music. Paula scanned the crowd but saw no sign of Dane Markham. A voluptuous waitress came to take their order. "What time does the entertainment start?" Paula asked her.

"You mean the music? Whenever Dane shows up."

"What time will that be?"

"Lord, who knows? Depends."

"On what?"

The waitress looked her up and down. "On a lot of things a lady like you wouldn't want to hear about. Sometimes he doesn't show up at all. You never can tell about Dane." Then she walked away.

Fifteen minutes passed, then twenty, and still the bandstand remained empty. Jim was getting restless, Verna looked nervous, and Paula conceded that if Dane didn't show up and start singing pretty soon, the three of them probably would be leaving.

The thought no sooner formed than there was some commotion in the back of the bar, then whistling and clapping, and Dane made his way through the throng and stepped up onto the stage, grinning and waving. He soon was joined by another guitarist, a man who made Willie Nelson look like an investment banker, and then by a piano player. Dane gave his guitar a few licks, and the evening's entertainment began.

Paula marveled at how rapidly the deafening din subsided. Dane's voice seemed to have a soothing, tranquilizing effect on the raucous crowd, and after listening only a few minutes, she felt it soothing her, too—and she wasn't easily impressed by musicians. His first song was "Born to Lose," surely a classic in country music, and his version was as smooth as maple syrup. Her immediate impression was that Dane sounded marvelous with the simplest kind of musical backup, so she couldn't help but wonder how he would sound with a full studio band. And if tonight's selections were any indication, he favored traditional country music, which was just the ticket these days. None of that crossover stuff. The applause after each song was enthusiastic and sustained.

She studied him with an objective, practiced eye, thinking what the right people could do with his image. He wore faded jeans, a nondescript denim shirt, and he needed a haircut, but in a crisp shirt, starched jeans and a Stetson sitting low on his forehead, he could be an attractive man—in a fresh-off-the-farm

sort of way. He had a lot more going for him than a lot
of the unknowns Justin and Lou had transformed into
attractive, polished pros. The right people could turn
him into a performer who would be as popular with
teenage girls as he was with their mothers, and that
rarely happened in country music.

Yes, he was good. Not just pretty good but real
good. Better than Tommy Lord had been. How could
a man with his wretched background sing so elo-
quently of lost love, unrequited love, newfound love?
She searched for the cold-eyed man she had met on the
riverbank, then realized that he changed when he was
onstage, became looser, freer. He warmed to an audience and received energy from the spectators' reac-
tions. The good ones always did. There was a
haunting, poignant quality to his voice that had the
potential to drive women crazy.

At one point, as Dane's eyes roamed over the
crowd, they met hers. He looked mildly surprised,
then amused. His next song was "Tears I've Shed in
Vain," and he sang it directly to her, bringing a lump
to her throat and causing tiny flutters in the pit of her
stomach, an odd sensation for a woman who was
fairly blasé about musicians.

He sang for perhaps twenty minutes before taking
a break. Jim squirmed impatiently. "Okay, you've
heard him. Can we go home now?"

"Just a minute, Jim, please," Paula entreated. She
was intent on watching the evening's feature attraction, who was heading straight for their table.

"Dane, you amaze me," Verna said when he was
standing in front of them. "If it hadn't been for Paula,
I'd probably never have known about your voice."

"Yeah, well..." His gaze shifted to Paula. "Thanks for coming, but I'm surprised you did." He waved a hand to indicate their surroundings. "Not exactly the country club, is it?"

Paula ignored that. "I wouldn't have missed hearing you sing," she said. "I guess I'm not the first person who's ever told you that your voice could take you places."

"As a matter of fact, you are. And coming from Justin Steele's widow, it's quite a compliment." The words were polite, but the wariness in his eyes was back. The man was definitely the suspicious type.

Impulsively, she reached into her handbag and withdrew the little case holding her business cards. Handing him one, she said, "If you ever decide to do something serious about music, get in touch with me. My home address and phone number are on that, too. I might be able to help you. I know a lot of people in the music business."

Dane glanced at the card, then at Paula. "You're a corporation vice president?" he asked incredulously.

"Yes."

"What does this Hamilton House do?"

"Owns restaurants...a lot of them."

"Well, I'll be damned!"

Paula and Verna exchanged amused glances, then Paula got to her feet. "Come on, Jim. Fair's fair. I know you're itching to get home."

Jim breathed a hearty sigh of relief, and he and Verna stood, also.

"Do you have to go?" Dane asked quickly. She would have no way of knowing it, but he had sung better tonight than he had in months. Just knowing she was in the audience had seemed to inspire him.

"The boys and I are just getting cranked up. Sometimes these gigs go on half the night. We really get smokin' later on."

Actually, Paula would have loved to stay. Not half the night but for another set or two. But she knew that her friends didn't share her enthusiasm for that sort of thing. She was just grateful that she had heard Dane Markham, and she really did hope he would try to do something with his music. "I'm sorry, but we have to go. I enjoyed it, though. Goodbye, Dane."

"Goodbye? Maybe I'll see you at the farm Monday."

"No, I have to get home. I'll be leaving tomorrow. You give some serious thought to that voice of yours. You're very talented. And I'd like to put something in the kitty." She pressed a twenty-dollar bill into his hand.

Dane stared at it as though he'd never seen a twenty before. "Thanks, but aren't you being a little too generous?"

"I don't think so. I enjoyed it that much." Turning, she followed her friends to the door.

Outside, as Jim was unlocking the car, Verna looked at Paula. "Is Dane really that good?" she asked.

"He really is. If Justin had been here tonight, I just know his ears would have been twitching. He probably would have written a contract on a napkin. I've seen him do it before."

"Then it's a real shame," Verna said with a sigh.

Paula frowned. "A shame?"

"That Dane will never be able to do anything about it."

"Why not?"

"Because of his dad. Dane wouldn't leave him, not for fame or fortune or anything. The man is totally incapable of taking care of himself."

Paula slid into the back seat. "Well, that is too bad. Justin helped many kids who weren't nearly as good as Dane is."

Verna had gotten in the front seat. She swiveled to look at Paula. "Dane Markham is no kid."

"True," Paula conceded. "And it's generally believed that if you haven't made it by thirty-five, you aren't going to make it, period. But I don't agree with that. Maybe he will someday. I hope so."

IT WAS PAST 2:00 A.M. when Dane drove his battered pickup across the wooden bridge and into the grove of pines where the trailer stood. There weren't any lights on, and he fervently hoped his father was home and in bed. To hope his parent also was sober was asking too much on a Saturday night. He parked at the side, near two rusting garbage cans, and walked around to climb the rickety front steps and push open the door. It was never locked. Anyone desperate enough to steal from the ratty old trailer was welcome to whatever he could find. How he hated it!

Dane flipped on a couple of lights and went into the back bedroom. It was empty. *Goddamn you, Dad!* If his old man had gotten himself thrown into the drunk tank again, he could stay there until morning. But where in the hell did his father get the money for booze? Dane saw to it that the man never had more than a few dollars on him at any time. Sadly, he had to surmise that there were a few Cro-Magnon types around who got their jollies by feeding the town drunk rotgut whiskey, then watching him make an ass out of himself.

Uttering a sound of the utmost disgust, he went back through the trailer to the front bedroom, which was his. He hadn't made the bed that morning, and it stood there, rumpled and uninviting. He emptied his pockets and counted the night's take. The crowd had been large, drunk and more generous than usual. He'd made sixty bucks tonight. That, added to yesterday's pay from the Greggs, meant he'd have a fairly comfortable week. When that happened, he always meant to start his "getaway fund," but he never did.

As he spread his pocket's contents on the scarred built-in dresser, he noticed one twenty-dollar bill among all the ones and the loose change. So he'd made forty dollars that night and been given twenty by a beautiful woman who doubtless spent twenties the way he spent quarters. Almost simultaneously his gaze fell on the business card she had also given him. For a minute he felt sick, then the numbness he usually could call upon at will overcame him.

Goddam you, too, Mrs. Steele! How dare she appear out of her safe, comfortable world and suggest that there existed a means of escaping the perimeters of his squalid one. Perhaps there had been a time when he'd had dreams—a wife, kids, a decent job, a future—but they had faded into such bleak oblivion that they were impossible to recall. He was stuck, unable to leave his father, without the means to move on even if his father hadn't been a problem, and as long as he remained here he never would obtain the means. It was a vicious cycle. He had nothing to offer a woman, so there wouldn't be a wife. The knowledge lay soddenly on his brain, leaving a bitter taste in his mouth.

How many times had he thought about running away—just packing up, getting in the truck and leaving? Too many to count. He would roam from place to place, work odd jobs until he had enough money to move on. He'd see the whole country, meet people who knew nothing of his past. Maybe he would create a new identity. Dane Markham simply would disappear from the face of the earth, and there wouldn't be a soul alive who would mourn his demise. The idea was deliciously appealing.

He'd never do it, though. Whatever force inside him that compelled him to stay with a ne'er-do-well parent was too strong to be ignored. Inherent, he supposed, although he couldn't imagine from whom such tenacity could have been inherited. Certainly the mother he didn't remember hadn't had it. From all accounts, she had been able to leave her husband and her son without a backward glance. Whereas Dane would stay where he was and work for the Greggs, or someone like them, until he dropped.

And he would stay angry. It seemed to him that he had been angry most of his life, not at anyone or anything in particular, just the whole damned world. That anger was as much a part of him as the color of his hair. It was, he thought, what kept the adrenaline flowing, the blood coursing through his veins. He rarely felt pain or discomfort, pleasure or contentment. Had it not been for the anger, he would have been numb.

The image of Paula Steele flashed through his mind, and he heard her speaking. *Your voice could take you places.* And she'd actually come to hear him sing. A woman like that!

Give some serious thought to that voice of yours. You're very talented. Was he? The notion that there was anything in the least remarkable, even admirable, about him was as foreign to him as knowledge of everyday life in Sri Lanka. What would Paula Steele do if he actually did show up on her doorstep?

Suddenly Dane gave a growl of self-disgust. *I'll tell you what she'd do, pal. She'd call the palace guards and tell you to haul ass. She was slumming. She probably gets a kick out of seeing how the peasants live.*

Dane shuddered. He experienced the urge to tear up her card, but for some reason he didn't. Instead, he undressed quickly and fell into bed, clearing his mind until it was as empty as his spirit.

CHAPTER THREE

IT WAS EARLY Sunday evening when Paula arrived in Nashville, bone weary and relieved to have the long drive behind her. Though her adopted hometown was Music City, U.S.A., to legions of country music fans around the world, the citizens who resided in the hushed splendor of Belle Meade estates much preferred Nashville's other sobriquet: Athens of the South. Those culturally elite Nashvillians chose to tell visitors about the city's replica of the Parthenon and Vanderbilt University. In fact, they openly sneered at the industry and artists who had made the city famous, referring to that Nashville as ''Nash Vegas,'' the last word in plastic glitz and decadence.

Still, it was in Belle Meade that Justin Steele had chosen to live as soon as his success permitted, and it was to the antebellum-style home that Paula had come as a bride. She turned onto the sweeping, curved driveway and parked at the foot of the front steps, giving two short beeps on the horn as she did. Mitch Fletcher was out on the veranda in less than a minute.

Mitch was a big brute of a man, almost intimidating in his stature, but underneath the burly exterior was a heart made of marshmallows. His wife, Rona, was petite, crisp, efficient, and she presented quite a contrast with her huggy bear of a husband. Paula did not remember a time when Mitch and Rona had not occupied the lower level bedroom near Justin's in-home recording studio. Rona had been Justin's secretary and Mitch his majordomo and bodyguard. Now their affections, which were deep, had been transferred to Justin's widow. They ran Paula's home and as much of her life as she would allow. There was no doubt in her mind that either would gladly do anything she asked them to, no matter how foolish.

Paula pushed the button in the glove compartment that opened the trunk, and Mitch lifted her heavy suitcase with the ease with which she picked up her handbag. "Glad to see you home safe and sound," he said. "I was getting nervous with that sun going down. How was the trip?"

"The trip was uneventful, and the visit with Verna was restoring. She sends her love. Any news from here?"

"Rona has a couple of messages from you, but I don't think any of them require immediate attention. Lou's waiting in the den."

The best thing about getting away for a few days, Paula thought as she stepped into the gleaming tiled foyer, was coming home. For all its elegance, the big house managed to convey a feeling of homeyness, and it always smelled of soap and polish and good things cooking. She paused to thumb through the pile of mail that had been left on the foyer table and to admire the stunning bouquet of fresh flowers in a brass urn. Flowers had been one of Justin's passions, and for years he'd had a standing order with a local florist to replenish the urn on a regular schedule. Paula had continued the custom, partly because it served to keep her husband's memory alive, but mostly because flowers gave her a lift, too.

Pivoting, she walked down the hall to the den in the rear of the house. The moment she entered the room, a tall, impeccably groomed man in his mid-fifties put down the newspaper he was reading and stood, smiling at her. "Good!" he exclaimed. "You're home."

"Hello, Lou."

"Tired?"

"A little," Paula admitted, thinking how wonderfully polished the man always looked. In a business where casual untidiness was the usual dress code, he dressed like the chairman of some very important board.

Lou Howard had been her husband's best friend and personal manager from the inception of Justin's career. Both men had wandered into Nashville in the early 1950s from rural backgrounds, and both had harbored vague hopes of doing something with the kind of music they loved so much. Their friendship had been formed over drinks at Tootsie's Orchid Lounge, and it had remained steadfast through the years. It had often seemed to Paula that Lou's feelings toward Justin had bordered on worship. The minute Justin had hit it big, Lou had dropped his own ambitions to manage him. As time passed and Justin had grown into a legend, Lou gradually had taken on other clients, many of whom now were Nashville's brightest stars. He'd never married or had much in the way of a private life that anyone knew about. His work was his life. He poured vast reserves of energy into it and in so doing had become a powerful broker in talent who could make or break careers. His contacts were widespread and numerous. His influence was considerable and, to those artists whom he favored, invaluable.

"Are you staying for dinner?" Paula asked.

Lou closed the space between them and placed a light kiss on her cheek. "If I'm invited."

"Since when do you need an invitation? As a matter of fact, I would insist you stay tonight. I want to talk to you."

"Oh?"

"While I was in Alabama I heard a singer, a very good singer. I want to try to get him up here so you can listen to him."

Lou regarded her seriously. "A new protégé, Paula?"

"Maybe." She turned and walked toward the window, lifted the curtain and stared out at the evening sky. The thought had taken hold at some point during the day's long drive. She had tried to dismiss it, but it had refused to let go. Then she'd realized the only reason she'd wanted to dismiss it was that Justin hadn't been there to hear him. If he had been, she knew they would already be doing something about Dane Markham—and the first thing Justin would have done was contact Lou. Paula had been denying her own instincts, something Justin had told her never to do.

She had begun arguing with herself. Dane might not want success. Hadn't Verna said he was without ambition? No one backed in the door. To succeed, he would have to want it more than he'd ever wanted anything and be willing to work like hell. That required dedication and discipline. Would he want to go to the trouble?

Could anyone really say no to the chance for fame and fortune?

Assuming Dane couldn't, he might not be person-able enough to attract a following. Paula recalled those cold, cold eyes. He had good looks that could be enhanced, but nothing she had heard about him, certainly nothing she had seen, indicated that he was capable of warmth and charm. That transmitted itself to an audience. Fans liked to believe that their idols were nice people.

He wouldn't be the first performer who was a complete ass offstage.

What did she know about him, about the kind of person he really was? Nothing except what Verna had told her, and none of that was good. He might be a thoroughly unpleasant man.

Justin had brought home plenty of people she hadn't been wild about. The talent was the thing.

What about his father?

That she didn't know. She supposed that would be Dane's problem.

And so it had gone throughout the trip. By the time she had reached her driveway she had come to the conclusion that she was going to try. Justin, she conveniently decided, would want her to. And it wasn't as though she would actually have to do much herself. If Dane would come to Nashville, even for a few days, she hoped she could simply turn him over to Lou. She wouldn't get heavily involved the way Justin always had. She couldn't; she had Hamilton House.

"He's very talented," Paula continued, turning from the window. "More so than a lot of people I could name who should bless you and Justin all the way to the bank. The talent's natural. He's never sung professionally except at some local joint."

Lou shrugged, knowing that talent often was found in some unlikely places. He was intrigued. Paula would recognize real talent when she heard it, so he took her word for it that the singer was good. Furthermore, she knew he handled only heavyweights, so she wouldn't waste his time with anyone mediocre. On top of that, in all the years he'd known her, she'd never asked a favor of him. But he did wonder why she was going to the trouble of helping the kid from Alabama. Since Justin's death, it had seemed to Lou that Paula had lost interest in the music business. "Sure," he said, "I'll be glad to listen to him if you can get him up here, but I can't help wondering why you're doing it."

"Funny. I wonder why myself. I guess I've missed that sort of thing, all those bright-eyed hopefuls." She paused. Dane Markham was anything but bright eyed, and she had no idea if he was hopeful or not. If, as Verna had said, he really did have the ambition of a worm, he wouldn't be willing to do what would be expected of him. "Life's too quiet, Lou. This might be an interesting project."

Lou pulled thoughtfully on his chin. "You want to live the way you did when Justin was alive. I guess we'd all like that, but it's not possible. I'm not sure you ought to take on another protégé without his help."

Paula shot him her most engaging smile. "But I have you."

"And I have a full roster of clients, at least one of whom expects more from me than it's humanly possible to give."

"I have to assume you're talking about Dottie."

"Mmm-hmm. Dear Dottie seems to think she's my only client."

Dottie Crowe was generally believed to be the heir apparent to the Tammy-Loretta-Dolly crown. Frankly, Paula couldn't understand the woman's incredible success. To her way of thinking, Dottie only had a so-so voice, but she was a blond knockout, and the fans seemed to love her. In only a few years she had become the most expensive act to book in country music. Even Justin had thought she was wonderful, so Paula assumed it was she who was out of step.

"I think when you hear Dane Markham, if you do, you'll find room for him," she told Lou. "Then I'll step aside and let you take over."

Rona entered the den just then, but when she saw Lou she stopped. "Am I interrupting something?"

"Not a thing," Lou said, walking to the bar at the far end of the room. "Paula's unearthed a new singer she wants me to hear."

"Really?" Rona grinned. "Hi, glad you're back."

"Hi," Paula said, returning her smile. "It's good to be back. Any important messages?"

"Not really, but Cynthia Caldwell called to remind you about some charity event you and Lou promised to attend."

Paula nodded. "Weekend after next."

"How's Verna?" Rona asked.

"Great, as always."

"There must be something to all that fresh air, sunshine and healthy living junk. Want a drink?"

"Not really. I sure could use some food, though. I'm starving."

"Martha's running a little late tonight," Rona said, referring to the Steeles' longtime cook. "She wasn't sure when you'd be in."

"That's such a long drive. No wonder I don't go see Verna more often than I do."

"Tell me about the singer."

"There's not much to tell," Paula said, "except that he has this voice, this incredible voice. It gave me a flutter or two, and I've heard the best."

"Is he anything to look at?"

"There's a certain attractiveness, yes, but he's had a hard life, and it shows. With a little sprucing up and some nice clothes, he probably would be a good-looking guy. Of course, our friend over there—" she nodded in Lou's direction "—is a past master at creating images. My main concern is whether or not Dane will want any help."

"Sure he will. Who could pass it up?"

At that moment Mitch poked his head in the door to say dinner was ready, and for the remainder of the evening the four friends passed a congenial few hours. It had often amazed Paula that she, Mitch, Rona and Lou had grown even closer since Justin's death. He had been their patriarch, the head of the clan, and they had closed ranks when he left them. They had their differences, of course, but for the most part each was respectful of the others, and they functioned as a family unit. Paula thought Justin would have been pleased that the people he had been closest to had remained close.

Later, she pleaded fatigue and went upstairs to her room. It was the room she and Justin had shared for twenty years and was more like a suite than merely a bedroom. Besides the sleeping quarters, there was a

sitting room that served as her home office and a huge
bathroom with a sunken tub and whirlpool, the one
ultramodern touch in the otherwise traditional house.
Mitch, she noticed, had placed her suitcase at the foot
of the bed, but she didn't feel like unpacking. Strip-
ping off her clothes, she took a long, leisurely bath,
then wrapped herself in a terry-cloth kimono and went
into the sitting room. There she dialed Verna's number in Alabama.

The phone rang twice, and Verna answered.

"Hi," Paula said. "Thought I'd let you know I'm
home safe and sound."

"Good. The trip went smoothly, I hope."

"Yes, thankfully. Has Jim forgiven me for ruining
his Saturday night?"

Verna chuckled. "The man doesn't hold grudges.
He probably enjoyed it more than he let on."

"Listen, friend, I want you to do a favor for me.
When you see Dane tomorrow, ask him to call me."

If Verna thought that was odd, and Paula imagined she did, she didn't say anything. "I don't know
when I'll see him again, Paula. His dad got himself
killed in a brawl last night...or rather, early this
morning. One of those awful places out on the highway."

"Oh, my God, Verna! How tragic!"

"Yeah, but I wonder if it wasn't inevitable. You
can't live the way he did and expect to reach a ripe old
age."

"But murder!" Paula shuddered. "How is Dane?"

"Hard to say. He's not one to show his emotions.
He called this afternoon to say he wouldn't be in tomorrow and wasn't sure when he would be. I might
never see him again. If I were in his shoes, I might

hightail it out of here as fast as I could. This place isn't exactly full of fond memories for him.''

"That's too bad. I wish I could have gotten in touch with him. I might have been able to help him.''

"How?''

"Oh...never mind. Just an idea I had. I'm not sure anything would have come of it. Anyway, I'm home. I enjoyed our visit tremendously. Now you and Jim have to come to Nashville.''

"You know I can't get Jim away from this place.''

"I know. You come.''

"One of these days I just might do that.''

"I'll believe it when I see it. Good night, Verna.''

"'Night. And, Paula, if I do happen to see Dane, I'll give him your message.''

After hanging up, Paula stretched and yawned, then stood up and got ready for bed. Verna probably was right; Dane would leave Alabama the minute he could. Now she wished she had made her decision about helping him at The General Store last night. It might have eased this difficult time for him. No matter how big a problem his father had presented, he had to be feeling wretched about now.

Then it occurred to her that if Dane had kept her card, he just might come to Nashville after all, provided he had the wherewithal. She hoped so. It was fun to think about giving Dane Markham the chance of a lifetime. But if he didn't show up, she imagined there would be someone else somewhere down the line. There was always such a pang of parental satisfaction associated with watching an unknown talent take his or her first step onto a stage, knowing that the chance to do so had come from your efforts.

As she crawled between the covers and switched off the bedside lamp, she chuckled. The image of Dane's dark, suspicious, wary face came to her mind. Feeling parental toward that man would take some doing.

A PINE BOX in the poorest section of the cemetery was the best Dane could do. He had not expected to feel sad, but he did. There were hot tears in his eyes and a lump in his throat the size of a golf ball. His temples throbbed, and he was overcome with a sense of despair. His father had been born, lived and died in poverty, which wasn't right. And Dane was the only mourner, which wasn't right, either. It all seemed so bleak and useless. No life should count for so little.

Once the preacher the funeral home had sent finished with his prayers, Dane walked down the gentle rise, got into his truck and drove to the farm adjacent to the small plot of land where the house trailer was parked. The man who answered his knock was Caleb Wells. Seeing Dane, he scowled.

Caleb had loathed the Markhams with fierce intensity for years, labeling them the worst of poor white trash. He regarded their proximity to his farm as a personal affront and had tried again and again to get Dane to sell the property to him. Dane had always refused, saying it was his father, not he, who owned the trailer and the plot of land it stood on. Since Caleb wouldn't speak to Dane's father under any circumstances, the farmer had been forced to live with his hatred and endure the Markhams. Now, however, things were different.

There were no words of greeting from Caleb, and Dane didn't bother with any, either. "You still want that piece of land my old man owned?"

"Reckon I do."

"Three hundred dollars, right?"

"Yes."

Dane reached into his pocket and withdrew the deed. "It's been signed. You got the money?"

"Wait here."

He was gone only a few minutes, and when he returned he handed Dane six fifty-dollar bills. Dane stared at them, and to his alarm he felt his eyes sting again. Six fifty-dollar bills. His father's estate. His own inheritance.

"Whaddaya want me to do with that eyesore of a trailer?" Caleb asked.

"I'll be out of it tomorrow. Then you can burn it for all I care." With that, he stepped off the porch and returned to the truck.

A few minutes later Dane walked through the door of the trailer. For once he didn't notice the worn linoleum floors, the peeling walls or the exposed pipes. For a fleeting minute he considered calling Verna Gregg, then decided against it. No goodbyes. He hadn't meant much to the Greggs, and they hadn't meant much to him. No one ever did.

For the first time in years, he had plans. Maybe they wouldn't materialize, but he was going to try. His mind made a rapid inventory of the place. Anything he wanted to take with him would easily fit in the small suitcase under his bed. He would hock his guitar. The salvage yard down the highway would buy his truck for parts, and with luck, someone there would drive him to the bus station. When he got to Birmingham, he'd get off, buy some clothes, then catch another bus.

And this life would be over. He would eradicate it from his memory. Maybe the next one wouldn't be all red-hot, but anything had to be better than the one he had been living.

THE FIRST FEW DAYS after Paula returned to work were filled with all the myriad matters her position entailed. First she called Vanessa Hamilton in Dallas to let her know she was back in the office. Then she tackled an enormous stack of paperwork. She had been gone only a week, but it was amazing how many things could pile up in five working days. The chief reason was that no one was willing to make decisions in her absence, a gripe shared by all the division vice presidents. It was human nature, she guessed, to pass the buck as far as it would go.

On the fourth day she worked at the office later than usual. When she finally walked through the front door of her house late that afternoon, she was almost knocked over by Rona, who had come running as if some sort of emergency were in progress. "Paula, there is a man in the den!"

"A man? Well, he didn't break and enter, did he? Someone must have let him in."

"I had no choice except to let him camp on the veranda. He refused to leave."

"Who is he?"

"I have no idea. I've tried quizzing him, but he refuses to talk, too. He just says you invited him here."

"Then let's go find out who our visitor is."

Paula walked briskly down the hall and into the den. Dane Markham got to his feet.

"For goodness' sake!" Paula exclaimed. So he had come, after all.

"Is it all right?" Rona asked anxiously.

"Yes, it's fine."

Rona breathed a sigh of relief and hurriedly left the room.

Dane stood as still as death, his heart pounding erratically. Of all the dumb things he had done in his life, and there had been many, coming here now seemed the dumbest. Paula's home had been a shock to him; he found it almost impossible to believe there were people who lived amid such luxury. But the mistress of the manor was an even bigger shock. He wasn't sure he would have recognized her if he had seen her somewhere else. She wore a soft crepe dress of dusty rose, and there were pearls at her neck. She was considerably taller than he remembered, but then he noticed the high heels. With her hair sleeked back into a French twist, she looked cool and sophisticated, easily the most beautiful woman he'd ever seen—and the most foreign. Women like Paula Steele didn't even speak to men like Dane Markham.

He could feel his nerve crumbling like clay. What in hell had gotten into him? What had made him think for a minute that he would be welcomed into this world of the megarich? Paula probably had been making small talk when she'd told him to look her up if he ever got to Nashville. It had been a long time since he'd felt so self-conscious, so inarticulate, so damned uncomfortable.

Still, he reminded himself, she *had* told him to look her up, and here he was. If she hadn't meant what she said, this would teach her a lesson about being too free with invitations. Now, what did he say?

"I had to try this," he said tersely. "I wanted to find out if you were serious or just making chin music."

A small smile lifted the corners of Paula's mouth. His eyes were as coldly wary as ever, but she could sense his nervousness, and that made him seem vulnerable, even appealing. He wasn't nearly as tough as he wanted the world to think. She noticed that he'd had a haircut, and the scruffy attire was gone. He was wearing tailored trousers and a sport shirt. She'd bet they both were brand-new. He looked nice, very nice.

"I don't make chin music, Dane," she said softly. "I wouldn't know how. Sit down. Would you care for a drink?"

CHAPTER FOUR

DANE RELEASED his pent-up breath; it escaped in a hiss. "Thanks. I'll take a beer if you have one."

"Sure."

He couldn't seem to take his eyes off the scissoring motions Paula's legs made as she crossed the room to the bar. Classy lady, he thought. He'd never known a truly classy lady before, and now one was getting him a beer.

"I'm very sorry about your father, Dane," Paula said, opening the door to the bar fridge.

"Thanks. He...didn't have such a great life. Maybe he's better off now."

"Still, it must have been terrible for you."

"How did you know about Dad?"

"I called Verna when I got home Sunday night. She told me."

"I feel kinda bad about leaving town without saying goodbye to Verna and Jim."

"I'm sure they understand."

Paula came out from behind the bar carrying a can of beer in one hand and something in a tall frosted glass in the other. After handing the beer to Dane, she took a seat on the sofa opposite him, sipped at her drink, then regarded him seriously. "The main reason I called Verna that night was to have her tell you to get in touch with me."

"Oh?"

"Yes. I had made a momentous decision during the drive home, and I wanted to talk to you about it."

Dane's brows lifted slightly. "You wanted to talk to *me* about a decision you'd made?"

"I suppose I should explain. You see, for years my husband and I opened this house to promising unknowns who were trying to break into the music business. Some of them have gone on to become enormously successful. Of course, they couldn't have done so without talent and hard work, but I like to think Justin's efforts—and, to a lesser extent, mine—helped, too. Frankly, I miss all that. The minute I heard you sing I knew your voice was special, and on the way home I decided to help you the same way Justin helped so many others. I can't do as much as he could, but I think I can do enough. I have to assume you're here because you've decided to do something with your voice."

"It was a thought."

"Good. I'm glad."

Dane searched her face, for what he wasn't sure. He wondered if she really was glad or was just being nice. She sounded sincere, but why would she care one way or another? It didn't make sense to him.

Paula took another sip of her drink before turning all business. "First of all, I want to make sure you're serious, that pursuing a musical career is what you want to do more than anything in the world. Are you serious enough to do exactly what you're told to do?"

Dane hesitated. His life up until now hadn't been anything to write home about, but it had been relatively free and unstructured. For the most part, people had ignored him, which meant they left him alone.

For sure there hadn't been anyone telling him what to do, and he'd always thought he liked it that way.

But the result was that he'd never done much, and what little he had done had been insignificant. "Sure," he said. "Sure I am."

"Okay. I hope you mean that. The life looks glamorous, but very little of it really is. Mostly it's just a lot of hard work. Now, let me tell you what I'm going to do. Lou Howard should be here soon. He was Justin's manager, and he's a powerful man in the business. Lou can get things done and get them done fast. I've already told him about you, and he's agreed to listen to you."

"That's it?" Dane had been expecting something more dramatic and much more difficult.

Paula smiled. "This town is full of people who would kill in order to get Lou to listen to them. He handles the biggest names. No unknown can just walk in and get his ear. But he'll listen to you because I asked him to."

"Then what?"

"That will be up to Lou. If he likes you, and I'm sure he will, he'll get in touch with someone at one of the record companies. My guess would be Owen Brewster at Heron Records. It's a middling-size independent label, which is good for a first record. It's so easy for an unknown singer to get lost in a big company's computer. Owen will arrange a recording session. Once the record is released, Lou knows where to set out the saucers of milk."

Dane frowned. "What?"

"He'll call every country music DJ he knows, and that's just about all of them, and tell them to play the heck out of it. If it's a chart climber, there'll be an al-

bum and maybe another hit single off the album. Then
maybe some big label will make you an offer you can't
refuse. Who knows how far it will go? You'll be in
good hands. Like I said, Lou can make things happen. That's one reason I'm sending you to him. Another is that he's scrupulously honest. He won't let
you sign anything you shouldn't. You have no idea
how many unknowns have signed agreements with
agent-managers only to discover after they'd become
successful that they'd signed something giving said
agent-manager the right to steal every dime they'd ever
make.''

Dane listened to her in a daze. She spoke with such
authority and sounded as if she knew what she was
talking about. But then, he had to remember that she
had lived with the man who practically invented
modern country music.

He couldn't believe he was sitting in an opulent
Nashville mansion, calmly discussing agent-manager
agreements and chart-climbing records with the widow
of a legend. Paula's easy assurance astonished him.
She seemed to be saying he could have a career in music with a shove in the right direction, and she was so
convincing that he was beginning to think maybe he
could, too.

Then his inherently suspicious nature intruded. He
did not find it easy to trust people. Why, he wondered, would this woman go out of her way to help
him? What was in it for her? No one had ever lifted a
finger to help him do anything. No one but a few reg-
ulars at The General Store had ever cared if he could
sing. Legions of people could have walked through
those woods that morning, heard him singing and
nothing at all would have happened. Paula didn't ring

true because he'd never met anyone like her, and Dane's usual method of dealing with people who didn't ring true was to stay away from them. The notion that someone of means might derive pleasure simply from helping someone else was totally alien to him. He felt himself tense, a lifelong reflex action when faced with something he didn't understand.

"If all this actually happens," he said, "what are you going to expect from me? What are the dues?"

"Dues?" Paula looked startled for a minute, but when she saw the distrust in his eyes, she understood. Dane no doubt hadn't had any experience with a helping hand. It would take some time for him to learn that the world did contain charity and benevolence, even if they had eluded him so far. One day he would discover that not every kindness had to be repaid. "What do I expect from you? Nothing but your best effort, of course. Make the best record you can."

Paula sensed he didn't believe her, not entirely, not yet, but that didn't matter. Perhaps he would in time. Once again, doubts sprang into her own mind. She really didn't know anything about him except that he had that incredible voice. He probably was thoroughly undisciplined. What if he turned out to be too wild and unmanageable to build an impressive track record? The bigwigs in Nashville preferred some humility in newcomers, and Lou refused to handle anyone who couldn't keep his act clean. If she called Lou into this and Dane disappointed her, she would lose credibility with a man who thought the world of her. Not that Lou would blame her; he had been through plenty of wasted auditions and one-hit "stars" in his time. But if Dane didn't live up to his promise, if he wouldn't play by the rules, Paula knew she would think long and hard before ever asking Lou for another favor.

She was trying to think of a tactful way to tell Dane all that when Lou strode into the den. Anything else she had to say was put on hold. "Ah, Lou, come here," she said. "I want you to meet someone. This is Dane Markham, the singer I told you about."

The welcoming smile on Lou's face faded slightly. He had been expecting a kid, and Dane Markham wasn't a kid. He looked as if he'd been around the track a few times and had found the race tough going. But when Dane stood and offered his hand, the older man shook it firmly and murmured the usual acknowledgment.

"Fix yourself a drink and join us," Paula went on. "Would you believe that Dane simply showed up on my doorstep? Talk about a stroke of luck. I was afraid I'd never see him again."

"I'm anxious to hear you, Dane," Lou said. "Paula's enthusiasm is contagious."

"I'm thinking we just might have ourselves an audition tonight. After dinner? How does that sound?" Paula addressed the question to both Dane and Lou.

Lou shrugged. "It's fine with me."

A wave of panic washed over Dane. They were so damned casual about everything. What would he sing? He didn't have a guitar. He hadn't unexpected anything like this, and he felt woefully unprepared. Was he supposed to just open his mouth and burst into song?

"Dane?" Paula prompted.

"What? Oh . . . well, okay, I guess."

Rona sailed into the room just then, was formally introduced to Dane, then took a seat next to Paula on the sofa. Lou sat down, and the three of them slipped into easy conversation. Paula related an anecdote from the office, which reminded Rona of something, and that in turn reminded Lou of a story. Dane sat in silence, feeling like an outsider who was eavesdropping on a secret tribal rite. He was uneasy and out of his element, but he discovered it was a pleasure to watch Paula talk about nothing in particular and make it sound interesting. Several times she tried to integrate him into the conversation, but he couldn't seem to answer in anything but monosyllables. Still her charming manner didn't falter. He wondered if she had ever found herself in an awkward or uncomfortable social position or if she'd ever said or done an ungracious thing in her life. He doubted it.

A few minutes later another man walked into the room, a burly hulk named Mitch. He announced that dinner was ready, and everyone stood. As easily as if she had done it hundreds of times, Paula tucked her hand into the crook of Dane's elbow. "I hope you're excited about this," she said softly. "I certainly am."

"Excited? I'm paralyzed. Listen, it's nice of you, but I really can't stay for dinner."

"Of course you can. There's always plenty. Martha is a superb cook, and she doesn't know how to make just a little bit of food. Also, you have to be here afterward to sing for Lou. We'll hold the audition downstairs in Justin's studio. Would you like to do a voice-over?"

"A what?"

"Do your vocal over a recording of Justin's band. We have hundreds of tapes."

"I . . . don't think so. I've never done anything like that before."

"Well, perhaps it would be best to let Lou hear just the voice." She smiled at him so warmly that Dane felt his insides melt. He supposed she could talk anyone into doing anything. Feeling almost hypnotized, he walked beside her, and they followed the others into the dining room.

Stepping into that room was like being plunked down on another planet. Although Dane would not have known its name, what he was experiencing was culture shock. The long dining table had been set with linen, china, silver and crystal. A plate of food that looked like a still life was set before him; only the tiny new potatoes cooked in their red jackets were familiar, but whatever it was that he began eating was delicious. He discovered he was ravenous, which surprised him. He'd always been rather indifferent about food, grabbing something whenever the notion struck, sometimes existing solely on hamburgers and fries for days at a time. At Paula's table, on the other hand, food not only was enjoyed, it was discussed, savored, appreciated. The wine they were drinking especially inspired a lively discussion about "balance" and "aroma" and "crispness." Dane didn't have the slightest idea what they were talking about.

Through the meal he watched Paula carefully. One didn't have to be around long to decide she definitely was head of the household, the one the rest of them turned to, even though she was younger than the others. At least he guessed she was younger. She certainly looked it, and that made him wonder for the first time just how old his benefactor was.

His benefactor! The word rolled over and over in his mind, eliciting a foolish grin that he hid behind his napkin. Assuming that all these wonderful things actually took place—and there was plenty of doubt in his mind that they actually would—he assumed Paula would be his benefactor, or patron, or whatever the proper word was.

Once again he glanced toward the far end of the table, and this time his eyes met hers for a brief second. She smiled before returning her attention to whatever Rona was saying. Paula looked beautiful and gentle, vulnerable and delicate, but Dane had a feeling that when the occasion demanded, she could be as delicate as a pit bulldog. What kind of background instilled that kind of confidence in a person? he wondered. Maybe she'd been born that way. Long ago he had learned that the world contained a handful of people who were meant to lead the vast majority around by the nose, and Paula definitely belonged with the handful. What an incredible evening it had been, and the best—or worst—was yet to come.

Merely thinking about auditioning for the man named Lou caused Dane's stomach to do another flip-flop, and his food stuck in his throat, causing him to swallow with difficulty. All his life, whenever he had been faced with something unknown or unpleasant, he usually had shrugged and walked away from it. He was having a hard time handling this.

Then dessert and coffee were being served. That meant the moment of truth was almost upon him, and he was quite sure he had never been this nervous in his entire life. He had forgotten the words to every song he'd ever known, and he experienced an overwhelming urge to stand, thank Paula kindly and get the hell out of there.

Paula glanced his way and saw the expression on his face. She felt sorry for him, but she knew he would be fine once he started singing. It was the waiting that had his stomach in knots. She was beginning to get a little impatient, too.

Finally dessert was finished. Paula clapped her hands excitedly. "All right, everybody. Bring your coffee with you if you want. We're going downstairs to the studio. It's show time!"

As everyone stood and began filing out of the dining room, she hurried around the table to Dane's side. "Try not to be nervous. I know that's easier said than done, but this really isn't so different from The General Store. In fact, this audience probably isn't nearly as tough as that one was. Just remember all those nights when it was only you up there pickin' and singin' half the night."

"I think I'm going to be sick."

"No, you're not. You're going to be wonderful. Come on."

His feet felt as though they weighed ten pounds each as he followed her out of the room, down the hall and to a staircase leading down. From the street the Steele mansion looked to be two stories, but it was built on a rise and actually was a trilevel. The stairs led down to a long hall with several doors opening off it. Paula paused at the third door and motioned Dane inside. The room they entered was a full-fledged recording studio with a soundproof booth, microphones all over the place and the very latest in sound and mixing equipment. A tape library occupied one entire wall.

Dane murmured an awed "Whew," then Paula thrust a guitar in his hands. He looked at it. "Was this your husband's?"

"One of them. His favorite, the one he used while performing, is in the Hall of Fame. I thought you might like to play this one."

"I couldn't!" The idea was almost irreverent.

"Why not? Guitars are meant to be played."

Dane picked up the instrument and strummed it gingerly. Never would he have thought he would touch such a guitar, let alone play it. The sound it made put a lump in his throat. Paula watched him, smiling at the look on his face. She guessed there hadn't been many special moments in Dane's life, and it delighted her no end to be the one who had given him this one.

The others were already seated. Paula pulled a stool out into the center of the room, patted Dane's arm reassuringly, then went to take a seat next to Lou. If her old friend sent out vibes, she wanted to be able to feel them. On the surface she radiated calm and confidence, but her insides were churning much the way Dane's were.

Dane glanced at Lou. "Is there anything special you'd like to hear, Mr. Howard?"

"Nope. Just sing until I tell you to stop," Lou said. "All you have to do is impress the hell out of me."

Dane swallowed away the lump in his throat and took a deep breath. *Get it in perspective, pal,* he told himself. *The world isn't going to end if the guy doesn't like you. You came here with little hope, and you can leave the same way. These people mean nothing to you, remember?* He'd take Paula's advice and pretend he was back at The General Store on a night when the audience was cool and no one else showed up to play. Settling himself comfortably on the stool, he strummed the guitar twice, then started to sing.

Lou leaned back in his chair and folded his arms across his chest. Then he closed his eyes. Right now all he was interested in was the voice. Dane Markham's stage presence, or lack of it, was something that could be worked on later. So could his image. Just the voice right now.

Lou had been handling the great and almost great for a lot of years, but he still felt like a kid in a toy store when it came to discovering new talent. In the past, when someone had really impressed him, he had practically taken the performer to raise. He was a rare creature in the music business, a man who had never become jaded. During auditions he always found himself cheering the performers on, hoping they'd be good, wanting them to be good.

And Dane Markham was. Lou could feel his pulse start pounding the way it did whenever someone new got to him. He hadn't heard "Tears I've Shed in Vain" sung that well since Justin used to do it. That song, more than any other, almost moved him to tears. Usually when he heard someone else do it, he compared it unfavorably with Justin's version, but not this time. When the song ended, his eyes were still closed and he said nothing, so Dane immediately swung into another standard. Lou let Dane sing four songs before asking him to stop.

"Okay, okay, I've heard enough. Well, you did it. You impressed the hell out of me. Yeah, Paula, you were right. He's got it."

Paula's stomach settled down, and Dane's mouth dropped an inch. "I . . . don't know what to say, Mr. Howard . . . except thanks."

"Don't thank me yet." Lou leaned forward and spoke to Dane as if they were the only people in the room. "You already know, I'm sure, that this isn't an easy town to take by storm. If you've got any old-fashioned notions about all-night drinking and picking sessions in honky-tonks, get rid of 'em. Nashville today is solid careerism. Nobody wants a problem child to take care of, and everybody wants a platinum record. Now, platinum is commonplace in rock—but not so common in country. Still, everybody's got blockbuster on the brain. So we're eventually gonna give 'em one. From this minute on, you don't listen to anybody but me, understand?"

"Y-yes, sir."

"First, I'm going to call Owen Brewster at Heron Records. He'll put together the best studio band he can find, which'll be damned good, and you're going to cut a record. 'Tears' might be a good song to do since it hasn't been on the charts in thirty years. Then I'm going for a maximum P&D, which is promotion and distribution, in case you don't know. Every station in the country will play it. Folks hear a record often enough and they figure it's a hit, so they go out and buy it and make it one. There are a lot of people out there who owe me some favors, so back-scratchin' time is upon us."

Shock waves shot through Dane. He felt as though he were watching a movie, something that had nothing to do with him. He'd experienced more emotions today than he had in all the thirty-six years of his life put together. Lou Howard didn't seem to have any doubts that all this was actually going to happen.

"Then we'll cut an album and send you out on the road," Lou went on. "No clubs or dance halls, though. You're going to play civic centers and sports arenas, places where people come to listen. You'll be opening for other acts for a while, but your day as a headliner is coming, mark my words. If that doesn't happen, I need to be in another line of work.''

"Mr. Howard, I—''

"Call me Lou. Now, let me tell you something about this crazy business. There are a whole lot of people in it who honestly believe that the only real good country music is made outside the rim of success. Once a performer gets popular, the feeling goes, the music suffers, and I can't say there hasn't been some truth to that. Some kid comes out of the Kentucky hills with a sound so pure it makes you cry. Five hit records later he's singing about leaving his heart in San Francisco, and he's carrying more strings with him than Mantovani. A lot of stuff is produced in this town that has about as much in common with real country music as clam chowder does with chili. But I've long wanted to prove that it doesn't have to be that way.''

Lou paused to rub his chin and let what he'd said so far sink in. "I'm a talent broker. That's what I do for a living. And I don't handle anything but successes. I wouldn't spend two minutes with you if I didn't think Halley's Comet was about to appear in the country music firmament. I plan to take you and show the skeptics that a singer can be successful, even commercial, and never forget to dance with the one he came with. You keep your nose clean, stick with me, and you're liable to wind up in the Hall of Fame.''

Lou leaned back and folded his arms across his chest again. "Okay, now if you want to, you can thank me.''

Stunned, Dane looked at Paula. She just beamed.

HALF AN HOUR LATER, Lou had left to keep one of his endless appointments, Mitch and Rona were upstairs watching television, and Paula was still in the studio, listening to Dane sing and strum Justin's guitar. He was too keyed up to wind down, and she enjoyed listening to him. But there were plans and arrangements to be made, so when he finished his song, she asked him a question. "Dane, how much money do you have?"

"A few hundred bucks."

"What's 'a few'?"

"Maybe three."

Paula frowned. "That's not very much."

"Maybe not to you, but it's a fortune to me. I know how to make three hundred dollars stretch from here to Christmas."

"Not if you have to pay for a room and three meals a day," Paula said practically.

"I don't need three meals a day. Two will do. And I don't eat fancy stuff, either. Don't worry, I'll make do."

"You need a roof over your head," she insisted. "That costs money."

"So I'll get a job. At a gas station, maybe. I'm a pretty fair mechanic."

She considered that. "I'd really prefer you not get tied to anything until we know what's going to happen. Tell you what—you stay here until Lou gets something going."

"Here?" he asked in astonishment.

"Yes, that's what the other bedroom is for. We almost always had someone staying in it. You haven't made other arrangements, have you?"

"No, I got off the bus and came straight here."

"How?"

"Took a cab."

"For sure three hundred dollars won't last long if you take taxis. Transportation for you is something we'll have to work out. There are a lot of things that need working out, but we'll start by giving you room and board for a while."

Dane shook his head in disbelief. These people weren't for real—they couldn't be. "I . . . don't know what to say."

"Thanks is always nice."

"Thanks."

"You're welcome. Come on, I'll show you the room. Where are your belongings?"

Dane fell into step beside her. "I have a suitcase. I guess the other lady . . . er, Rona, put it somewhere."

"I'll find it. Here's your room."

The bedroom looked the way Dane imagined a nice hotel room would—subdued colors, completely comfortable and tasteful. The decor was neither too masculine nor too feminine, and his feet actually sank down into the plush carpet. A palace wouldn't have seemed more luxurious to him. To bed down in a room like this was a fitting finish to what had been, from start to finish, an unbelievable day.

Maybe this wouldn't last. He doubted it would. Personally, he expected someone to let him in on the joke any minute now, but until they did, he intended enjoying every minute of this.

"I think you'll be comfortable here," Paula said. "At least we never had any complaints. There's the bathroom, and that's the closet. Just make yourself at home. Mitch will bring your things down soon. Breakfast is served at seven-thirty because I like to leave the house around eight. If there's nothing else, I'll see you in the morning."

She turned to leave, but Dane touched her arm. "Paula, I . . ."

"Yes?"

"What am I supposed to do around here until whatever is going to happen happens?"

"Don't worry. Mitch will keep you busy. Verna told me you're handy, so he ought to enjoy having you around. With a big house like this, something always seems to need doing."

Was that the catch? Dane wondered. In return for helping him, they got an unpaid lackey? Well, what the hell? It wasn't a bad trade-off—some manual labor for a chance to be somebody. And if even half of what Lou Howard had said to him was true, he wouldn't be around here long.

He knew he should say something to Paula. Even if she had ulterior motives in doing this, she had gone to some trouble to help him, and no one else ever had. The trouble was, he didn't know what to say. He was still suspicious. He couldn't help it; life had turned him that way. But there was another feeling gripping him tightly, and he didn't know its name. Gratitude? He'd never been grateful to a soul. If anyone had ever tried to tell him something like this could happen to him, he would have laughed in his or her face. "I . . . uh, really don't know how to say what I'm thinking."

She smiled. "You don't have to. I know . . . and again, you're welcome. Justin once told me that the feeling he experienced when he gave someone a leg up was like none other on earth, impossible to describe.

Now I know what he meant. Tonight has been wonderfully exciting for me, too.''

She sounded sincere. That might be hard for him to accept, but she sounded so damned sincere. That was the kicker. If he thought about it too much, he might burst out in hysterical laughter. Three days ago, "home" had been a broken-down trailer in the Alabama woods; now he was here. And all because Paula Steele had chanced to hear him singing on a riverbank.

But Dane didn't put any faith in fairy tales, and this one might contain all sorts of witches and monsters. For a minute he simply stared at her. Then, in a voice that was too humble to be his own, he said, "Lady, I can truthfully say I've never met anybody like you before."

Paula's smile broadened. He probably would have been appalled if he could have seen the look of wonder on his face. He was fighting accepting it all. "Good night. Sleep well."

"Good night." Dane watched her leave and felt the wariness creeping back in. He couldn't shake the notion that there was more to it than this. These people were going to want something from him. The life he'd led up until now had been governed by the "tooth for a tooth" precept, and it hadn't been a bad way to live. At least you always knew where you stood in relation to others. He had no idea where he stood around here, because he'd never associated with their kind.

But even if he couldn't believe, he could appreciate this unexpected interlude. He began to inspect his new quarters. Although compared to the other rooms in the house that he'd seen, his bedroom was rather plain, to Dane it was dazzling—a kaleidoscope of blues and beiges and rusts. Everything complemented everything else—a figurine here, a work of art there. Colorful pillows were tossed on the bed, and a knit throw lay at its feet. In the small bathroom were the thickest towels he had ever touched. A linen cabinet behind the door held more, along with soap and lotion, toothpaste and shaving gear. When he opened the closet, he found a portable television set on a roll-around cart. In the main room, the bed was firm, its spread thick and quilted. He pulled it down and felt the sheets; they were as smooth as silk. Above all was the feeling of cleanness. He imagined that in this house, nicks, tears, smudges and dust were not tolerated.

Then he sank into the big easy chair and propped his feet on its ottoman. So this was the look and feel of money, he thought. How easy it would be to get used to living this way, and how difficult to give it up.

CHAPTER FIVE

PAULA WOKE EARLY the following morning, as she normally did, and also as usual, she didn't immediately get out of bed. She lay awake, arms propped behind her head, thinking. It was her favorite time of day; she used it to tick off items on her agenda, to plan ahead. This morning, however, all her thoughts were on Dane. He presented a unique challenge.

In the past, she had employed different methods of dealing with the young people who had stayed in the house. On the few occasions when their young hopeful had been female, it had been easy and natural to slip into the role of big sister, the all-knowing expert on hair, clothes, makeup, manners and men. The frustrated parent in her had found that fun, and she had been good at it. She'd never had much personal contact with the men; that had been Justin's job. This time things would be different. Justin was no longer around, so that meant she would have to take a greater interest in Dane. There wasn't anyone else to do it.

And that might be a problem. He was a lot older than any of the others had been, too old to fit the mental image the word *protégé* conjured up—a young person who was malleable, curious and eager to learn. He probably was curious, and he might even be eager to learn. But malleable? Paula doubted it. She couldn't forget that look on his face last night. If he was human at all, he had to have felt excitement, but his look had not been one of pinch-me wonder. He was suspicious, cautious, distrustful and wary. Dane no doubt would balk at being told what to do too often.

So how would she smooth the rough edges, turn him into someone who could ingratiate himself with an audience? Maybe she wouldn't be able to, but therein lay the challenge.

From downstairs came sounds of the household beginning to stir. Getting out of bed, Paula began her unvarying morning routine. When she walked into the dining room some forty minutes later, she was dressed for the office—sleekly elegant in a jade silk draped-neck blouse and beige pleated skirt, every inch the professional woman.

"Good morning, everybody," she greeted cheerfully.

Dane swore he felt his nerve ends tingle. She was the only person he'd ever met who could alter the entire atmosphere of a room simply by walking into it. She had...he guessed the word was *presence*. And he wondered how long he would have to be around her before the mere sight of her no longer rendered him awestruck. He was wholly confused, having never reacted to a woman in such an odd way, and he couldn't say he particularly enjoyed the effect she had on him. It set him off balance and made him feel vulnerable, a feeling he despised above all.

As Martha bustled around the table, filling juice glasses and coffee cups, Paula asked, "What do all of you have planned for today?"

This was the way every weekday began. Paula liked staying on top of the household operation—difficult to do when she was away from the house so much of the time. She didn't recall that either she or Justin had ever said, "Rona, you do this" or "Mitch, this will be your job." Their areas of responsibility had evolved according to their respective talents and likes. Thus, Rona functioned as a secretary/bookkeeper, handling Paula's personal correspondence, finances and social invitations, as well as the residual business from Justin's career. Mitch was the housekeeper. He oversaw the servants and the gardeners, took care of repairs, ran all the errands, did most of the shopping and in general created a serene atmosphere for Paula to come home to each evening. Though each received a handsome salary, Paula never thought of them as employees. They were family.

Intrigued, Dane listened to their conversation. Their lives seemed to him so full, so well-ordered, and he vowed that if he ever had money, this was the way he was going to live. Not on such a grand scale, of course, but meals would be served on a dining table, and it would be covered with a tablecloth. There would be no cereal boxes or milk cartons in sight. Plates would match and so would glasses. He didn't realize it, because he had yet to think of himself as ever being part of this environment, but he was receiving a lesson in the art of living with success. Already his world had begun to expand.

Promptly at eight, Paula got to her feet, wiping daintily at her mouth with a napkin. "Well, I'm off to the mill. Have a good day, everyone." Her smile included Dane.

Mitch stood up instantly. "I'll bring the car around," he said, and hurried out of the room.

"See you this evening," Rona said as she, too, left. "Dane, if you need me, I'll be in the office."

"Where's the office?" he asked.

"Just past the studio, downstairs."

Paula picked up her handbag and tucked it under her arm, giving Dane another of her dazzling smiles. "The upcoming weeks can be very exciting for you if you take advantage of them, Dane. Please make yourself at home. Use Justin's studio if you like. Work on your songs, listen to tapes. Some of the equipment is pretty sophisticated, so you might want to get Mitch to show you how to use it. And listen to Mitch and Rona. They've both been around the music business a long time. You can use this time to observe and learn, if you choose to.'

She sounded like a damned schoolteacher, Dane thought. There was such an air of authority about her, and an authoritative woman was virtually unknown to him. As with anything unfamiliar, her manner sent a flash of irritation sweeping through him. He half expected her to reach out and pat him on the head.

The irritation passed quickly, however, and he fell into step beside her, following her out the front door and onto the long, covered veranda. Mitch had just pulled her car to a halt at the foot of the steps. He watched as she descended the steps, then paused to exchange a few words with Mitch before getting in the car. As she drove away, she threw Dane a jaunty little wave.

He folded his arms across his chest and glanced around at the unfamiliar surroundings. The Steele residence and its grounds were magnificent. Back home there had been a few families whose homes had seemed to him the ultimate in luxury, but they were sharecropper cabins compared to this place. It was like goddam Tara. A slow smile spread across his face as he thought of the reaction of some of The General Store patrons had they known where he was and what he was doing. No one he'd ever known would have believed it.

Mitch bounded up the steps with amazing agility, given his sheer size. "How strong are you?" he asked.

"Pretty strong," Dane assured him.

"Good. I can use some help. Paula wants the furniture in her bedroom rearranged. Let's go."

That wasn't exactly the way Dane had envisioned spending his morning, and it was no small chore, but he enjoyed being around Paula's most personal things. A lot could be learned about a person from seeing his or her private place. Everything was so tidy. Once, when Mitch opened her closet door to give himself some elbowroom, Dane got a glimpse inside. Everything—her clothes, shoes, handbags—was arranged as precisely as an efficient secretary's filing cabinet.

Above all, Paula's bedroom was utterly feminine. The bedspread was about a foot thick and covered with lace-trimmed pillows. There were plants and silk flowers, perfume flacons and jewelry boxes. The room even smelled good—sweet and clean, like Paula. A framed photograph of Justin stood on her dresser, and their wedding portrait hung on the wall. Without these objects, it would have been difficult to imagine that a man had ever lived in the room.

But perhaps she had redecorated after her husband's death...or changed rooms altogether, Dane decided. God knows, there were enough of them to choose from.

REARRANGING PAULA'S BEDROOM took most of the morning, but after lunch Dane was left to his own devices when Mitch had to run some errands. It had been on the tip of his tongue to ask the big man if he could go along for the ride, but he quickly decided against it. In the world he'd come from, you didn't insinuate your company on someone who hadn't asked for it. Instead, he prowled the quiet house, soaking up the feel of luxury.

For want of more exciting diversions on a lazy Friday afternoon, he browsed through the library. Dane had never been much of a reader, chiefly because he'd never had money to spend on books. Once, when he was seventeen and going through a phase of wanting to better himself, he'd gone so far as to get a library card. Unfortunately, he'd lost the first book he'd checked out, which had cost him seven precious bucks. After that, he'd contented himself with magazines and books other people had given him.

He noticed that some of Paula's books were pretty heavy, but there was some entertainment, too. He chose a Western and a spy thriller, which he carried down to his room for bedtime reading. He was about to head for the studio to make a little music, but the open door at the far end of the hall beckoned. Peeking inside, he saw Rona seated at a long table that was laden with stack after stack of papers. He tapped the door, and she looked up.

"Hi, come on in."

"I don't want to interrupt anything."

"You won't. I'm not really working."

Dane strolled into the room. "Then what are you doing?"

"Cataloging Justin's sheet music collection. I've been at it for over a year, and the end is nowhere in sight. He started collecting thirty years ago, and Justin never did anything halfway. There are boxes and boxes of the stuff I haven't even opened yet."

"Why do you have to catalog it?"

"One, there are collectors who would pay a princely sum for some of these pieces, so we ought to know what we have, right? Two, Paula wants to donate part of the collection to the Hall of Fame, and they need to know what they're getting." Rona picked up another sheet, studied it, then let out a low whistle. "Look at this!"

"What is it?" Dane asked.

" 'The Soldier's Sweetheart,' " she said in awe.

"Important?"

"I'll say. That was the first song Jimmie Rodgers ever recorded. Nineteen twenty-six...or maybe it was '27. Wow!"

Dane was certain that a great deal of the significance of Rona's discovery was lost on him. "If the collection's so valuable, why don't you sell it?"

Rona smiled. "Oh, Paula's never sold one thing that belonged to Justin. She's given certain things to people who would appreciate them, but she'd never sell this collection."

"I guess I don't understand giving away something you could get a lot of money for."

"Look around, Dane. Paula's not exactly hurting for money. She's got more than she'll ever be able to spend, even if she lives to be a very old lady."

"Must be nice."

"Well, you listen to Lou and do what he tells you to do, and maybe you'll have more than you can spend someday."

Dane found it impossible to envision a lot of money. He often talked about how nice it would be to have it, but when he got right down to it, what would he do with it? Having had so little in his life, he'd never cultivated expensive taste—despite his newfound admiration of linen-covered dining tables. He'd like to have a house he could be proud of, but he didn't have anything like this place in mind. The idea of having an entourage to look after him held little appeal. He wasn't a clotheshorse or a jewelry buff or a car nut or a gourmet. Even if he could afford to, he wouldn't know how to order a four-course meal in a fancy restaurant or shop in an exclusive men's shop. He had never made airline, restaurant or hotel reservations, nor did he feel particularly deprived because he hadn't. He liked to sing and fish, in that order, and he supposed he'd still drink beer even if he could afford the finest brandy.

"I don't know, Rona," he said thoughtfully. "I was born poor, and I'll bet I die poor, no matter how much money I have. It has a lot to do with the way your mind works."

"We'll see," Rona said with a knowing smile. "We'll see."

At that moment the phone at her elbow rang. She picked it up, exchanged a few words with the caller, then placed the receiver on the table and got to her feet. "Mitch needs a phone number, and it's upstairs in the library. I'll be right back."

While Rona was gone, Dane idly scanned the unimposing, utilitarian office. Though well equipped, it was the one inelegant room he'd seen. Then his eyes fell to rest on the strewn tabletop. On his right were two tidy stacks of sheet music, the items Rona already had recorded in a big ledger. On his left were six or seven piles left to be cataloged. It occurred to him that it would be incredibly easy to pick up a handful of the sheets and stash them somewhere for selling at a later date. No one would even know they were gone because no one knew what was there.

Yet, he—a virtual stranger whom none of them knew much about—had been left alone with the valuable collection, trusted without question for reasons Dane couldn't begin to fathom. Nothing in his past had prepared him for that kind of trust. It was just another incredible incident heaped upon a whole string of them.

Maybe he was being put to some kind of test, he thought. Maybe they were feeling him out, seeing if they could trust him.

Rona returned with a small address book in hand, read a number out of it to Mitch, then hung up the phone. When she was seated, Dane said, "Maybe I could give you a hand with this. It looks like quite a job."

"Thanks, Dane, but I have my own system. Besides, I imagine you're going to be much too busy before long to have time for this. I'm doing it mainly to keep Paula from trying to tackle it. She has more important things to do."

A minute of silence passed before Dane sat down in a nearby chair and asked, "How long have you known Paula?"

"Twenty-one years, since she married Justin. I was his secretary."

"She must have been just a kid."

"Not really. She was out of college and had been working a couple of years when they met. If I remember right, she turned twenty-four a few months after the wedding."

Dane's eyes widened. That would make her...forty-five? He couldn't believe it. She didn't look a bit older than he did—maybe not as old—and he was thirty-six. But then, a life of comfort and ease, free of the hills and valleys most people had to contend with, held the wrinkles and gray hairs at bay. He was unwillingly fascinated with Paula, which was unusual. People rarely interested him for longer than a few minutes. "How did Paula meet Justin?"

"She was working for a publication in Birmingham. Justin was in town to do a show, and Paula was sent to interview him. They had dinner, and after that, Birmingham suddenly became Justin's favorite city in the whole world." Rona chuckled. "Fairy-tale stuff."

"Funny. I thought she'd probably been a society girl."

"Not Paula. She grew up in that little town you hail from."

"Sylacauga?" Dane grew more surprised with each answer. "I wondered how she came to know Verna Gregg."

"They've been close since they were kids."

"What about Paula's family?"

"Her dad died when she was six or seven. Her mother supported them by taking in sewing and doing alterations for some of the local shops. Paula worked her way through college, even had to drop out for one entire semester when the funds got low. Once she and Justin were married, she saw to it that her mother never wanted for a thing the rest of her life. She was a devoted daughter. In fact, 'devoted' is a good word to use to describe Paula. It was a lucky day for you when she heard you sing, young man. She won't rest until your success is assured."

"If she was just a working girl when she met Justin, how the hell did she ever get to be a vice president of a big corporation?"

Rona eyed him speculatively. "So many questions."

"Can you blame me for being curious about the only person who ever lifted a finger to help me?"

"And it doesn't hurt that your benefactor is a wealthy, beautiful widow, right?"

Dane tensed at the dig, then decided it would be prudent to let it roll off him. Cultivating Rona's friendship would only score him points. "Is she beautiful?" he asked with a grin. "I hadn't noticed."

"Sorry. That remark was uncalled-for, but you'll discover that Mitch and I are terribly protective of Paula. I don't know why. She certainly knows how to take care of herself."

"Her job?" he prodded.

"Oh, yes. Well, Paula went to work for Hamilton House not long after she and Justin got married. She was used to working and didn't want to sit around waiting for her husband to come home. The job wasn't much, just another girl Friday-type thing for the woman who was marketing director. Paula wasn't looking for a career at that time. She expected to have kids and be a homemaker. But the kids didn't come along, so she kept working and kept getting promoted. Even today she swears she finds it hard to think of herself as the corporate type. But she's smart, she's organized, and she knows how to manage people. She simply inched up the ladder until she came under the watchful eye of Vanessa Hamilton herself.''

Rona sighed, and a faraway look came to her eyes. "Justin was so proud of her, so enormously proud. And crazy about her. Insane. She was his foot on the ground. So was Marjorie, his first wife. Justin was one of those men who don't function well without a strong woman in their lives.''

Dane would have liked nothing better than to keep pumping Rona for information about the first truly intriguing person he'd ever met, but he sensed she was tiring of the conversation. He waited a minute or two before getting to his feet and ambling into the adjacent studio. At least now, for the first time, he understood why a woman like Paula Steele would help someone like him. She must have remembered what it was like to have nothing.

WHEN PAULA RETURNED home that evening it was with a beaut of a headache and a worry that wouldn't be resolved without a trip to Atlanta. Once she'd checked the mail on the foyer table, she went straight up to her room to change and gulp down a couple of aspirin before going in search of Dane. On her way through the den she stopped at the bar for two cold beers, then went downstairs.

He was in the studio, as she hoped he'd be—sitting on a stool in front of a dead microphone, strumming Justin's guitar and singing along to the accompaniment of a recording of Justin's band. For several minutes Paula stood in the doorway listening to him, much as she had that morning on the Alabama riverbank. His voice sounded even clearer and stronger than it had then, the result, perhaps, of some rest and good food. She didn't know much about his previous life, just the bits and pieces Verna had told her, but it didn't sound as though clean living had played a predominant role in it.

Dane caught sight of her and stopped singing. She stood framed in the doorway, dressed in slacks and a short-sleeved blouse, looking far more the way she had the first time he saw her. He unstrapped the guitar and propped it against the stool as she stepped into the room.

"Hi," Paula said, handing him one of the beers. "How was your day?"

"Not too bad. Yours?"

Sighing, she plopped down in a nearby chair. "I've had better."

"Problems?"

"Uh-huh. Unfortunately, that means a trip to Atlanta I hadn't counted on."

"That's no big deal, is it?"

"It is if I have to end up firing someone." Paula frowned. "That's one part of the job I hate. When I have to let someone go, especially a longtime employee, I feel terrible for days."

Dane took a hefty swig of the beer. It tasted wonderful. "Strange," he said. "I've been fired a bunch of times in my life, and I don't recall that anyone doing the firing seemed to feel all that bad about it. What did this guy, or gal, do?"

"It's more what he hasn't done. He hasn't cleared up a problem that the Atlanta restaurant has been having for far too long, so that means I'm going to have to do it for him. I get very upset when I have to drop whatever I'm doing to go do someone else's job.''

"What's the problem?''

"The customer comment cards. Each of the restaurants has a box at the door where patrons can drop them. The boxes have special combination locks on them, and only I have the combination. The reason for that is obvious—if the boxes weren't sealed, the managers could go through the cards and remove the really unfavorable ones. Anyway, every other Friday the boxes are shipped to me. After I read the cards, I send them to the home office in Dallas. Atlanta has been getting too many rotten ones lately. The ones that came in today were the worst yet. I've got to put a stop to it.''

Dane listened with mixed degrees of interest. Business bored him, but in spite of himself, he was interested in almost anything about Paula. He still couldn't see himself ever fitting into this world, this culture, but a nagging inner voice kept telling him he should absorb as much of it as he could while he could. "Paula, tell me something—why do you keep working? You have everything. You could do anything you wanted. You've already climbed to the top, so you don't have a point to prove. Why put up with the hassle?''

"Pray what else would I do?''

He shrugged. "I don't know. Anything. See the world.''

"Flit, you mean. I know so many women who do, Dane—wives of Justin's friends and business associates. Their husbands are successful and driven. Their kids have flown the nest. Unless they have an all-consuming hobby or do scads of volunteer work, they're bored out of their minds. They shop. They play cards. The lunch at the club with 'the girls.' They give parties to celebrate everything from Cinco de Mayo to Bastille Day. They travel, usually alone because their husbands are too busy to go with them, and they've become bored with all the fashionable places. Some of them drink too much. Some of them feel neglected by their husbands, so they get involved in unsatisfying, dead-end affairs. It's sad, really. I've worked all my adult life. I'll work until I drop or am put out to pasture, whichever comes first. It's the only way I know how to live."

"Takes all kinds, I guess. Now, me, I think I could stand having all the money and all the time in the world to just do whatever I wanted, whenever the notion struck."

A little ping went off inside Paula's head. *The man has the ambition of a worm,* Verna had said. He wouldn't last long without the drive, the hunger. He seemed to be trying to learn, but she hadn't had much experience with his type. Perhaps he was only taking what he could get for as long as it was offered. If so, she was going to a lot of trouble for nothing.

Paula shoved the disturbing notion aside. "No, you couldn't," she said decisively. "You'd hate it. Trust me. You would. My mother used to say that everyone's entitled to a little poverty in life."

"I was standing first in line when that was handed out." Dane took another drink of beer, watching as she sipped hers. "You know, sometimes you talk to me like I'm a kid."

Paula looked taken aback. "Do I? I don't mean to, but...I suppose I do feel considerably older than you. Not surprising since I am, you know, by quite a bit."

"Nine years isn't all that much."

She cocked her head, eyeing him. "How do you know how old I am?"

"Rona told me. I mean, she didn't come right out and say, 'Paula's forty-five,' but she told me you married Justin twenty-one years ago and turned twenty-four not long after the wedding. Even I can figure that out."

Paula chuckled. "There's always someone around who knows exactly how old you are. Forty-five! It sure got here quick."

"Does your age bug you?"

"No more so than it bugs any woman over forty."

"You shouldn't even think about it, because if you didn't blab it all over the place, no one would ever know. You sure don't look forty-five."

Paula would have vowed to the heavens that she wasn't a woman who doted on compliments. Most sounded insincere to begin with. So why, then, did Dane's simple remark send such a warm flush of pleasure through her?

Perhaps because he said it as though he meant it. She imagined Dane never wasted breath saying things he didn't mean...or in doling out compliments, either. She really hadn't figured him out yet, and she didn't suppose there was any reason she should. She was extending a hand to him, not taking him to raise. "Thanks, but I don't blab it. Far from it. I try to ignore it."

He grinned. It did bug her, and that was refreshing. It made her seem more human, less perfect. "So, when are you going to Atlanta?"

She considered a minute. "I guess I'll have to wait until a week from Monday. I can't go next week. It's scheduled down to the minute. And Lou and I have to

attend the charity ball Friday night. That's a must."
Suddenly she stopped and snapped her fingers.
"Maybe we should take you with us."

"Me?"

"You'd make some really great contacts. It's black-
tie, but we could rent you a tux."

"Me at a black-tie affair? You gotta be kidding. I
wouldn't know how to act. I wouldn't know what to
say."

Paula brushed that off with a little wave of her
hand. "You say what everyone else does. When you
make eye contact with someone, just say, 'Hello. Nice
to see you again.' And you can bet your bottom dollar he or she will say, 'Nice to see you, too,' because
they won't remember whether they've seen you before or not."

She was really serious, Dane could see. He couldn't
have been more surprised...or appalled. "I really
would rather not," he said. "I might embarrass you,
and I'm sure I'd embarrass myself a dozen times before the night was over."

Paula considered that. If he really would be uncomfortable, making a few contacts might not be
worth it. Maybe she, Lou and Owen were enough for
now. "All right. If you feel that way. It was just a
thought." Getting to her feet, she drained her beer and
tossed the can into a nearby wastebasket. "Guess I'll
go see what Rona and Mitch are doing, and it won't be
long until dinner. Coming?"

Dane's empty can joined hers in the trash as he, too,
stood and followed her out of the studio.

THE ENSUING WEEK was like something out of a
storybook for Dane, although he kept looking over his

shoulder, waiting for the ax to fall. Paula talked to him about "challenge" and "stimulation" and seemed to be interested in what he thought, in what he wanted. That was a new one. In the past his relationships with women had been strictly physical, so he had no idea how to relate to one on this new level. He didn't even know how to be friends with a woman, and Paula seemed to want them to be friends.

Maybe she just had a soft spot in her heart for impoverished waifs. Maybe he'd never figure her out. He wondered why he didn't stop trying. Why couldn't he just relax, enjoy the days as they came and stop thinking about tomorrow?

Then Lou stopped by Tuesday night with the news that Owen Brewster was in the process of setting up a recording date, so Dane and his manager holed up for a couple of hours, working on an arrangement of "Tears I've Shed in Vain." Justin's original, recorded in 1958, was smooth and ballady, an early crossover hit. But crossover no longer was the thing. Everyone wanted "real" country, if there was such a thing, so Lou decided they should add twin fiddles, plenty of steel guitar and do it upbeat. When Brewster himself called on Friday afternoon to say the recording session had been set for the following Wednesday, Dane, at last, let himself believe, that maybe, just maybe, it all might actually happen.

But as head spinning as these experiences were, one was even more so: he had been allowed access to a world he wouldn't have dreamed of in his wildest flights of fancy, and those who had allowed it had done so as if it were the most natural thing in the world. Mitch, Rona, the servants—all treated him as if he'd lived there for years. It was never far from his mind that he owed every bit of it to Paula. And he was just as aware that it all could end as quickly as it had begun.

Still, he was only human. Though he didn't want to let his guard down completely, he felt the first twinges of excitement begin to spew inside him like a geyser. When Paula got home Friday evening, Dane all but collided with her in the foyer. "Brewster called," he announced. "Wednesday's the day."

Her face broke into a delighted smile. "Oh, Dane, that's wonderful! Didn't I tell you Lou could make things happen?"

"I think you're more responsible than anyone."

"I didn't do much, not really." She idly glanced through the mail, favored him with another dazzling smile and headed for the stairs. Dane detained her by placing a hand on her arm.

"Look, I've been here over a week, and I haven't spent so much as a dime of that three hundred, so... what say you let me take you out to dinner to-night... to celebrate?"

She sighed ruefully. "That would be fun, but I can't. The charity ball, remember?"

He stepped back; a mask fell over his face. "Oh, yeah, I forgot."

Paula hated disappointing him. Actually, she would have genuinely enjoyed having dinner with him, but she doubted he believed that. "Another night. Give me a rain check."

"Sure."

She glanced at her watch. "Oops, I'd better get a move on. Lou's picking me up at seven, and I need a major overhaul. Maybe I'll see you before I leave."

Ah, what the hell? Now he felt foolish for even asking her to go out to dinner with him. Paula was the kind of woman who went to charity balls. Dane shoved his hands into the pockets and ambled down the hallway to the den. No one was there. He looked out the big picture window to the gardens where Mitch and two yardmen had been working earlier, but he saw no one. Rona, he knew, was still working in the office, and he didn't want to disturb her. There didn't seem to be a damned thing for him to do. This was the time of day he usually spent with Paula, and though he hated admitting it, he missed rehashing his day with her. He finally went into his room to morosely wait for dinner.

The meal was delicious, as usual, but Paula didn't join them. When he inquired about her, Rona informed him that the ball also included a sit-down dinner for hundreds. Then, just as the three of them were leaving the dining room, the doorbell rang, and Lou, resplendent in his tuxedo, was ushered into the house. Rona whistled appreciatively as she swept past him. A moment later, Lou uttered the same sound as his eyes rose to the head of the stairs. Dane turned, and his mouth fell open. Paula was coming.

He'd never seen anything so gorgeous in his life. She was wearing a floor-length rose-colored gown, cut something like a Grecian toga. Her hair had been done in an elaborate cluster of plump ringlets that were held back from her face, while tiny curled tendrils sprang loose here and there. A diamond teardrop fell from each earlobe. Dane realized he was gaping, but he couldn't help it. She was a vision.

He wanted badly to say something memorable, something profound that would make an impression on her, but he'd never been so tongue-tied. "You look...beautiful," he stammered.

"Why, thank you, Dane," she said with another of those stunning smiles.

"You really do, Paula," Lou agreed, stepping toward them. "Heads are going to be turning tonight."

Over one arm Paula carried a short cape that matched the dress. She held it out to Lou, and he draped it around her shoulders—but not before she turned, giving Dane a glimpse of a startling amount of her creamy smooth back. The dress swooped down to only inches above her waistline. Though demure in front, the garment was damned provocative from behind. Watching the appreciative expression on Lou's face did something odd to Dane's stomach, and he wondered if there was more than friendship between Paula and her late husband's friend.

Now Dane wished he had agreed to go with them. He would have felt as out of place as cabbage in a rose garden, and he probably would have made a complete ass out of himself before the evening was over, but it might have been worth the risk. At least he could have spent the night looking at Paula.

It was too late for that now, though. Paula and Lou were making their exit. Once the two party goers had swept grandly out of the house, Dane prowled like a caged tiger, itching to do something after eight days of living like a Mormon missionary. Since arriving, he had been out of the house exactly twice, both times to run errands with Mitch. He had lived a more exciting life back home. He was in Nashville, for Pete's sake! Out there was a city where one could walk into almost any eating and/or drinking establishment and hear music being made, some of it by tomorrow's stars, and so far the only music he'd heard had come from himself or Justin's recordings. Resolutely, he went in search of Mitch.

"Did you mean it when you said I could use your car anytime I wanted to?" he asked the big man. Mitch's blue Camaro seldom got driven. If he and Rona went somewhere together, they went in her Buick. While working, Mitch usually used a white pickup that had belonged to Justin.

"Sure, help yourself. You've got a driver's license, right?"

"Right. I just thought I'd like to hear some music being made by someone other than myself for a change."

"You won't have to go far for that." Mitch heaved himself out of the chair. "I'll get the keys." Returning a minute later, he handed the keys to Dane and said, "There's a house key there, too. If it's music you're after, Justin used to be particularly fond of a place called Miller's. I hear it gets a little rowdy sometimes, but I guess you can handle that. Musicians like it because the audience tolerates anybody's music, at least for one song. I'll get a city map and show you where it is."

"Sure appreciate this, man. I'll top off the tank before I come home."

"Just bring it back without any new dents," Mitch said, then left to get the map.

A few minutes later, when Dane had been shown how to get to Miller's, he thought of something. "Say, would you like to come along? Rona, too, if she'd like."

"Thanks, but no thanks," Mitch said. "I lost my taste for nightlife a long time ago, and Rona never did like it. You just go and have a good time."

"Okay, see you later."

Dane walked out the front door, stepped off the veranda and headed for the parked car in the driveway. The mere act of leaving the house, knowing he was going to do a little bar hopping and see something of Music City, U.S.A., should have eased the restlessness inside him, but it didn't. Today had been a momentous one for him. He actually was going to make a record; big shots in the music business were going to listen to *him* sing. What once had been only a tantalizing possibility, therefore unreal, now was within his grasp. He should have been whistling, kicking up his heels, singing... something. Where was the sheer elation?

He slid behind the wheel of the Camaro, shoved the key into the ignition, and it came to him. The person responsible for everything that was happening wasn't with him, and that took the edge off.

Dane gave a growl of self-disgust as he backed out of the driveway. *Not tonight, not any night, pal. Paula doesn't go bar hopping, and you don't go to charity balls. Best remember that.*

CHAPTER SIX

THE CHARITY BALL was one of the major social events of the year, so the turnout was tremendous. Tuxedoed gentlemen and gowned, bejeweled ladies thronged the ballroom, where sixty tables for eight had been set up. Photographers lurked everywhere. An army of white-coated waiters passed champagne and canapés. The ball represented the "other" Nashville at its swanky best.

After seeing and being seen, Paula and Lou slipped away to a relatively quiet corner. Paula plucked a canapé from a passing waiter's tray while Lou lifted two flutes of champagne. "So, how's the boy wonder been this week?" he asked as he handed Paula one of them.

"Dane?" She smiled. "Like a kid turned loose in a candy store one minute, suspicious as the devil the next."

"I'm going to do some big things with that fella, provided he cooperates."

"He will," Paula said decisively. "I'll see to it."

Lou frowned slightly. "He's not a kid, Paula. You're not dealing with raw clay there. He's bound to have some firmly ingrained ideas and habits, things are not easily gotten rid of. You don't have time to hover over him like a mother hen, and he'd probably balk if you did."

"I know. The life he's led doesn't breed submissiveness. But I sense that he's trying very hard. Sometimes I catch him studying us—our manners, the way we talk, the things we talk about. I seriously doubt that anyone has ever helped Dane in any way, so this is all new to him. I don't think he's really accepted that it's actually happening."

"How long do you intend letting him stay at the house?"

Paula sipped her champagne, looking at Lou over the rim of her glass. Slowly she lowered the crystal flute. "As long as necessary, I imagine. Why?"

Shrugging, Lou said, "Oh, no reason."

"Come on, Lou. What's on your mind?"

"Like I said, he's no kid."

It took a minute for Paula to digest his meaning. "I hope you're not worried that my virtue will be compromised."

"He's a man."

Paula chortled delightedly. "And a decade younger than I am. What in the devil would he want with me when the woods are full of pretty young women?"

"Don't you have a mirror?"

"Lou, you have absolutely made my day." Slipping her arm through his, she gave him a little hug, then looked out over the sea of heads in the ballroom. "Maybe we should start trying to find our table. This is some crowd."

Lou reached into his pocket and removed a card he had been handed at the door. "Table three, not that that tells us much. We're sitting with Marty Oliver's party."

"Oh, wonderful! I haven't seen Marty in ages."

The nice-looking, baby-faced man rose to greet them, flashing a smile that had charmed millions. Marty Oliver was a certified country music superstar, the most famous of Justin's "finds." He was also one of Nashville's most solid citizens. Besides being a top-money performer, he and Owen Brewster owned Heron Records and a booking agency, and Marty's philanthropy was legendary. He was the kind of man the industry pointed to with pride when outsiders accused it of being populated by crazy airheads.

But what had most endeared Marty to Paula was his unswerving loyalty to Justin. He seized every opportunity to give Justin Steele full credit for his success, something not all of their ex-protégés still bothered to do. Paula greeted Marty and his wife, Alicia, warmly, then acknowledged the introductions made around the table. Lou was acquainted with everyone, while she knew none of them, though all were heavily involved in the music business. That served to make her realize just how out of touch she had become.

Lou rounded the table to sit beside Alicia, while Paula sat beside Marty. "What's this I hear about your unearthing a new singer?" he began.

"He's very good, Marty. I can hardly wait for you to hear him."

"Owen tells me he's going to do 'Tears.' Nobody's ever done that song as good as Justin did, though God knows, forty people have tried to."

"Dane's doing 'Tears' was Lou's idea...and you know how possessive Lou is when it comes to Justin and his songs."

"Mmm." Marty rubbed his chin. "This kid, this singer, doesn't have any problems, does he? Booze, drugs, that kind of thing?"

"I sure haven't seen any signs of it."

"That's good. Heron tied up a lot of time and money in Tommy Lord's career, only to see it washed away in a sea of Jack Daniel's."

"I don't think you'll have any problems with Dane. By the way, he's no kid. He's thirty-six."

"Where in hell's he been?"

As succinctly as possible, Paula told Marty everything she knew about Dane.

"If he hits it big, that'll be a great rags-to-riches yarn to feed the media. The fans love it when a new idol comes from the ranks of the impoverished.... Lord, you're a sight for sore eyes, Paula. Don't make yourself so scarce from now on. I miss you."

"You're a sweetheart, Marty. You always have been."

At that moment waiters swooped through the ballroom, distributing shrimp cocktails, and abruptly the food became the focus of everyone's attention. Paula thought about what Marty had said. Rags to riches in the entertainment industry had become such a cliché. She would much prefer Dane's publicity package to lean on another line.

Her thoughts braked. That was out of her hands, something for Lou to handle. She'd done all she could do for Dane, all she *should* do—more than she'd meant to do. Already she could detect in herself a twinge of possessiveness toward him and his career.

And that, my dear, she thought as she speared a shrimp, *is a no-no.*

ARMED WITH Mitch's directions, Dane had no trouble finding Miller's. It was the kind of place that had been around since three-digit phone numbers. A pool table and a long bar completely filled one wall. Tables for four were scattered helter-skelter throughout the huge room, and six ceiling fans put forth a valiant but losing effort to circulate the smoke-laden air. The menu on the sign behind the bar leaned heavily toward burgers and fried things. There was no stage, but an area off to one side was cleared, and a five-piece band was holding forth. As crowded as the place was on Friday night, Dane managed to find a stool at the bar. He ordered tap beer and settled back to listen.

The band's music was whiskey raw, gutbucket honky-tonk, the kind of thing Ernest Tubb and Hank Williams and Lefty Frizzell once had made *the* sound. Dane could have listened to it six days running. It got his blood flowing again. He listened to a couple of numbers, polished off his beer, then swiveled to order another. That was when he first saw the blonde seated on the stool next to him.

She must have just sat down, he thought, because there was no way in hell he could have missed her earlier. She was in her early twenties, he guessed, and she was built the way women were meant to be built. Her breasts strained against her lipstick-red T-shirt. She definitely fell in the "looker" category, with enough curly hair for two people, pouty lips and predatory eyes. She also wasn't shy. "Hi," she said.

"Hi."

"I'm Trudy."

"Hi, Trudy. I'm Dane." He signaled the bartender with a raised index finger.

"You come in here often, Dane?"

He shook his head. "First time."

"Where do you usually go?"

"I've only been in town a week."

"You a musician?"

"Yeah, guess you could say that."

Trudy's eyes rolled to the ceiling. "One of these days I'm gonna ask some guy in this town that question, he's gonna say no, and I'm just flat dab gonna fall down in a dead faint. Whaddaya play?"

"I sing."

Trudy's eyes rolled again. "You and every third guy I've met since I got here."

Dane grinned, shoved some money toward the bartender and picked up his fresh beer. "You got something against musicians?"

"Not really, but it sure would be nice to meet an insurance salesman or something."

"Aw, you wouldn't be sitting in a joint like this if you liked insurance salesmen." He noticed she wasn't wearing a ring, but a guy couldn't go by that. "You married?"

"Nope. Are you?"

"Nope. Engaged?"

"'Fraid not. Pretty single and pretty apt to stay that way, from the looks of things."

Then and only then did he feel safe in asking, "Can I buy you a beer?"

Trudy pretended to give it consideration. "I guess that'd be okay."

Dane signaled the bartender again, this time tapping the bar in front of Trudy.

"Don't suppose you're from around here," Trudy said.

"Nope. Alabama."

"No one's from around here. Did you ever notice that? You take a poll of this place, and everybody's from somewhere else and has written a song. Somewhere there has to be someone who was born and raised in Nashville."

Dane was beginning to feel congenial, and he wondered if Trudy would be worth cultivating for a night's diversion. He hadn't been with a woman in some time and was beginning to feel the itch. But hell, he couldn't keep Mitch's car out all night. Maybe just half the night. "Where are you from, Trudy?"

"Laurens, South Carolina. Nice place to be from, I guess. Lemonade on the front porch on summer nights. 'Skeeters a hummin' in the honeysuckle vine. A vegetable garden out back. Real nice. Lord, I wanted out of that town so bad I thought I was gonna die."

Dane smiled sympathetically and paid for Trudy's beer. "So, what brought you to Nashville?"

"My voice." Trudy snorted derisively. "Or so I thought. I was a pretty big deal in Laurens and surrounding towns. Sang in church, at weddings, at ball games. Lots of ball games. Football, baseball, basketball. I figure I've done 'The Star-Spangled Banner' more often than the Marine Corps Band. But singers like me are a dime a dozen in this town. I'm beginning to think you're better off getting discovered someplace else and then coming here." She indicated the band with a toss of her head. "Whaddaya think of that bunch?"

Dane swiveled to give the band his attention once again. They were finishing a rollicking Cajun holler. When they were done, the fiddle player swung into "Orange Blossom Special." The crowd began to whistle and stomp. "Damned good, seems to me" was his verdict.

Trudy sighed. "I hope so."

"Why?"

"'Cause the drummer's my boyfriend."

Dane blanched slightly. Scratch Trudy. "I thought you said you were unattached."

"You asked me if I'm married or engaged," she reminded him. "And I said no, which is the livin' truth. But if the band makes it big, Lonny says he's gonna marry me. If that happens, I'll send you a telegram."

Dane felt an instant communion with Trudy. She had no illusions about life, love or anything else. They were birds of a feather, kindred souls. "Well, when I hit it big, maybe I càn give them a leg up. Then you can have your vine-covered cottage...or whatever it is you want."

"Sure. Of course," Trudy said with a smirk. "You've been in town a whole week, so your big break ought to come along any day now."

Dane couldn't resist doing a little bragging. "As a matter of fact, I'm making my first record next week."

"Come on. Tell me another one."

"It's a fact. Of course, I had a little help. A lady I know introduced me to somebody important."

Trudy looked skeptical. "Who?"

"I don't think I ought to tell you that."

"Sure, I understand," she scoffed. Still, she looked interested. Maybe she thought he just might be telling her a little bit of truth. "You any good?"

"That lady I was telling you about seems to think so."

"I was talking about your voice."

"So was I."

The band chose that minute to take a break, and the drummer homed in on Trudy. He was a tall man who wore a black cowboy hat and sported a drooping auburn mustache. He reminded Dane of an extra in a Western movie.

"Wheredya get the beer, sugar?" the drummer asked Trudy.

"This gentleman here was nice enough to buy it for me."

She could have talked all night without saying that, Dane thought ruefully. The look the drummer shot him was downright hostile. The way to handle this, he decided, was to be puppy dog friendly. "Hi," he said, sticking out his hand. "I'm Dane Markham."

"Lonny Sloane." He took the offered hand, but his expression didn't warm perceptibly.

"Nice to meet you, Lonny. Trudy was just telling me about you." Dane turned to signal for another beer. "How about letting me buy you one, too?"

"No, thanks," Lonny said. "I never drink while I'm working."

"That makes you a mite unusual in the world of music, doesn't it?"

Lonny's expression turned menacing. "Listen, friend, I'd appreciate it kindly if you didn't buy Trudy no more beer. She has a problem with the stuff, you know."

Trudy, in unladylike fashion, kicked Lonny in the shin. "Don't be such a jerk, Lonny. The only 'problem' I've got is you're too cheap to buy me more than a couple."

Lonny ignored her, keeping his eyes squarely on Dane. "I'd also appreciate it if you'd go sit somewhere else."

Actually, nothing would have pleased Dane more than to go sit somewhere else, but he'd be damned if he was going to do it to please Lonny. "Guess I must have missed seeing the reserved sign on this stool."

Trudy punched Lonny on the arm. "Don't be such a jerk. You oughta get friendly with Dane. He's only been in town a week, and he's already got a recording session set. How long have you and the band been here? You still don't have one."

Dane fervently wished Trudy would go powder her nose or something. She was baiting her boyfriend, which wasn't doing a thing for the man's disposition.

Lonny glared at Dane. "You don't say? After only a week, huh? Who're you cuttin' it for, friend?"

"Heron," Dane said tersely.

"He knows somebody important," Trudy offered.

Lonny's eyes never left Dane's. "Who?"

"That, pal, is none of your business."

Lonny snorted and turned to Trudy. "Sugar, you gotta be the dumbest broad I've hooked up with in some time. That's the oldest line in the book."

A prickling sensation began at the nape of Dane's neck and spread. Slowly he swiveled to face Lonny squarely. "Are you calling me a liar?"

"No, I'm calling you a damned liar."

Dane knew discretion was the better part of valor. He also knew he had little to lose by ignoring the taunt and getting the hell out of here. After all, he was acquainted with not a soul on the premises, while Lonny no doubt knew many. He'd never see the blonde or the drummer again, so what difference did it make that his integrity had been challenged?

Anger, however, clouded his judgment, and discretion was something Dane had seldom practiced. His fist cracked across Lonny's chin as he came up from the stool.

A four-year-old could have predicated what happened next. Dane found himself surrounded by the other members of the band, and more punches were exchanged. The bartender, who also happened to own the joint, saw Dane strike the first blow. Having recently paid the bills resulting from another Friday night fracas, he didn't hesitate to pick up the telephone. The police dispatcher located a patrol car only a block away. To Dane's utter consternation, he quickly found himself a guest of the City of Nashville. The charge: creating a public disturbance and resisting arrest. A humorless desk sergeant informed him he could make one phone call after the requisite hours in jail.

Dane gave serious thought to staying in jail rather than making that phone call, but after a couple of hours he changed his mind. He hated it more than he'd ever hated anything, but there was only one person he could call.

PAULA WAS LIVID! She had been home and asleep for an hour when the call came. She grabbed for her bedside phone before the ringing could wake the entire household, then listened in disbelief as Dane poured out his story. Dressing hastily, she started downstairs, only to encounter Mitch coming up.

"What's up? Who was on the phone?" he asked.

"Dane. He's in jail. Seems he got in a fight in some bar."

"Great. Just great. I'll go bail him out."

"I'll go, too. You'll have to drive your car home since I have no idea what condition Dane's in. He didn't sound drunk, but you never know."

Together they drove to the police station. Once Paula paid the fine and bailed out her bedraggled boarder, they rounded up Mitch's car, still parked near Miller's. Mitch drove it, and Dane slumped dejectedly in the passenger seat of Paula's Mercedes. The only outward sign of his encounter with the boys in the band was a cut over his right eye and an angry red splotch on his chin. The wounds to his pride, however, went deeper. To have Paula bail him out of jail was the ultimate humiliation.

Paula was too furious to even talk to him, but by the time they got home, she had found her voice. Dane had been hoping the confrontation he knew was coming would wait until morning, but no such luck. When Mitch walked off to return to his room, Paula said, "Dane, come into the den. I want to talk to you."

Sighing resignedly, he turned to follow her.

"Sit down," she said, her mouth pinched into a tight line, her eyes snapping.

"I'd rather stand, if you don't mind."

"I do mind. Sit down!"

He sat, as docilely as a schoolboy summoned before the principal.

Paula looked away for what seemed forever but could only have been a minute or two. When she finally spoke, she struggled to keep her composure. "First of all, were you drunk?"

"Hell, no! I only had a couple of beers."

"I can't tell you how disappointed I am in you."

"It wasn't my fault!"

"Did you or did you not throw the first punch?"

"The jerk called me a damned liar."

"Oh, God!" Paula raked her fingers through her hair. "So you had to defend your honor regardless of the consequences?"

"Where I come from, any man who calls another man a liar expects to get decked."

Paula's composure gave up the fight. "This isn't where you came from! This isn't rural Alabama! You can't go around punching anyone who says something you don't like." She took a deep breath. "What brought on tonight's altercation in the first place?"

"I bought a lady a beer. Her boyfriend didn't like it. Or maybe he didn't like the way I comb my hair. I don't know what his problem was. I was trying to be friendly."

"Aren't you smart enough to know not to cozy up to a strange woman in a bar without first determining if there's a husband or boyfriend on the premises?"

"Hell, yes! I established that she wasn't married or engaged. She…didn't tell me about the boyfriend until it was too late. Paula, I was just minding my own business, having a couple of beers and listening to some music. For that I wind up in jail. Go figure it."

"Oh, Lord, this will probably be in tomorrow's paper," Paula said, more to herself than to Dane. "Let's just hope neither Lou nor Owen sees it." Sighing tiredly, she walked to Dane, her arms folded across her breasts. "You're a step away from the big time—do you realize that? A step! Lou and I told you the first night you were here that you were going to have to work your butt off and keep your act clean. Do you want success, Dane? Do you?"

He simply stared at her a minute. "Yeah," he finally said. "Yeah, I want it."

"Then from now on you're going to be a model of exemplary behavior. And so help me God, if you ever pull another stunt like tonight's while you're in this house, I'm washing my hands of you and telling Lou to do the same. All of us went through one experience with a talented but thoroughly unmanageable singer, and we won't do it again. Is that clear?"

"Yes, ma'am," he said sarcastically. There wasn't a doubt in Dane's mind that she would do exactly as she said. "But I wish you would understand that I didn't go in that place with any thought of making trouble. I was . . . a victim of circumstance."

"Maybe. And maybe you should stay out of places like that. Trouble just seems to find some people, and you might be one of them."

Dane wondered if she was right. Looking back over his life, he seemed to have been in trouble at least half of it, but it had come looking for him, not the other way around. He'd never gone out looking for anything but a good time . . . or just something to take his mind off his bleak existence.

"Now, I'm going to be gone most of next week," Paula said. "Can I trust you?"

"Yeah, you can trust me. Hell, Paula, I didn't do anything tonight."

"Nothing except get thrown in jail!" she snapped, then took a deep breath. "Never mind. What's done is done. We'll just forget this happened. Get some sleep."

Thank heaven for small favors, Dane thought. Getting to his feet, he headed for the stairs.

"Good night," Paula called after him.

He stopped and turned. "Believe it or not," he said contritely, "I'm really sorry about this."

"I believe you. I don't think you went out looking for a fight. But don't be so quick with your fists from now on. Stop and ask yourself what you actually proved." Paula's voice softened. "Dane, the popular conception of the Nashville music scene is that it's one big happy family, a lot of good ol' boy folksiness wrapped up in a southern drawl, but nothing could be further from the truth. There's an establishment here, men like Lou and Owen Brewster and Marty Oliver, and they want performers who will play by their rules. I'm not saying you can't be successful without them. Some big names are, but they usually find they have to make their music somewhere other than Nashville. It'll be a whole lot easier for you to be a success in this town if the establishment is in your corner. Attaining stardom is one thing—maintaining it is something else." She squared her shoulders. "We won't mention tonight again."

Dane nodded numbly and headed for the stairs again. Paula stared after his departing figure. When he had disappeared from sight, she turned off the lights and went upstairs to her own room. Shrugging out of her clothes, she slipped her gown over her head and crawled back in bed, only to lie awake and stare at the ceiling.

She felt like a parent who wanted to believe her kid was only high-spirited, not the hell-raiser everyone accused him of being. It came to her with something of a start that she was going to be the most disappointed person alive if Dane turned out to be too undisciplined for success. She wanted him to hit it big—she hadn't known how much she wanted it until tonight. But she certainly didn't know why she wanted it so much. Perhaps it had something to do with protecting her own credibility with Lou and Owen and Marty.

Or perhaps the reason was something more complex. She had begun to like Dane, to like having him around. Oh, he still had a small chip on his shoulder, but it had slipped a bit. If he still harbored wariness and distrust, he had learned how to hide his feelings. He was unassuming, unimpressed with himself, charmingly wry at times. His humor was self-effacing. He often made remarks about his unfunny past that were downright hilarious, and the remarks always poked fun at himself. Mitch and Rona liked him; Paula would have known if they hadn't. There were people who were easy to be around, and Dane had seemed to be one of them. Paula hated thinking that perhaps her judgment was way off base, that he wasn't the person he'd seemed to be at all.

But everyone deserved a second chance, and she intended giving Dane one. One, that was all.

DANE FRANKLY DREADED the next day. He half expected to be sent packing and was trying to decide where he would go if that happened. So he couldn't have been more surprised when, at breakfast, Paula said, "You've been here all this time and haven't seen any of the things people come to Nashville to see. Would you like me to give you the grand tour?"

She certainly was one peculiar lady. Last night might never have happened. "Well..." He gulped. "Sure."

Like most inhabitants of cities that other people save all year to visit, Paula took Nashville's attractions for granted. She'd never considered spending a day seeing the Ryman Auditorium, where the Grand

Ole Opry had originated, or Printers' Alley or Music Row, but that day she did all of it. The sight-seeing was fun for her because Dane enjoyed it so much. When hunger struck, Paula took him to a hole-in-the-wall café that served things like country ham, squash casserole and fried okra. Then the afternoon was devoted to the Country Music Hall of Fame and Museum.

The last time Paula had been there was when Justin was inducted into it. She and Dane spent hours going from Merle Haggard's pardon from prison to Elvis's gold Cadillac, and somewhere in between, Dane decided he easily could have spent a week in the place. Paula thoroughly enjoyed it, too, and made a silent vow to come back more often—even though she knew she probably wouldn't.

Time flew. A visit to Opryland was out of the question that day, but on the way home Paula had an idea. "Would you like to see my office?" she suddenly asked.

Dane didn't care where they went or what they did. He was just having a good time. "Sure."

The building that housed the corporate offices of Hamilton House, Incorporated, Southeastern Division, was impersonally modern, perhaps a tiny bit more attractive than most structures. But Paula's own executive suite looked less like an office than anything Dane could imagine. There was a desk, but the focal point of the big room was a long table around which stood eight lambskin-upholstered chairs. Apparently that was where Paula liked to hold her staff meetings, a far cry from the usual austere conference room. In one corner were two fawn-colored sofas, both of them strewn with print pillows. A lacquered coffee table sported a stunning silk flower arrangement and several glass figurines. Vertical blinds covered the room's six windows, and tall mirrors made the office seem larger than it actually was.

"Whew!" Dane exclaimed. "You work here all day and then go home to that mansion at night. I guess you don't know the meaning of the word *tacky*."

Paula laughed. "Vanessa always encouraged us—by 'us' I mean the six vice presidents—to furnish our offices the way we would furnish our houses. I've noticed that the men stick with a more businesslike look, but this feels like my office, not the vice president's office."

Dane strolled around the room, studying the paintings and accessories, while Paula sat on one of the sofas and watched him. He clearly was impressed by all the subdued elegance. He stopped at her desk and stared at the three framed photos of herself and Justin. Then he picked up the model of Justin's private plane, fingering it carefully. "Your husband's?" he asked.

"Yes, the manufacturers presented that model to him the day the plane was delivered. We logged many an air mile in that."

"You traveled with him?"

"When I could."

"Where's the plane now?" Dane asked, setting the model back in place.

"I gave it to the pilot."

Dane looked at her incredulously. "You gave it to the pilot?"

"Yes. His dream was to start his own charter service, and I knew he'd have a hard time affording the first plane. I thought he, more than anyone, would appreciate having Justin's plane. After all, he knew it inside and out.''

Dane shook his head in disbelief, although nothing he learned about Paula's generosity really surprised him anymore. Crossing the room, he sat on the other sofa, where he could face her. "You know, I can't imagine living with someone twenty weeks, much less twenty years. But I really can't imagine what it would be like when that person suddenly was gone.''

Paula studied a fingernail. "No one can tell you what that's like, Dane, not unless you've experienced it personally... and then no one has to tell you.''

"Do you mind talking about Justin?''

"No, no, I don't. Not at all.''

"He was such a larger-than-life figure to those of us who loved his music. What was he really like?''

"Kind,'' Paula said simply. "A very gentle man. I've known a lot of stars, but Justin behaved less like one than any of them. He was living proof that nice guys don't always finish last. He often was billed as Gentleman Justin Steele, and the label fit him to a T.''

"He died of a heart attack, didn't he?''

Paula nodded. "He took ill on the golf course. It was sudden—completely unexpected since he'd never had any heart trouble. Still, he was sixty-four and hadn't led the most prudent life, certainly not in his younger years. I guess he did his fair share of hell-raising before he married Marjorie, and maybe a bit of it after she died. During the last seven or eight years of his life, all of us tried to get him to change his ways, but he cooperated only to a point. He would drink two cocktails instead of four and eat whatever Martha set before him—for maybe two weeks. Then he'd balk. He'd say something like, 'My daddy never ate a can of tuna packed in water in his life, and he lived to be ninety!' Of course, he conveniently forgot to mention that his daddy worked like a pack mule until he was in his late seventies and never touched a drop of alcohol.''

Paula smiled fondly at the memories. Then she regarded Dane solemnly. ''Keep that in mind. If Justin had mended his ways when he was your age, he'd still be alive today.''

Dane's eyes narrowed. ''There you go again—talking to me like I was a kid.''

''Sorry. Maybe it goes with all this.'' Paula's arm made a sweep to indicate the office. ''I spend all day telling people what to do. I'll try to watch it from now on.''

''I don't mind it when you tell me what to do. I need that. But I do mind when you talk down to me. I don't consider myself your equal by any means, but I like to think we're at least contemporaries.''

Paula truly was dismayed. ''Good Lord, Dane, I never meant to talk down to you. And of course you're my equal. To think you aren't is absurd. And as for being contemporaries . . . well, you are a great deal younger. . . .''

''Not a great deal.''

''Ten years is quite a difference.''

''Nine,'' he corrected.

''That seems like a lot of years to me.''

''It isn't.''

Paula laughed and threw up her hands. ''Forget it. But don't forget to remind me if I ever start talking down to you again.'' Pushing herself to her feet, she said, ''I suppose we should head on home. It's getting late. Dinner will be ready soon, and there are several things I want to do before leaving tomorrow.''

"You have to leave tomorrow."

"Uh-huh. I want to be there first thing Monday morning."

"I'm . . . going to miss you." Dane sounded embarrassed to be saying it.

"Why, thank you, Dane," Paula said, truly touched. "Do you know something? I'm going to miss you, too." The incredible thing was, she meant that.

As they left her office, they passed her desk, and Dane once again looked at the photos of her and Justin. "Paula, do you think you'll ever remarry?"

The question took her by surprise. "I don't know. I'm certainly not adverse to the idea."

Dane stepped ahead to hold the door for her. As Paula started to go through it, she paused and looked up at him. "You never married, did you?"

"No. I never had anything to offer a woman."

"Did you ever come close?"

He shook his head and grinned. "Back home the ladies didn't exactly consider me a good catch."

"What a shame they weren't perceptive enough to look below the surface. You can be very charming, you know. Those ladies don't know what they missed."

It was a lighthearted remark. Paula couldn't possibly have known the impact it had on Dane. To receive a compliment like that from a true lady like her sent his pulse racing. He had to fight to keep the smile of satisfaction off his face. He felt he'd reached a landmark today—the first fragile beginnings of a true friendship with this classy lady. He didn't even known why it meant so much to him to have Paula accept him. He didn't know how to nourish and foster such a friendship so that it would grow. All he knew was, he felt damned good.

And Paula felt wonderful. The day had been one of those rare interludes when everything was fun, and Dane had proved to be the nicest kind of companion. She had gotten tiny glimpses of his shy charm, an eagerness to please and a southern-gentleman kind of courtliness. He called every woman he didn't know "ma'am," and he was a great opener of doors and holder of chairs. His kidlike enthusiasm during their tour of the Hall of Fame had been contagious. Could a person change so much in such a short time? The wary stranger with the cold eyes she had encountered on the Alabama riverbank seemed to have vanished altogether. Her faith in Dane had been restored.

Happily, so had her faith in her own judgment. She truly regretted having to leave town, but then, she always did. The travel was one of the few aspects of her job that Paula disliked. Airline service taxed her patience to the limit. Even the finest hotels and restaurants lost their appeal very quickly. No matter how artfully packed, clothes out of a suitcase never felt or looked right, somehow. The homebody in her always longed for her own house, her own bed, her own familiar things.

But this time her reluctance to leave was more pronounced than ever. Of course, she was going to Atlanta to handle an unpleasant chore, but that was only part of it. What she regretted most was being gone Wednesday. After giving Dane his chance at the brass ring, she wouldn't even be with him the day he made his first record. Somehow that just didn't seem right.

CHAPTER SEVEN

PAULA WENT TO ATLANTA hoping that the restaurant's problems wouldn't prove to center on Russell Powell, the manager there. She liked Russ, and he had done a great job for years. But she couldn't afford to be sentimental. She was determined to straighten out Atlanta before Vanessa had to call her on the carpet.

Given her ability to sift through the trivial and get right to the heart of problems, Paula had barely been in the restaurant two hours Monday morning before she zeroed in on the source of its troubles: Freddie LaCosta, the head chef.

A temperamental artist who had trained in France, Freddie had come to Hamilton House from a stint as assistant chef at a swanky Boston restaurant, and he expected to do things his own way. Hamilton House policy was to encourage chefs to be innovative, provided the innovations fell squarely within the context of what Vanessa Hamilton wanted, and what she wanted had been decided years before. The word *yuppie* hadn't been invented when Vanessa determined that her restaurants would appeal to the twenty-five to forty set, people who were young, successful, had disposable incomes and followed food trends and fads. Through the years Hamilton House had happily embraced nouvelle cuisine, the Tex-Mex explosion, the

Cajun craze and the grill-everything phenomenon, and the patrons flocked to the restaurants.

Freddie, on the other hand, wanted classic cuisine, with its elaborate concoctions and complex sauces. He balked at the simplest instruction or restriction, and when Freddie balked, everything else—the food, the service, the patrons—became secondary. Paula briefly wondered why Russ couldn't manage him better, but after observing the chef in action for two days, she realized that King Solomon himself would have had a difficult time managing Freddie. On Tuesday night, after the dinner crowd had thinned out, she and Russ had dinner off his desk in the manager's office and talked about it.

"Russ, I guess you know that Freddie might have to be sent packing," she said.

"I hope we don't have to do that, Paula. I hate to say this since the man infuriates me half the time, but Freddie really is a genius in the kitchen."

"But if he's a disruptive influence, he'll have to go. I actually saw him threaten one of the waiters with a meat cleaver. The poor man was terrified, and terrified waiters seldom give good service. The restaurant's reputation is suffering, and I can't have that. You've got to take charge of him."

Russ sighed. "Chefs! The bane of my existence. If they're good, they become prima donnas. If they're so-so, they can't summon the excitement necessary to turn out the kind of food Vanessa wants. When I first got into the business, I thought hiring and keeping good waiters would be the chief personnel problem, but I was wrong. It's those damned chefs. All most of them can think about is opening their own restaurant anyway, so what do they care about the fate and fortunes of Hamilton House?''

"There's not a manager in the organization who doesn't have the same gripe, Russ. I'm going to have a long talk with Freddie before I go back to Nashville, but if he doesn't shape up, can I trust you to get rid of him? I noticed the assistant chef seems bright and eager to learn. Well trained, too. Perhaps he could take over.''

Russ groaned. "He's only twenty-five. He's too young to take over a large kitchen.''

"How old is Freddie?''

"Thirty-four.''

"He acts eighteen sometimes," Paula said pointedly.

"I know," Russ conceded. "All right. Have your talk with him, and if it doesn't do any good, I'll let him go. I suppose I can do the cooking if it comes down to that.''

Paula smiled. "I know it's tough. No one likes to fire anyone, but something has to be done about those customer comments or Vanessa will let both you and me go.''

Russ looked up from the veal piccata he was devouring with such relish. "That reminds me—what do you hear from the home office these days?''

"From Dallas! Nothing. I haven't talked to Vanessa in a couple of weeks, and I rarely have occasion to talk to anyone else. Why?''

"No juicy gossip?''

"At the risk of sounding immodest, Russ, I'm a little too high up on the ladder to hear much company gossip, juicy or otherwise.''

"Well, this tidbit comes from pretty high up the ladder, too. To be specific, from the office of Dolph Wade."

Paula's eyes widened slightly. She didn't want to appear eager in front of Russ, but she was interested. Dolph Wade was executive vice president, number two in command. He had started out with Vanessa and Stuart Hamilton all those many years ago, and now that Stuart was gone, Vanessa relied heavily on Dolph. It was generally assumed he one day would be the company's C.E.O. Paula had been with Hamilton House too long not to be interested in anything that happened in the upper echelons. One never knew when office politics might affect one's own position. "What about Dolph?" she asked nonchalantly.

Russ pushed his plate away and folded his arms on the desk. "You heard about the buy-out offer from Barrington International, of course."

"Of course. I gave it maybe three minutes' thought. I knew Vanessa would never sell the company."

"It seems Dolph encouraged her to do just that."

"Dolph? Come on, Russ. That doesn't make sense. Dolph knows Vanessa better than anyone. Who did you hear this from?"

"Mary Linden."

Paula scoffed. "Mary has the biggest mouth in the company. Who needs a newsletter when Mary has a telephone at her elbow?" Yet, she thought, Mary was Dolph's secretary and had been for years. She might be an incurable gossip, but she was usually right on top of everything that went on at Hamilton House, chiefly because she made it her business to be so. "I can't believe Dolph would advise Vanessa to sell out. What could he have been thinking of?"

"Don't ask me, but scuttlebutt has it that Vanessa is, to put it mildly, steamed...maybe to the point of giving Dolph the heave-ho. They no longer speak, and Dolph's nervous."

"Good grief." Paula thought about that a minute, then shook her head. "No, Vanessa would never get rid of Dolph just because he gave her advice she didn't want to hear. He would have had to do something more than that."

"Maybe he did." There was a pause before he added, "How do you think you would like living in Dallas?"

"What?"

"Face it, Paula. Vanessa's nearly eighty. She's always seemed indestructible, but no one is. If Dolph really is out of the picture, she's going to have to name her successor. Why not you?"

Paula waved that aside with a grin and a flourish of her hand, but a light flashed inside her head. Assuming the gossip proved to be true, assuming Dolph wouldn't be the next C.E.O., Russ was right—Vanessa would personally choose her successor. The woman was far too protective of her business empire to leave its future to chance. And in the corporate chain of command, the six division vice presidents were immediately under Dolph. At the home office, everyone else was too specialized. Out in the field, the V.P.'s were supposed to have the big picture. She slowly sipped her wine, pretended to savor it, then set down the glass. "This wine is excellent," she said. "Let me see that bottle again. New to the list, didn't you say?"

Thus Paula easily steered the conversation in another direction, but later that evening, back in her hotel room, she thought of it again. A corporate shake-up was something she wouldn't have imagined in her wildest dreams. Vanessa had always run such a tight ship. Paula had guessed the company would change hands with no more of a ripple than the United States changed presidents—and with a tenth as much fanfare. But Dolph's fall from grace would send shock waves throughout the entire organization.

What could he possibly have done? More than display poor judgment—Paula would bet on that. More than give unwanted advice. Vanessa wasn't a hard-nosed matriarch who tolerated no opinion but her own. Poor judgment would earn Dolph nothing but a slap on the wrist, but if he had been disloyal in any way, he could hang it up. Vanessa prized loyalty above everything, even competence.

Paula made a valiant effort to push aside all thoughts of what might happen, but human nature intervened. Giving in, she then thought of her colleagues—the other five vice presidents.

If she herself had to name Vanessa's logical successor, she would have chosen Roger Burroughs in Hartford. The oldest of the six, Roger had been a vice president the longest. But his very age could be a problem, as could his family. Their roots were deeply embedded in New England soil. His wife's ancestors had come over on the *Mayflower,* and the entire Burroughs clan was heavily involved in local and state politics. Somehow Paula couldn't picture Roger packing up and moving to Texas.

Sharon Carpenter in Kansas City was too new on the job. Hugh Reeves in Houston had already announced his retirement. But there was Grady O'Connor in Mississippi. Vanessa adored Grady, and Paula had to admit that Grady's innovative ideas had been invaluable to the company. Still, he was in charge of Hamilton House's vast agricultural operation, and he didn't look, act or think of himself as a businessman.

So that left Matt Logan in San Francisco...and herself. Paula had no trouble envisioning Matt sitting in Vanessa's chair. Handsome, sophisticated and ambitious, Matt looked the part of the C.E.O. He had everything going for him, including his fierce loyalty to Vanessa. Yes, Matt could very well be the one.

But, giving credit where it's due, so could I, Paula thought candidly. *Assuming, of course, that all this actually happens, which is assuming quite a lot on the strength of gossip.*

Until that night she'd never given a minute's thought to the top spot in the corporation. Dolph had always been the heir apparent, and everyone had known it. Now, however, until something was actually announced, until the rumors were proved true or false, she supposed she wouldn't be able to help thinking about it, at least occasionally.

THE NEXT DAY, Wednesday, Paula scarcely let Freddie out of her sight. She was unobtrusive about her surveillance, watching him out of the corner of her eye while pretending to be absorbed in other things, but nothing the chef did escaped her notice. She wanted to be fair, to give him every chance, but he was impossibly vain, close minded and tyrannical; he ran the kitchen like a serfdom. By the end of the dinner crush, she had determined that Freddie's days with them were numbered unless he got rid of his "I'm the star" attitude and adhered more closely to what Vanessa wanted.

She decided, however, that her talk with him would have to wait for the following day; Paula didn't want to linger at the restaurant that night. This had been Dane's big day, and she couldn't wait to hear how the session had gone. At eight o'clock she was back in her hotel room, reaching for the phone.

Rona answered the call. "Oh, hi, Paula. How are things going there?"

"Not too bad. Is Dane around?"

"Yeah, and he's cooking on all burners. Let me see if I can find him. He might have soared off into the stratosphere by now."

Paula guessed that meant things had gone well. She noticed he sounded out of breath when he came on the line.

"Paula?"

"How did it go?" she asked without preliminaries.

"The recording session?"

"*Of course* the recording session. I've been thinking about it all day."

"Lou said it was great."

"How did you feel?"

"Like a fifth wheel, if you want the truth. I was the only one there who didn't know what the hell he was doing. Well, maybe not the only one. The band Owen assembled had too many strings and too many backup singers. I swear, it looked like a damned choir. Lou spent half the morning trying to lose the strings and half the singers, which led to a gigantic argument with Owen—who's a heck of a nice guy, by the way."

"Yes, he is," Paula agreed, "and don't give the argument another thought. Lou and Owen argue half the time, anyway. It's the way they do business with each other."

"Then, when we were finally ready to start, another singer showed up and claimed he was supposed to have the studio today. Turns out there really had been a mix-up, so Lou and Owen left to find another studio. But all in all, I guess things went pretty good. Lou liked the results, and that has to count."

"In a big way. Oh, Dane, I have so many good feelings about this. I hated it that I wasn't there today."

"Yeah, so did I. Didn't seem right that you weren't. When will you be home?"

"Hopefully, tomorrow night. If not, early Friday."

A pause followed, then Dane said, "Paula, maybe we could do something Friday night. Let me take you to dinner. I know that's not much of a way to show my appreciation, but—"

She interrupted him. "I once told you that thanks aren't necessary, and they still aren't. I've been eating out since Sunday night. Do you know what I really want to do when I get home? Soak in my own tub, eat Martha's cooking, then maybe go down to the studio and listen to you sing and sing and sing."

"That'll be easy to arrange."

"You have no idea how much I'll enjoy it. Tell everyone there I miss them and can hardly wait to get home."

"Will do. Good night, Paula."

"Good night, Dane."

Paula replaced the receiver in the cradle and stood. Peeling off her clothes, she went to take a shower. She was beginning to wish she hadn't been in such a hurry to leave the restaurant earlier. It promised to be a long evening. She knew of few things she disliked more than solitary nights in hotel rooms; she was definitely a lousy traveler.

As she stepped under the shower's spray, an unexpected thought hit her: *What if you were president of Hamilton House?* Before age had slowed her, Vanessa had been on the go constantly, often making so many trips in a month that Paula wondered how she knew where she was half the time. And when she wasn't traveling or working, she was doing civic or charitable work, scheduling her life down to the second.

Had it all been necessary? Paula wondered. Probably. Little that was worthwhile in life was attained without sacrifice on the home front. Paula's life away from the office, on the other hand, had always been so unhurried and unstructured—just the way she liked it. As she lathered herself, then rinsed under the shower's stinging spray, she realized that she could barely remember living anywhere but Nashville. Leaving would be a wrenching experience.

Turning off the water, she smiled sheepishly. Who said she was going anywhere? Good grief, one tiny morsel of gossip and she was packing her bags! She was only one of six. Chances were good that one of the others would get the nod. Chances were even better that Vanessa would get over being miffed at Dolph, and things would go on as before. Her immediate concerns were getting her unpleasant little chat with Freddie over as early as possible tomorrow, then getting home. She could hardly wait to hear Dane tell her every single detail of what must have been an incredible week for him.

PAULA RETURNED HOME the following afternoon feeling pretty good about her mission to Atlanta. At least she knew Freddie understood a little better that Hamilton House food was fresh, light and lively, that if he wanted to cook with lots of butter, cream and sauces, he would have to do it somewhere else. Frankly, she doubted the chef would stick around long since he was passionately committed to classic French cuisine, so she had told Russ to intensify the young assistant's training. But all in all, she guessed she had accomplished what she had set out to do, although she wouldn't know how truly successful she'd been until she'd seen the next batch of customer comments.

She also returned home to the startling news that Dane's professional career was going to begin sooner than any of them had expected. One of the scheduled guests on the Friday night edition of the cable TV show *Today in Nashville* had been forced to cancel because of illness. The said guest was one of Lou's clients, so the agent had phoned the show's host, Tony Grant, and asked if Dane could fill in. Grant had said fine. Thus, tomorrow night the unknown singer was going to appear before millions. Paula found her protégé in a state of semishock, vacillating between heart-thumping excitement and mind-paralyzing terror.

Thrilled for him, she tried to put him at ease. "You were going to begin performing soon anyway, Dane. It just happened sooner than we thought."

"All those people!" was all Dane could say.

"Forget the people out in television land. Concentrate on the studio audience. It's not all that much larger than the bunch you used to sing for at The General Store. You've probably seen the show. You know how laid-back it is. Tony Grant can make anyone feel at home. Please try to relax and enjoy this.''

"Everything's happening so fast," Dane said, raking his fingers through his hair as he paced back and forth. "Too fast. I make my first record one day, and two days later I'm on *Today in Nashville*. I don't think my mind can adjust."

Paula smiled sympathetically. Had she been in his shoes, she was sure she would have felt shell-shocked, too, but she didn't want him to know that. "Sometimes it happens that way. The annals of the music business abound with fairy tales. I know one young man who was a fry cook one year, watching the Country Music Awards on a TV in the café's kitchen. The next year he was walking across the stage to receive the Horizon Award for the most promising new artist. All it takes is one record . . . or someone on the inside giving you the right shove."

"But . . . on the show . . . what do I say, what do I do?"

"Do your song, then answer Tony's questions truthfully. He'll probably ask where you're from, how you got to Nashville, that kind of thing."

"You don't mind if I mention you?"

"Not at all. I'll say it again—enjoy this. And thank your lucky stars."

Dane stopped his nervous pacing and fastened her with a look she couldn't interpret. "That's easy. I only have one."

"What?"

"You. You're my lucky star. So . . . thanks."

"Why, Dane . . . how nice." To Paula's amazement she actually felt a flutter or two in the region of her heart. The sensation was all the more peculiar for its unfamiliarity. She couldn't remember experiencing anything exactly like it. Since the relationship she and Justin had shared had not been of the heart-fluttering variety, maybe she never had.

Just as amazing to her was how glad she'd been to see Dane when she'd arrived home earlier. She hadn't realized how thoroughly he had ingratiated himself with her, with all of them. During dinner Paula noticed the camaraderie that had been established among Dane, Rona and Mitch. He might have lived with them for months instead of a couple of weeks. It occurred to her that when he was gone, Dane, more than any of the fledgling performers before him, would be missed.

AFTER DINNER it was decided that the first order of business was the way Dane would look on camera and in front of the studio audience. Paula went through his closet, inspecting every garment. "Starched jeans," she finally decided. "Starched shirt, too. This one." It was a long-sleeved cotton sport shirt, white with gray pinstripes. "A belt with a big silver buckle. Straw cowboy hat. Boots."

"I don't have any of those things," Dane protested.

Paula looked him up and down, measuring him. "You know, you're just about Justin's size. Maybe an inch taller, but that doesn't matter. What size shoe do you wear?"

"Nine D."

"You may have to wear two pairs of socks. I think Justin wore a nine and a half. Come on upstairs with me."

A lot of Justin's things had been stored in a walk-in closet in one of the spare bedrooms upstairs. Paula didn't know why she had kept so many things. She simply had stored them in the closet and forgotten about them. "Justin was a compulsive buyer," she told Dane. "I don't think he ever wore some of this stuff."

When she opened the closet door, Dane let out a little whistle. There must have been three dozen pairs of cowboy boots, none of them the garden variety, either. And at least as many hats filled both top shelves. After much consideration, they chose a hat and a pair of ostrich-skin boots that fit after a fashion. A belt was no problem. A dresser drawer yielded plenty of those. "What we want is your basic clean-cut young cattleman's look," Paula said authoritatively as they left the bedroom and went downstairs. "Go put these things on. Model them for me, so I can see if the look is right. There won't be time after I get home tomorrow afternoon."

Dane did a double take when he saw his reflection in the mirror. Could clothes really transform a person so much? He was still staring in disbelief at his image when Paula tapped lightly on his bedroom door and asked if he was ready.

"Yep. Come on in."

She entered the room, and he turned toward her, a sheepish grin on his face. Paula's eyes widened in appreciation and approval. "Oh, Dane," she breathed, placing a hand on her chest. "You look... wonderful!"

"Howdy, ma'am. Now if I just had a horse."

Paula crossed the room and placed her hands on his upper arms, looking him up and down for what seemed forever. "Yes...yes, it's perfect.

Just . . . perfect.'' She was a little taken aback by the effect he was having on her.

Just as Dane was stunned by the look on her face. No woman had ever reacted to the sight of him this way. He experienced the overwhelming urge to slip his arms around her waist and just hold her. The thought shook him, and when she left the room a minute later, he realized his heart was pounding so frantically it sounded like the beating of a hundred drums. He'd better watch it. One false step and he could be banished from this Eden. He had no business thinking about Paula the way he was thinking about her now.

FRIDAY EASILY QUALIFIED as the longest day of Dane's life. When Paula got home from work and took a good look at him, she worried that he might be a basket case by the time it was his turn in the spotlight. He picked at his dinner, and during the drive to the studio he was so quiet that she anxiously glanced sideways at him several times. Nothing she said could put him at ease. He was petrified. Fortunately, Tony Grant was capable of carrying on a thirty-minute conversation with a statue; if anyone could draw Dane out, Tony could.

The show aired from a studio at Opryland, Nashville's glittering amusement park. It was Tony Grant's task to give each of his guests a turn to shine, and he did that masterfully. He often reminded Paula of Walter Cronkite, though he was folksier, much more approachable. Mainly the host came across as the world's biggest country music fan, and he treated the guests on his show, newcomer and headliner alike, with courteous interest.

Usually, however, the show had at least one guest who was a bigger star than the others, someone who could dominate on the strength of his or her name alone. That night it was Dottie Crowe, currently Lou's most famous client, and there was nothing subdued about Dottie. She was all over the place in her tight leather pants and flowing blonde locks. Mild-mannered Justin and sophisticated Lou had created the flamboyant creature. Dottie had been a shy, almost mousy young woman of twenty-one with zero stage presence when they had taken her under their collective wing. They had chosen her songs, put together her band, taught her how to walk, talk and dress to please the fans. Now she was a seasoned pro who both startled and delighted fans with her lusty voice and outrageous clothes. Tonight, besides singing two songs, she traded wisecracks with Tony and with the audience, and in general made the evening hers.

Finally Dane was introduced. Paula thought she might have been more nervous than he was as she watched his debut on a backstage monitor, but his appearance went off beautifully. She had never worried about his talent—the man could sing!—but she had wondered how he would interact with an audience. Happily, he put forth just the right amount of humility and shy charm. The applause after his song was enthusiastic. Then Dane went to sit on the curved sofa next to Dottie, and Tony conducted a brief interview with him. Dane thoughtfully mentioned both Paula and Lou as being responsible for his being where he was.

At the very end of the show, Tony always asked his guests where they would be appearing in the near future. Dottie rattled off a month's worth of personal appearances. The spokesman for an up-and-coming country-rock group mentioned dates at several state fairs and a rodeo. When it was Dane's turn, he looked surprised and said, "I just made my first record. I'm not appearing anywhere."

Tony Grant, bless him, countered with, "I doubt you'll be able to say that much longer."

Paula went limp with relief when the credits finally rolled and Dane was walking toward her with a grin on his face as big as Tennessee. He was only a few feet away from her when Dottie Crowe herself approached, stopping him dead in his tracks.

"You've been signed by Lou Howard, is that right?" the star asked Dane.

"Y-yes, ma'am," he replied.

Dottie favored him with a dazzling smile. "And you don't have any appearances scheduled as yet?"

"No. Like I said, I'm new at this."

"Tell you what, Dane—the band and I are leaving on a five-city tour in a couple of weeks, and my opening act just got himself a headlining date. How would you like to open for me?"

Dane's mouth dropped, and he turned to Paula, eyes quizzing. She urged him with a nod of her head. Dane faced Dottie again. "I . . . er, Miss Crowe . . ."

"Dottie, please."

"Ah, Dottie . . . I just made my first record. I don't have a band or—"

"I have a band," Dottie cooed.

"I don't have an act."

"How many songs do you figure you know?"

"Oh . . . a couple hundred, I guess."

Dottie smiled. "Nine or ten will do."

Paula stepped forward and placed a hand on Dane's arm. "It's a wonderful opportunity," she said softly. "We can get you ready for it. You know we can. Look how far you've come already."

Dottie's expression altered and was replaced by a slightly frosty smile. "Hello, Paula."

Paula offered a cool smile of her own, as puzzled as always by Dottie's strange reaction to the sight of her. She couldn't imagine what there was about her that aggravated Dottie so, but something definitely did. Paula could count on the fingers of one hand the times the two of them had actually engaged in anything resembling conversation, but each time the same feeling had persisted: Dottie didn't like her. That didn't particularly disturb Paula, nor was it something she ever thought about, but she did think Dottie's animosity toward her was more than a little strange. They didn't even know each other. Maybe the source of it all was Lou. Dottie was terribly possessive of her manager, so maybe she resented his close friendship with Paula. If so, that was pretty ridiculous.

"Hello, Dottie," Paula said as pleasantly as possible. "You're looking well."

"Thanks. I understand the music world has you to thank for Dane."

"All I did was introduce him to Lou. You, more than anyone, should know what he can do for a performer." Paula hadn't meant it as a dig, but perhaps it had come out as one. She saw Dottie freeze, so she smiled and returned her attention to Dane. "Jump at this chance, Dane. It'll be a wonderful boost for you. You'll be seen by thousands of people."

He looked doubtful but nodded numbly. "I...okay, Paula, whatever you say. Thanks, Dottie. I appreciate this."

"Don't mention it," Dottie said, her smile returning. "I'll talk to Lou tomorrow and be in touch. Bye, Dane."

"Goodbye."

"Goodbye, Paula."

"Goodbye, Dottie."

Dottie swept out of the studio, trailed by her entourage, in a manner befitting her superstar status. Paula dismissed her without another thought, turning on Dane. "You were wonderful!" she enthused.

His smile was boyishly appealing. "God, I hope I didn't look as nervous as I felt."

"No, I was watching the monitor, and you were perfect. The audience was tuned in to you—I felt it."

It had been a memorable night. Things were galloping along, changing with breakneck speed. A lot of people were in Dane's future now—Lou, Owen, even Dottie Crowe. In fact, in the years to come, Paula thought, most people would probably only remember that he had begun his career as Dottie's opening act, so she would get the credit for discovering him. Which was fine. The only time Paula was ever mentioned in music circles anyway was as Justin Steele's widow, and vanity was not one of her shortcomings. She would always know who discovered him and so would Dane...she hoped. She also hoped he would turn out to be the kind of star Marty Oliver was—a solid citizen, a true gentleman who never forgot those who had helped him. She especially hoped he someday would extend the same kind of helping hand to a deserving unknown.

Impulsively—and Paula was not an impulsive person—she stepped closer, threw her arms around him and hugged him, managing to place a sound kiss on his cheek in the process.

Dane almost fell down. There had been a time in the not too distant past when he couldn't have envisioned a woman like Paula even speaking to him, much less touching him. He knew she was only reacting to the special energy of the night, that the gesture was prompted mainly by exuberance, but he responded strongly, without thinking. His arms went around her, and he buried his face in her sweet-smelling hair. He held her tightly for so long that she pulled back in astonishment. Confusion registered in both their expressions. Embarrassed, Dane released her abruptly, took her arm and led her out of the studio.

They barely exchanged half a dozen sentences on the way home. Dane was overcome with excitement, disbelief, gratitude and a dozen other emotions he couldn't give names to. He especially was overcome by the memory of having actually held Paula in his arms.

Paula, too, was preoccupied—aware of her accelerated heartbeat and shifting all too unusual sensations. She also was aware of the reason for those sensations. She chided herself for letting something as simple as a hug get to her, but she had to go back many, many years to remember the last time she'd felt, even fleetingly, a young man's firm body.

CHAPTER EIGHT

TWO WEEKS LATER, Vanessa Hamilton sat at her desk in the paneled study of her estate north of Dallas, studying the dozens of legal documents spread out before her. There were times when great wealth could be nothing but a nuisance, she thought. For months now, she and her attorney had been working on her revised will, yet scarcely a day went by that something new didn't occur to her. So many details. When one had a fortune and no heirs, it was difficult to choose the most worthy recipients of one's fortune. There were pet charities, of course. Local museums would receive her extensive art collection. Certain treasured friends would be remembered with certain treasured items. Then an estate sale would be held.

But the biggest treasure of all was the presidency of Hamilton House, Incorporated, and only she could decide to whom that plum would go.

Vanessa's eyes dulled as she thought of Dolph Wade, her once trusted associate, the man whom she long ago had chosen as her heir apparent. What a fool he had been to scheme behind her back, allowing avarice to cloud his judgment. One might grudgingly admire a clever schemer, but his chicanery had been astonishingly inept. He had chosen money over power and influence and would live to regret it. Dolph as yet was unaware that she had discovered his duplicity and had taken steps to circumvent it. She did not want him to know until she had named her successor. By then he would be powerless and of no further value to the company. Good riddance.

So back to the immediate. As shocked and hurt as Vanessa had been over Dolph's disloyalty, she had not allowed it to interfere with her work. She never allowed emotion to dictate her actions, and that had saved her from disaster many times in her long life. Months ago, immediately after discovering Dolph's scheme, she had determined that she would select the next president of Hamilton House from among her six vice presidents. Several months ago she had summoned Matt Logan from San Francisco to Dallas, and, frankly, she was tempted to choose Matt and be done with it. He was charming, sophisticated and a dedicated company man. He would make a capable, loyal C.E.O., and she was tired of the whole affair.

But fair was fair, and others were deserving, too. None was more deserving than Paula Steele in Nashville. Like Matt, she was capable, and her loyalty was unquestioned. Vanessa's eyes flicked to the calendar, then to her antique clock. Friday night. Monday morning was as good a time as any for a visit with Paula. She reached for the telephone.

DURING THE PAST TWO WEEKS Dane had become an integral part of Paula's daily routine. She seemed to have spent almost as much time on his career as on her own. Occasionally her thoughts had drifted to the home office, to what might or might not be transpiring, to what Vanessa might or might not be doing. But as the days passed without word from Dallas, she decided Russ's remarks had been nothing but unfounded rumor. Mostly she was concerned with Dane and the upcoming tour.

They learned from Lou that appearances were scheduled for Memphis. Little Rock, Oklahoma City, Amarillo and Albuquerque. Dottie no longer played the byways but stuck strictly to cities where large turnouts were guaranteed. Three of the upcoming concerts were already sold out. Every night after dinner, Paula and Dane holed up in the studio, working on the songs that would comprise his act, on his stage manner and dress, on everything. She was grooming him for stardom.

After having lived with Justin so long, after listening in on countless conversations between her husband and Lou, Paula was very knowledgeable. Perhaps she knew little about P&D and risk-reward ratios, but she knew the values, mores and peculiarities of the business that had made Nashville famous, and she tried to impart that knowledge to Dane.

Thanks to her efforts, Dane actually could feel himself evolving into someone who could walk out on a stage and entertain people. In fact, he seemed to be undergoing a lot of changes, some of them welcome, all of them confusing. He didn't feel like the same person who had arrived in Nashville. Certainly he didn't feel like that angry, embittered man whose only pleasure in life had been singing at The General Store on Saturday nights. He supposed he also had Paula to thank for that.

Thinking of her always brought him up short. Since that night at the television studio, he had thought of her much too often, and not always in the mentor-protégé context. He guessed she was the first attractive woman he'd spent a lot of time with that he hadn't made a pass at. Not that he hadn't thought about it lately. Unwise, he cautioned himself constantly. Paula was a fantasy creature, almost exotic to a man like himself. Unattainable. If he dared, in his wildest imaginings, to long for something besides friendship between them, he had only to remember the temporary nature of their present circumstance. He would have to leave soon, and he would be out of her mind soon afterward. He didn't belong in her house and never would. To think otherwise was a waste of time.

Paula would have been astonished to know the surprising turn Dane's thoughts about her had taken, but she had noticed him changing. He was an eager, responsive student who assimilated every facet of this new world he found himself in. She wouldn't have dreamed he would turn out to be so receptive. He seemed to regard her every word and suggestion as the gospel, which bothered her to a certain degree. Though she was careful to offer no advice that hadn't been cleared with Lou first, she was aware that it was *her* knowledge, *her* approval that Dane sought most avidly.

Just as she was aware of the growing closeness between them. They had discovered they could communicate without benefit of words half the time. A glance between green eyes and brown often was all that was needed to understand each other perfectly. This special relationship wasn't something either of them had deliberately cultivated. Rather, it had developed gradually, a by-product of the hours they spent together. They got along well; it was as simple as that.

Rona had been the first to notice and comment on it. "You two certainly seem to mesh," she observed to Paula one day. "It's nice to have a friend like that, isn't it? All this has been good for you. The sparkle's back.''

And Mitch had told Dane, "If you have Paula for a friend, you don't need too many others. She's as loyal as a cocker spaniel. Look at her friendship with Verna."

Lou had also noticed the close relationship, but he didn't accept it as readily or as happily as Mitch and Rona had. It was, in his mind, unseemly for a woman like Paula to form such a close friendship with a man so much younger than she was, and he finally voiced his displeasure.

It was Friday evening, four days before the Crowe tour was to depart. Dane had spent the past three days rehearsing with Dottie's band. During the coming week, the troupe would perform in Memphis on Tuesday night, Little Rock on Wednesday and Oklahoma City on Thursday. Then there would be a one-day break; Dottie wanted to visit friends in Oklahoma before weekend appearances in Amarillo and Albuquerque. Dane would travel with the band. Dottie, of course, traveled in her custom bus, a conveyance that was outfitted like a luxury hotel and—in Lou's words—was "slightly smaller than Rhode Island." That Friday night Lou had come for dinner and a final pep talk with Dane. Later, though, he and Paula were alone.

"You're becoming far too attached to that man, Paula," he said bluntly. "Now, don't get me wrong. I don't have a thing against Dane. In fact, I like him quite a lot, and I think he's got a spectacular career ahead of him. But I'm not sure this relationship between the two of you is wise."

"Since when is friendship unwise, Lou?" she asked.

"Are you absolutely sure that friendship is what it is?"

"Of course I'm sure," she said, slightly peeved. "How can you think it's anything else?"

"I can't imagine." Lou's voice was tinged with sarcasm. "It can't have anything to do with his being a man and your being a woman."

"Lou, when you talk like this, all you do is flatter the hell out of me."

"You're very naive for a woman your age."

Lou's misgivings, Paula knew, stemmed from his thinking of her primarily as Justin's wife. As far as he was concerned, she had no business getting closer to another man, not even platonically. And if she ever became romantically involved with one, which wasn't beyond the realm of possibility, Lou no doubt would regard the relationship as almost adulterous. If anything was unwise, Paula thought, it was Lou's inability to accept Justin's death, to let go of his memory and realize that life had to be for the living.

But she would be the last one to knock loyalty, and few friendships were as enduring as the one Lou and Justin had shared. "Lou, dear, your concern for my well-being touches me, it really does, but I wish you wouldn't begrudge me my friendship with Dane. He considers me his mentor, his expert on just about everything. That won't last. As his career progresses and his self-confidence increases, he won't need me the way he does now. He's never, ever given me any reason to think he's interested in me in a man-woman sort of way. I'm just the first person he's ever trusted completely."

Lou digested that and seemed to accept it. "All right, Paula, if you say so. And if he really does trust you all that much, maybe you should have a serious talk with him. He's going to be getting his first taste of life on the road, and the road has ruined more than one good man."

Paula nodded solemnly, having given that very thing a lot of thought lately. Once Dane's career took off—she never thought "if," only "when"—he wouldn't stay the same person he was now. Change was inevitable. Hopefully, the changes would be for the better, but too often just the opposite was true. And to a man who'd never known much of the good life, the temptations might be irresistible.

When Lou left the house, Paula went in search of Dane. She expected to find him in the studio, but when she passed the open door to his room, she saw him sitting in the easy chair, reading, his feet propped on the ottoman.

"Dane, may I talk to you for a few minutes?"

He looked up, closed the book and started to rise. Paula hurried into the room. "Please don't get up. There are just a few things I want to mention to you."

"Sure." Dane pushed the ottoman toward her, and she sat down. "You look very serious," he said. "What's up?"

"First of all, I'm going to be talking to you like a favorite aunt, so I don't want you accusing me of treating you like a kid. I won't mean it that way at all. I simply have your well-being in mind."

Dane fought a smile. In spite of what she said, she had slipped into her schoolteacher stance, all prim, somber and instructional. "Okay. Forewarned. I'll keep my feathers unruffled."

She was seated squarely in front of him, and since he was leaning forward slightly, elbows on his knees, hands clasped in front of him, their faces were very close. She looked into his dark eyes, eyes that no longer were cold and wary but warm, smoldering, sexy. He was grinning at her in an endearing way. If he learned to use that grin onstage, someday his concerts would be female stampedes.

Paula took a deep breath. "You're getting ready to go out on the road, and there are a thousand pitfalls waiting for you. Everything imaginable will be available—booze, pills, hard drugs, even harder women. All that has turned more than one performer's head."

"So I've heard."

"I hope you listen and take heed. And later on, when you've had some hits and are headlining your own show, you'll face something else—pressure. Pressure to do two hundred shows a year, one-nighters, and no one can be up two hundred nights a year. But you don't want to disappoint the fans, so you try. More pressure. By then there'll be a bunch of people depending on you for their living, so you'll never feel you can just lie back and take it easy. Unless your head's really screwed on straight and your ego is firmly intact, you can go off the deep end quickly. So many people need a crutch to put up with it, and that's when they turn to one of the above mentioned, anything to get through just one more performance. This town abounds with horror stories. Sometimes it seems it's worse here than in Hollywood." She paused and focused on a spot beyond his right shoulder. "It kills me to think of that kind of thing happening to you."

For a minute Dane didn't move, not a flicker. He simply stared at her with a sort of bemused expression. Then he leaned back, folded his arms across his chest and smiled. "You're worried about me."

"Of course I'm worried about you. It's a crazy life—unnatural, really."

"You're the one who turned me on to it."

Paula bit her bottom lip and frowned. "I know. I hope I don't live to regret that."

Dane didn't know when anything had pleased him so much. Maybe nothing ever had. "Thanks for worrying. I don't think anyone's ever worried about me before, and it's a nice feeling." Suddenly he leaned toward her again, this time taking one of her hands in his and toying with her fingers. "I can see how some kid fresh off the farm might let it all mess up his mind, but as the saying goes—this ain't my first circus. I've been offered all that stuff you mentioned. Believe it or not, they're available back home, too. I've drunk an ocean of beer, known my share of women your mama wouldn't invite to tea, and I've even sampled some pills. But that was in younger years when my future looked as bright as a stormy day. As for hard drugs, I wouldn't touch 'em then, so I'm not about to now. Paula, the point is, I've walked over some broken glass on my way here, and I'm not about to do anything to louse up all the great things that are happening to me."

Paula's pent-up breath oozed out of her, and she gave a shaky little laugh. "Oh, Dane, I hope you mean that."

Giving his hand a squeeze for emphasis, she leaned forward and planted a kiss on his cheek, narrowly missing his mouth. Again it was an impulsive gesture, not rooted in thought, but Dane felt his throat constrict and his mouth go dry. It was over in a split second, but that was long enough for him to drink in the sweet fragrance of her, to feel the texture of her cheek as it brushed against his. He didn't now what he wished more—that she would stop these friendly little hugs and light little kisses, or that she would dispense them more freely. He was working very hard at being her friend, because he knew friendship was what Paula wanted and expected from him, but it wasn't easy. She intrigued him, inspired him, enchanted him. He thought about her all the time.

When Paula pulled back and saw the peculiar expression on his face, she decided she would have to curb her enthusiasm in the future. Some people didn't like such familiarity, even from friends. Dane probably wasn't on close terms with friendly touching.

But then he startled her by raising a hand and touching the side of her face. She pressed her cheek into his palm, and their eyes met. For a split second Paula felt herself falling under a strange, mesmerizing spell. Nervously she ran the tip of her tongue over her lips to moisten them, a movement that Dane seemed to find hypnotizing. *How odd,* she thought. *I'm actually thinking how much I would like for him to kiss me. I'm going dotty.*

But was that so strange, so unacceptable, after all? She and Dane spent a lot of time together. He was an attractive man, and she had been deprived of intimacy with a man for a year. She shouldn't feel guilty if an occasional errant thought crossed her mind. It was how one acted upon such thoughts that was important, and she would never put her remarkable friendship with Dane in jeopardy.

At that moment Rona's voice rang down the hall. "Paula, are you down here?"

Dane's hand dropped to his knee. Nonplussed, Paula jumped to her feet and went out into the hall. "Here I am, Rona."

"There's a call for you. Take it in the office. It's Vanessa Hamilton."

"Vanessa?" Calling her at home on Friday night? Paula was sure that had never happened before. Hurrying down to the office, she flipped on the light switch and reached for the phone.

"Vanessa? What a nice surprise."

"I hope I'm not interrupting anything, Paula. I realize this call is rather irregular."

"You're not interrupting a thing. How are you?"

"Oh, I'm fine, as well as can be expected, I suppose. Paula, I know this isn't giving you much notice, but I'm doing it with a purpose in mind. I'd like to see you here in Dallas on Monday, if you can manage it."

"Of course I can manage it." Paula's heart began to race. "I'll be there Sunday night."

"Let me know the time of your arrival so I can arrange to have someone meet you at the airport. There will be a reservation for you at the Anatole. It's close to the office. And prepare to spend three or four days with me."

"Fine." Three or four days? Her trips to the home office never lasted more than two. God, how Paula wanted to ask questions. Could this have something to do with what Russ had talked about? This was no ordinary business trip, of that she was sure. It didn't fit Vanessa's modus operandi, from which the woman seldom deviated.

"And I'll send a car around for you at nine Monday morning."

"I'll be waiting."

"I'm looking forward to seeing you, Paula. It's been a while."

"Yes, it has. Five months, right? I'm looking forward to it, too, Vanessa."

After she'd hung up, Paula stood at the desk, deep in thought. She could almost sense change in the air, and an unpleasantly tight feeling knotted in her chest. It came to her with utmost certainty that she didn't want change. She liked everything the way it was.

Impatiently she pivoted, turned out the light and left the office. She was overreacting, something she almost never did. There were dozens of things Vanessa could want to discuss with her.

For three or four days?

Dane was standing in the hall outside his room. She was so lost in thought she almost bumped into him. The frown on her face brought one to his. "Something wrong, Paula?"

"What? Oh...no, I don't think so. But I'm going to have to leave for Dallas Sunday afternoon."

"Another trip so soon?"

"I'm afraid so, and that means I have a lot to do tomorrow."

"How long will you be gone this time?"

"Three or four days. I'll definitely be back long before you are."

"But you won't be here when I leave."

She smiled. "I imagine you'll be too excited to miss me."

Wrong, he thought. Nothing on earth could excite him so much that he wouldn't miss her. Hell, he even missed her during the day when she was at work. "You weren't here when I made the record. You won't be here when I leave on my first tour."

"It can't be helped." Paula's smile grew wistful. He sounded like a little boy whose mother had just told him she couldn't attend his ball game. "When Vanessa beckons, I come running. I've got to go make my airline reservations. Good night, Dane. I'll see you in the morning."

As Dane watched her walk away, he was forced to remember her other life, the one that had nothing to do with him. Paula was so down-to-earth, so free of pretensions that it was easy to forget she was a vice president of a multimillion-dollar corporation—an important lady with important things to do.

Once again he reminded himself that he was little more than a transient here. He would make the first real money of his life on the tour, so he couldn't in all good conscience continue to accept Paula's hospitality. After he got a place of his own, their meetings would be brief and infrequent. And if he really did have the kind of career she and Lou kept insisting he would have, he would be on the road most of the time. The special relationship they had established would wither and die. Paula might even take on a new protégé and focus all her spare time and energy on the newcomer.

The thought was so disheartening that it shook Dane. He, who had lived thirty-six years without becoming attached to anything or anybody, had become far too attached to Paula, far too fond of her. And that was like becoming too fond of a distant star.

If Paula had seen the expression on his face as he stared after her departing figure, she never again would have said that Dane wasn't interested in her in a man-woman sort of way.

SATURDAY PASSED in a blur of activity, which was normal when an unexpected trip came up. Paula spent the morning at her office and most of the afternoon on the phone with her key staff. On Sunday morning she packed, and that afternoon, after lunch, Mitch drove her to the airport.

She had always enjoyed the sprawling power and energy of Dallas. Nashville in many ways still seemed like a big small town. Her arrival at the Dallas-Fort Worth airport Sunday night gave her just enough time to call Vanessa, have a light dinner, take a shower and fall into bed. Monday morning she woke feeling refreshed and full of curiosity about this unexpected summons from on high. At promptly nine o'clock the Hamilton House driver picked her up at the hotel, and fifteen minutes later she stepped into Vanessa's plush private office. The company matriarch was standing in front of the large picture window behind her desk. She turned, and her face broke into a radiant smile.

"Paula, how nice to see you."

"Thank you, Vanessa. It's good to see you, too. You're looking wonderful."

Vanessa Hamilton was and always had been a strikingly handsome woman. Paula imagined her youthful beauty had been quite breathtaking. When Paula had first begun with Hamilton House, Vanessa had been an arresting beauty of some sixty years who had looked a good twenty years younger than her age. Now that she was nearing eighty, she easily could have passed for a woman in her sixties. Naturally, her face was now lined and there were folds of skin at her neck, but the excellent bone structure and the alert, penetrating eyes remained. Her translucent complexion was enviable, and her silver hair was always expertly waved and stylishly coiffed. One of only a handful of wealthy Texas women who had made, not inherited, their fortune, Vanessa was a woman of means and power, and she looked the part. She was a motivational wizard who inspired near-fanatical devotion to Hamilton House in her employees. Even those who thought her too imperious and demanding—and there were many—admitted that her like seldom had been equaled. Paula quite simply considered her the most extraordinary woman she had ever known.

The two women met in the center of the office and lightly embraced. Then Vanessa held Paula at arm's length, studying her. *She's beautiful,* was her verdict. And the beauty was arresting, the kind that inspired second looks. Paula was not the kind of woman who got lost in a crowd; she dressed with style and flair, and she exuded self-confidence. The older woman liked that.

Vanessa had admired Paula for years, seeing much of her own spirit and resoluteness in her. From the beginning, when Paula had first begun breaking away from the pack and climbing the corporate ladder, Vanessa had thought her bright and capable beyond her years. Even then she had known the day would come when Paula would hold a position of significance. Vanessa had often wondered if perhaps, through the years, she had been more exacting of Paula than she had the others. She hoped not, but if she had, the younger woman had come through with flying colors, never disappointing her.

"How have you been, Paula? I mean, really."

Paula knew Vanessa was alluding to her widowed status. "You know how difficult it is. But all of Justin's old friends are still with me, and I have my work. Also, there's a new singer we're helping along.''

''Then your days are full?''

''Yes, very.''

''That's good. I've seen so many women fall apart after their husbands are gone.'' Instead of inviting Paula to have a seat, Vanessa made a move toward the door. ''Let's take a walk. There have been some changes since you last were here.''

Out in the corridor the older woman led the way to the elevators. Paula was quick to notice that they passed Dolph Wade's office without stopping to have a word with him. Always before, Dolph had been the second person Paula saw when she visited the home office. In fact, she did not see the man or hear his name mentioned the entire day. It was as though he no longer existed. Russ's gossip was beginning to look like fact.

What Vanessa had in store for her that day was a grand tour of the facility. Hamilton House, Incorporated, had grown from a small regional operation to a giant corporation that tentacled the nation, vastly different from the modest-size company Paula had gone to work for twenty years ago. A giant control board tracked the refrigerated eighteen-wheelers that crisscrossed the nation around the clock, rushing fresh food from the Mississippi-based agricultural complex to the restaurants. An enormous computer room enabled Vanessa to see at a glance every meal served in every restaurant every day.

Paula met with people in marketing, in distribution, in restaurant operations and in accounting. It was the Nashville operation times ten, only far more complex, employing hundreds more people and encompassing many more departments. Paula, for instance, knew next to nothing about distribution; that was handled here in Dallas. Nor did she know a thing about Grady O'Connor's agricultural operation in Mississippi. Vanessa had her finger on the pulse of every department and still seemed to know the name of every single employee. She was amazing.

The two women lunched in the executive dining room, where, not surprisingly, many of the dishes served at the restaurants nationwide were first conceived. Naturally the meal was excellent, and throughout it Vanessa never stopped spewing facts and figures, an accounting both fascinating and astonishing to Paula. Vanessa's mind was as keen and alert as ever. Nothing escaped her notice. Paula was beginning to realize she was being given a crash course in the home office operation. There had to be a reason for that, she knew, and though she'd always considered speculation and guesses to be a foolish waste of time, now she couldn't avoid guessing.

Until two o'clock that afternoon, Vanessa and Paula poked in and out of offices, chatting with men and women at various levels of the corporation. Then the older woman pleaded fatigue. "At my age I find I can't do without afternoon rest," Vanessa said. "Clark Jenkins in marketing will show you around for the remainder of the afternoon, but I'd like for you to have dinner with me at my place tonight."

"I'd love that," Paula said.

"My driver will pick you up at six-thirty, if that's all right."

"That's fine. I'm looking forward to it."

"There'll just be the two of us, so wear whatever you like. I have a great deal to tell you."

Paula could hardly wait to hear what it was.

THE INTERESTING AFTERNOON flew by, and when Paula got back to her hotel room, she had to hurry in order to be ready by six-thirty. That day she had spoken to just about everyone of importance in the home office, and more than one casually dropped remark had convinced her that Russ had been right—Dolph was on his way out. Then Paula had learned something else—Matt Logan from San Francisco had been in Dallas months earlier and had received the same indoctrination she was being given. So Paula finally accepted it as fact: Vanessa was searching for her successor.

It's strange, she thought. *I should feel more than I'm feeling.* She didn't know who else was being considered—surely Matt was—but even if all six vice presidents were, that still meant she had a good chance. She thought she should be feeling more excitement, more anticipation, more something. Instead, she just felt . . . uncertain.

It would mean so many changes. Her unhurried, unstructured life-style would vanish. She would have to give up Justin's lovely house. So many old, cherished friends might never be seen again. Would Mitch and Rona come with her? They had vowed to follow her to the ends of the earth, but would they really when push came to shove? Nashville had been their home far longer than it had been hers, and they had friends all over the state. Worst of all, Paula would have to follow the progress of Dane's career from afar. She would hate that. He was the last in a long line of protégés but the first who was hers and hers alone.

Which reminded her. She glanced at her watch, wondering if she had time to call home. Deciding she did, she picked up the phone and placed the call. Maybe she was being foolish, but she couldn't let him leave on tour in the morning without a parting word from her. Rona answered, they exchanged the customary pleasantries, then the secretary called Dane to the phone.

"Butterflies?" Paula asked gently.

"More like a hive full of angry bumblebees," he answered.

"They'll disappear once you step onstage."

"God, I hope so! The way I feel now I'd have trouble getting through 'Three Blind Mice.'"

Paula laughed lightly. "I'll be thinking about you. Knock 'em dead."

"I'll give it my best shot." There was a pause, then Dane said, "Paula, thanks a bunch for calling. I figured you'd be so busy doing important things in Big D that you wouldn't have time to think about me and the tour."

"There's no way I could be so busy or anything could be so important for that to happen. I wish I could talk longer, but I'm having dinner with Vanessa, so I can't be late. But tomorrow night my thoughts will all be of you. Only Vanessa could prevent me from being in Memphis to watch the show in person."

"That...really means a lot to me." His voice sounded clogged with emotion.

"Now, I've really got to hang up. Goodbye, Dane."

"Goodbye, Paula."

Hanging up, Paula jumped to her feet and rushed to finish dressing by six-thirty. Focus, focus, she kept telling herself. She shouldn't be thinking about anything but tonight's dinner with Vanessa. It could prove to be momentous. It might change her life. But, damn, she wished she could be in Memphis tomorrow night!

CHAPTER NINE

THE LAVISH ESTATE that Stuart and Vanessa Hamilton had built north of Dallas had once been far out in the country, a true pastoral paradise. It no longer was, since the city had marched relentlessly toward it. Only the vast amount of acreage Vanessa owned kept the beautiful place from being completely surrounded by development. The car drove through iron gates and up a sweeping driveway, coming to a halt in front of the imposing Mediterranean-style house, which was trimmed with lacy grillwork and set off by meticulously groomed grounds.

Inside, as an aproned servant led the way down a polished oak floor to the rear of the house, Paula's practiced eye took in every detail of her surroundings. Much of what she knew about fine furnishings she had learned from Vanessa. The house exuded refinement and a quiet, understated beauty, but its very simplicity was deceptive—the kind of understatement that could only be achieved by employing unfailing good taste and spending plenty of money.

"Please wait in here, ma'am," the maid said. "Mrs. Hamilton will be down in a moment."

The paneled study was a cozy, inviting room for its enormous size. Paula imagined it was doubly cozy in winter with a crackling fire blazing in the fireplace. Vanessa's good taste was in evidence everywhere, for the woman had spent a lifetime acquiring fine things and knew how to showcase them. Yet Paula's eye immediately fell upon an incongruous sight amid all the fine Georgian and Victorian antiques—a framed snapshot resting on a console. The picture, circa 1939, was of a small café with striped awnings and a neon sign. Vanessa liked to boast that Hamilton House had begun with five-cent coffee and thirty-five cent plate lunches. Paula marveled that such a modest café could have been the start of it all, just as she was amazed by the astonishing amount of time and energy Vanessa and Stuart had poured into their impressive business empire.

Vanessa sailed into the room at that moment, and Paula set the snapshot back in place. She smiled admiringly at the older woman. Tonight the matriarch looked regal, even aristocratic in her sweeping lavender dressing gown. A strand of perfect pearls adorned its neckline, and her hair was a blaze of silver around her slightly square face.

Paula herself wore what she referred to as "the dress"—her indispensable navy blue chemise, which could be dressed up or down as the occasion demanded. Tonight she had tied a vivid print scarf around the neck and cinched the waist with a leather belt.

"Ah, Paula, how lovely you look," Vanessa greeted her. "But then, you always do. I'm having sherry, but there's a lovely chardonnay in the ice bucket, if you would prefer."

"I think I'll try some of it, thanks."

"How was your afternoon?" Vanessa asked as she poured the wine.

"Informative. Hamilton House employs some very bright young people." She accepted the glass Vanessa handed her.

"You'll meet more tomorrow. Sit down and let's talk." Two matching sofas flanked the fireplace. Paula sat down on one, and Vanessa took a seat opposite her. "Before you leave here you'll have gotten a thorough look at the entire organization. It's growing by leaps and bounds."

"That's certainly the impression I received today."

"Obviously I have you here in Dallas for a specific reason."

Paula smiled. "That's also the impression I received."

Vanessa sat back, sipped at her sherry and grew very serious. "Paula, have you ever had someone very close to you disappoint you terribly?"

Paula fleetingly thought of her disappointment the night she learned Dane had been in a barroom brawl, but she doubted that was a good analogy. "No, I don't think I ever have."

"Good. It's a miserable experience. Now, for the reason I have you here. A very distressing thing has happened to me. It was months ago, so I've had time to recover from the initial shock, but betrayal is something one never forgets. I assume you heard about the buy-out offer from Barrington International."

"Of course."

"What did you think about it?"

Paula shrugged. "Actually, I don't think I thought anything about it. I would have been the most astonished person on earth if you had accepted it. I know how much Hamilton House means to you."

That seemed to please Vanessa. "Good. I would have thought everyone who knows me well would have felt as you did. However—" Vanessa's mouth compressed into a tight line "—Dolph urged me to accept the offer."

"Oh?" Paula assumed a this-is-news-to-me-attitude. She wondered if Vanessa had any idea of how company tongues already were wagging. Normally she would guess that the woman was aware of every single thing that transpired in the home office, but Vanessa was far too busy a person to concern herself with office gossip.

"Yes," Vanessa went on. "Everyone in the company knows Dolph advised me to sell, so they all assume that my frosty attitude toward him these days is because he favored the buy out. They also assume that I'll get over it, but they're wrong. There was more to it than just rotten advice. Much more."

I would have bet on that, Paula thought as she sipped her wine and remained silent.

"Not only did he urge me to sell, he was so vehement about it that I became suspicious as the devil. So I investigated. Actually, I snooped around Dolph's office one afternoon after everyone was gone." Vanessa shot Paula a smile of triumph. "There was a time when I thought Dolph brilliant, but during the Barrington matter he did something so incredibly stupid that I still find it hard to believe. Stupid and traitorous. It seems that my once trusted executive officer stood to profit handsomely if he could persuade me to sell."

Paula gasped and leaned forward, her expression rapt. "Do you mean the Barrington people offered him money?"

Vanessa nodded. "I see you're properly shocked. So was I."

"Vanessa, how do you know this?"

"Dolph taped a conversation between himself and the Barrington reps. I'm sure that was to prevent their trying to renege later. But I found the tape."

"Does Dolph know?"

"No. Only one person besides you and me knows about any of this. Matt Logan."

"Matt?" Again Paula pretended to be puzzled.

"Yes, I had him here some months back. But I'm getting ahead of my story. Obviously, Dolph is not going to take over Hamilton House when I'm gone. I can forgive stupidity and greed, but I can never forgive disloyalty. And I've given far too much of myself to the company to have power plays and infighting destroy it when I'm no longer around to protect it. So...I'm going to have to name my successor, someone I trust, someone who's never disappointed me. I'm considering several people. Matt, for one. And you. How do you feel about that?"

Paula sucked in her breath. "Do you need to ask? I'm flattered as I can be."

"Would you accept?"

"I don't know how I could refuse."

"It's a time-consuming job, Paula, impossibly so some days. There are times when half an hour to yourself is an unheard-of luxury. And being president of the company would require relocating to Dallas. I know how Matt feels about San Francisco, just as I know how Nashville has come to be your home. Also, I understand Matt is getting married this summer. A local woman. I wonder how she would feel about such an upheaval."

"Matt's getting married?" Paula asked, her eyes bright. "How wonderful for him! He's been alone such a long time."

"Yes, he has, and it *is* wonderful. But as I said, it will naturally affect his decision. And you mentioned helping a new protégé, just as Justin used to do. I'm afraid that being president of Hamilton House wouldn't leave you much time for such projects. I've tried to take all these things into consideration. I even thought about bringing in an outsider, but I can't risk that. I want someone I can trust. I'm passionate about this."

Paula clearly detected the fervor in her voice. Her own reaction to Vanessa's news was mixed. Even though she had envisioned this, hearing it put in so many words made her face the possibility of leaving all that was dear and familiar to her.

But to be C.E.O. of Hamilton House! Just knowing that the woman she thought so highly of was considering her was a thrill. "Little in life is ideal, Vanessa," Paula said. "I'm sure Matt feels the way I do. We've both given so many years to the company that neither of us could turn down a chance to stand at the helm."

Vanessa thought it remarkable that none of her six vice presidents had ever displayed the slightest bit of jealousy toward the others. They seemed to operate more like an exclusive fraternity than anything. And she was certain that whoever was chosen to take her place would enjoy the same support from the others that she had. But then, they were a remarkable group of people. She wouldn't have put them in their lofty positions if they hadn't been.

"I'm going to tell you something else," she now said to Paula. "The person who becomes president of Hamilton House will acquire far more than a fancy office, a title and a mountain of responsibilities. He or she will become the single largest stockholder in the corporation. That translates into money and power. Regardless of what people think about your ability or your looks or your personality, they can't ignore money and power."

A peculiar feeling rose up in Paula. She had known plenty of people who hungered for money and others who craved power over money, although the two seemed to go hand in hand. But she honestly didn't think she'd ever yearned for either, not really, not even when she was young. Now she had more money than she could spend, and the thought of enormous power was...well, frankly it was a little frightening.

"When Matt was here, Paula," Vanessa went on, "I extracted a promise from him, and now I'm going to ask the same of you."

"Of course."

"Nothing must happen to Hamilton House, and the wrong people could, in a few years' time, destroy what it took Stuart and me our lifetimes to build. I want you to promise that if you sit at my desk, you'll keep the company intact and pass it along to others who'll do the same. It so frightens me to think what a cartel like Barrington could do to it. The changes they admitted wanting to make were absolutely appalling."

"You have my solemn vow, of course," Paula said soberly. "And I won't even have to be sitting in your chair. The slightest whisper of a buy out, and I'll storm the ramparts...or whatever."

That, too, pleased Vanessa. "You and Matt and some others have been such stalwarts over the years. When Stuart died, I confess to having had more than a few moments of self-doubt and worry."

"You?" Paula laughed lightly. Self-doubt and Vanessa didn't seem to go together.

"Oh, I put up a marvelous front, but there were many times when I wondered if I could do it alone."

"Strange. I never doubted you could for a minute."

Vanessa smiled, then turned serious. "I intend taking my sweet time about making my choice. Ordinarily I wouldn't drag my heels. Stuart used to caution me about making snap decisions, but I've always believed there's divine interference that shapes our lives, so why agonize over every tiny detail? This time, however, things are different. This time my decision will determine Hamilton House's direction for decades to come. No detail must be overlooked, no question can go unanswered. But I've more or less promised myself I will reach my decision by my eightieth birthday. I've also promised to give myself a birthday party people will remember long after they've forgotten me. Now, enough of this. Let's have another drink, shall we?"

Paula was on her feet in an instant, reaching for Vanessa's stemmed glass. "Dinner will be ready soon," the older woman said. "Duck in the most divine plum sauce. I'm thinking of adding the dish to some of our menus."

In a few minutes dinner was announced, and the two women enjoyed a beautifully prepared meal while they gossiped about almost everything but business. It was after ten when the driver deposited Paula at the

Anatole. Up in her room she undressed hastily and fell into bed, but, not surprisingly, she couldn't sleep.

It had been a busy day, an incredible day, really. Over and over she reminded herself that Vanessa easily could choose Matt or someone else; still, she couldn't stop playing "what if." The challenge of running a multimillion-dollar corporation would put her capabilities to the ultimate test, but always there would be the sheer thrill of achievement.

Then self-doubt surfaced. Could she motivate people the way Vanessa did? Could she handle the pressure on her time? She'd always been a well-organized person, but as part of that organization she'd seen to it that she had plenty of hours to call her own. Could she still do that as president? Maybe, but it wouldn't be easy.

And how sad she would feel to leave Nashville, particularly if Mitch and Rona elected not to come with her. They had been such a big part of her life for so long.

Thinking of Mitch and Rona prompted thoughts of home, and thoughts of home brought on thoughts of Dane. By the time Vanessa made her decision, Dane's career would be steaming along and he no longer would be a very big part of Paula's life. The brighter his star shone, the more she would fade into the shadows, which was as it should be. Once he left the house, she would see him seldom, if ever. He might choose to live somewhere other than Nashville. Many did, particularly the ones who didn't mesh well with the country music establishment. And from experience, Paula knew that many protégés, once they became famous, forgot their mentors altogether. She didn't think Dane was like that, but success could do odd things to the nicest people.

There was a lot in her life that could change soon. Paula just hoped that when the changes came, if they did, she would be able to accept them with equanimity. She'd always been pretty good at handling whatever life threw her, good or bad; she wasn't one for brooding about the past. What was ended was ended—one went on to something else.

But, dear God, she would miss Dane. How in the world had she allowed herself to become so attached to him? She was a lot smarter than that. The others, Justin's kids, had not lingered long in her thoughts after they'd gotten their break and moved on or, in a few cases, given up. Looking back, they came together as a sea of eager faces, each indistinguishable from the other. It would be different this time, unpleasantly so. Dane wasn't just a face. She knew him; he was real. Maybe too real.

TUESDAY AND WEDNESDAY were full for Paula from waking to sleeping. Her mind spun from the myriad details bombarding her from all sides. Back in her hotel room at night, she wrote voluminous notes, reminders of all she had seen and heard that day. She spent Thursday morning in planning and development, being briefed on the company's plans for the coming decade: expansion into Canada and more restaurants for each division. Then, after lunch with Vanessa in the executive dining room, she was finished. She could go home, and home had never sounded so welcoming.

It wasn't until she was back at the hotel, trying to get her flight changed to an earlier one, that an idea took hold of her and refused to let go. She was two hundred miles south of Oklahoma City, and tonight Dottie's show was playing the Myriad Arena there. Why, Paula wondered, couldn't she fly home from Oklahoma City just as easily as from Dallas? She did so want to see Dane perform before a really large audience. Mitch and Rona weren't expecting her; not certain how long her business here would take, she'd merely told them to "look for me when you see me coming." She thought about it for a few minutes, then told the reservations clerk she'd changed her mind, to book her instead on the next flight to Oklahoma City.

Excitement began building inside her. Now she would see firsthand how Dane was handling being on the road. She wondered about so many things, especially how he was getting along with Dottie. Paula had heard stories about Dottie's ambition and determination, how she hired and fired band members on a whim and had reduced more than one young female singer to tears. Paula seriously doubted Dane had ever run into anyone quite like the superstar. Yes, it would indeed be interesting to see how he was meshing with the famous Miss Crowe.

DOTTIE CROWE LIKED MEN, and men liked Dottie. At thirty-two she already had acquired and discarded two husbands and a dozen lovers, and there always seemed to be another man waiting eagerly in the wings. They gravitated toward her, awed either by her looks or her success or a combination of both.

That she kept her men as long as she wanted was not surprising. Dottie was possessed of an untamed kind of beauty and a lusty sexual appetite. What for most women was a pleasure was for her a need. She simply could not be without a man for long, and there were plenty around to see to it that she never had to.

On a less amorous note, she also had a mind like a steel trap and the physical stamina of a bull elephant. Not for her the frequent bouts of depression and exhaustion that persistently felled country music's female singers. Dottie was a bundle of charged energy who left those around her gasping for breath. She kept an alert eye on every facet of her career and knew at any given moment how well her latest album was doing in, say, Cincinnati or Cheyenne.

Yet, these attributes did not make for especially good press in Nashville. So through the years she had carefully created an image designed to endear her to audiences. They lapped up her golly-gee-whiz drivel; she was very careful to be quoted as saying things like, "I'd rather be complimented on my biscuits than on my last record." Such quotes might make her acquaintances, who knew Dottie would be hard-pressed to boil an egg, roar with laughter, but the public loved them.

Little of what her fans thought they knew about her was based on fact, because nothing about her fit the standard mold. She hadn't "suffered." Both of her divorces had been amicable. In fact, she had remained friends with her ex-husbands, and they were friends with each other—a unique achievement. She hadn't come from the poor rural background that seemed a prerequisite for country music stardom. She and her mother had lived in a charming, affluent Nashville neighborhood, and Dottie had gone to exclusive private schools, graduating with honors. None of that, however, ever made it into her press releases.

Moreover, Dottie had never been forced to clerk in a store or wait tables or cut hair while hoping for her big break. Though there was a popular story circulating that had a young Dottie Crowe intercepting Lou Howard outside his office and forcing him to listen to her sing, not a word of it was true. After graduating from college, she simply had sent a demo tape to Lou; he had listened to it and he and Justin had made her a star, a position she had happily held for ten years. "Charmed" was a word the press used to describe her life. "Cute" was the way her fans described her. If anyone had it all, Dottie did. Everything she touched turned to gold. She always got what she wanted.

But she hadn't gotten to first base with Dane Markham, and that had graduated into something of an obsession with her. On the night they both had appeared on *Today in Nashville,* she had determined he would be her next conquest, but so far nothing had happened. He, of course, was in awe of her star status, which she loved, but he was also a true gentleman around her, and she didn't like that at all. She had offered to share her bus with him when they left Memphis; he had declined politely, saying it wouldn't sit well with the other members of the show. In Little Rock she had contrived to be alone with him, but finding no other members of the troupe with them, he had made an excuse and exited quickly. Dottie had unleashed her entire arsenal of feminine wiles and ploys on him, to no avail. Dane was, in fact, so immune to her considerable charms that she briefly wondered if he was gay.

Now they were in Oklahoma City and would be for two days. Dottie had planned to make a side trip to Stillwater to visit old friends, but if she could arrange something with Dane after tonight's show, the friends would have to wait until another time, another tour. He presented a challenge, something no man she'd ever met had.

AFTER THE SHORT FLIGHT from Dallas and a taxi ride from Will Rogers World Airport to Myriad Arena, Paula had to do some fast talking to convince the stage guard she was who she said she was and had every right to be backstage. The man finally decided she didn't look the part of a groupie and begrudgingly granted her entrance. Dane was onstage, midway through his act. Paula stood in the wings, watching him and experiencing a surge of pride. *I put him there,* she thought.

He had loosened up a little since that night on television, but she had to remember he had the Memphis and Little Rock concerts behind him. His self-confidence had to be growing with each passing day, with each completed performance. She was careful to stay back, hidden by the sound equipment, lest he turn and catch sight of her. He looked relaxed enough, but discovering she was watching might throw him off balance.

At last he swung into "Tears," his swan song, the one he hoped to make his signature number. The applause was vigorous, and Paula sensed that the audience would have welcomed an encore. There wouldn't be one, however. Dottie had made it clear that when he finished "Tears," no matter if they tore down the house, he was to get off so she could go on. Encores belonged to headliners, not opening acts. Everything and everybody on the show was there to showcase Dottie.

Dane was walking offstage, his head down, his face flushed with excitement. He stopped for a moment to lay his guitar near the sound equipment, where the road crew wouldn't miss it. Then he looked up, saw her and stopped dead in his tracks. "Paula!" he exclaimed.

She burst into laughter when she saw the startled look on his face, but Dane didn't join in. He was so stunned—and so pleased—to see her that he could hardly breathe, much less laugh. "Where...where did you come from?"

"Dallas, remember? I just decided to make a pit stop on the way home. You see, I heard about this new singer..."

For one long, tantalizing minute they simply stared at each other. That she had gone to the trouble to come to see him touched him deeply. He drank in the sight of her, wishing with all his heart he was more eloquent. He wanted to tell her she was the most beautiful sight he'd ever seen, but coming from his mouth, he feared, the words would sound grossly insane. All he could do was stare, and he wondered if he would ever acquire enough sophistication, enough polish to meet Paula on equal terms, to do something but stare at her.

When at last they moved, they moved simultaneously. The space between them narrowed, then closed altogether, and they shared their first true kiss. When they broke apart, Dane looked shaken to his toes.

"I can't believe you're here," he said.

"I'm so glad I got to see you. You were wonderful."

"You can stay tonight, can't you? Dottie's heading for Stillwater as soon as the show's over, and the band and I have rooms at a motel out on I-40. Surely you can get one there, too."

"I'm counting on it," Paula told him. "I have to stay somewhere. I have reservations on a flight home tomorrow afternoon. I rushed here straight from the airport. My luggage is on the band bus. The driver looked slightly askance, but I explained that I was a friend of yours."

Dane tucked her hand in the curve of his elbow and led her toward the stage door. "Come on, let's blow this joint."

"You aren't staying for the rest of the show?"

"My stint's finished. There won't be any calling me back to take a bow or anything like that. Believe me, Dottie never lets me forget I'm second banana. Let's take a cab to the motel. We'll get you a room, have a couple of drinks and then have dinner."

"At this hour?"

"None of us ever eats until after the show. Usually around midnight. Have you eaten?"

"I had a sandwich before boarding the plane, but I might be able to choke something down by the time midnight rolls around."

"Good. I've got a lot to tell you."

"I can hardly wait to hear all about Memphis and Little Rock."

Dane stopped and gave her a quick hug. "Damn, I'm glad you're here. This is the best surprise I've had in a long time. I can't even tell you how much it means to me."

Unaccountably, Paula felt as giggly as the shyest teenager, and that certainly was an unfamiliar sensation. She hadn't been very giggly even when she was a shy teenager. What had prompted such an unusual feeling? Maybe it was the expression of delight and wonder on Dane's face? And he kept touching her, as if reassuring himself she was real. That alone was worth the trip. "I'm glad I'm here, too. Let's go."

They slipped their arms around each other's waist and headed for the exit. Neither of them saw Dottie glaring after them. She had come out of her dressing room just in time to see Dane grab Paula and kiss her. Granted, it didn't qualify as the most passionate embrace Dottie had ever seen, but it had been a warm, lingering kiss. And she had seen the look on Dane's face, as though seeing Paula was the most exciting thing that had ever happened to him. She also saw the affectionate expression on Paula's face. If their relationship hadn't progressed beyond the mentor-protégé stage, it would soon. Those two had something going, no doubt about that.

Dottie felt her cheeks sting. It really was disgusting, Dane with that older woman. So that was why she hadn't been able to get through to him. There was someone else, and it was Paula Steele, of all people! The enormity of that injustice flailed at Dottie, causing her to seethe. Any other woman would simply have meant she would have to work harder, but there was something so damned aristocratic about Paula. How that queenly air would appeal to a country boy from the sticks!

Dottie fixed a leaden stare on the woman. Usually when she confronted Paula, she tried to ignore her, but now she studied her as though she were under a microscope. She studied her hair, her clothes, her shoes. She would have inspected the contents of her handbag if she could. Dottie wasn't assessing her competition; Dane had ceased to matter that much. But Paula mattered. She always had.

Hatred oozed from Dottie's pores. Her resentment of Justin Steele's wife was rooted in the past and of long standing. Fortunately, only one other person on earth knew of the reason for that hatred, and she could trust him. He, more than anyone, understood.

Suddenly Dottie was aware of the strains of her opening number. Squaring her shoulders, she pasted on her stage smile, adjusted her sequined jumpsuit and stepped forward into the glare of the spotlight.

CHAPTER TEN

PAULA AND DANE were blissfully unaware of the angry look that followed their departing figures. Outside, he got her luggage off the bus and informed the driver he was going back to the motel. Then they went out front and hailed a taxi.

"How much of the show did you get to see?" he asked Paula when they were on their way.

"About half. You're really looking good up there."

"It gets easier. I felt like a wooden Indian in Memphis, but things were a little better in Little Rock."

"How is working with Dottie?"

Dane grinned and scratched his chin. Dottie had been coming on to him during the tour. She'd even told him she could "do" things for him if she had a mind to, and she'd left no doubt just how he could persuade her to "have a mind to."

Rarely had he felt the need to employ restraint where women were concerned, but this time he did. Something about Dottie—he had no idea what—started a caution light blinking in his head. If anyone had told him he would ever be afraid of a woman, he would have laughed uproariously, but he'd never met a female quite like Dottie before. His instincts had told him to keep his distance, and his instincts, he discovered, were in good working order. Last night on the bus, he and the piano player had fallen into conversation. For some reason they had hit it off from the beginning. The pianist was an older man who'd been in the business a long time and had been a member of Dottie's road band since the inception of her career. Talk naturally had gotten around to the star of the show. "She's got the hots for you, son," the older man had said, "and you better be careful. That gal's poison. She chews up guys and spits 'em out. I know more than one ol' boy who wishes he'd never laid eyes on her."

Dane now told Paula, "Oh, not too bad. She's been nice to me, but I've heard stories about how rough she can be. The guys on the bus call her Her Highness. Not to her face, I might add."

Paula looked thoughtful. "Justin thought the world of her. So does Lou. I never really understood that, but what do I know? You certainly can't quarrel with success. Have the crowds been big?"

"Yeah, Dottie really packs the house. So, how was Dallas?"

"Busy." During the flight up, Paula had decided not to say anything about Vanessa's reason for summoning her. There was no need to get Mitch and Rona in a stew over something that might never happen. And right now Dane still looked to her for support and reassurance. That wouldn't last much longer if tonight's performance was any indication, but at the moment he needed her. He might panic a little if he thought there was even a possibility she would have to leave Nashville. So she was going to let everyone think this had been nothing but a routine business trip.

The taxi pulled up to the entrance of the motel; Dane and Paula got out. Then and only then did she realize how impulsive this trip had been. Why did she often behave so rashly where Dane was concerned? For most of her life, she had rarely strayed from her plans. But here she was in Oklahoma City when she should have been on her way home, and the strangest part of all was that she didn't regret coming. She just hoped the motel had a room for her.

It did. Just about everyone associated with the show was staying there that night, and with no show the next day, things promised to get lively before the evening was over. But for now Paula and Dane could be alone to talk.

He unlocked the door to her room and stood aside to allow her to enter. As he placed her suitcase on the luggage stand, he asked, "Do you want to go to the bar?"

"Oh . . . I don't think so. I'd like to just relax and visit before having dinner. If you want something, call room service."

"I really don't want anything, either. Only your company."

Paula kicked off her shoes, collapsed into an armchair in front of the window and tucked her feet beneath her. Dane took the other chair and grinned at her foolishly. For a minute neither of them said anything. Then Paula asked, "Has it been what you thought it would be?"

"I . . . I guess so. I didn't really have a lot of preconceived notions about the tour, none except for all those warnings you gave me. So far the pitfalls have avoided me. Maybe I'm too new and green. Maybe everyone's just feeling me out first, but I don't think so. Dottie's pretty straight laced when it comes to anything but men, and she expects everyone else to be, too. The guys tell me she doesn't even drink beer."

Paula nodded. She'd heard Dottie was the straight-arrow type. She certainly would be if Lou had anything to say about it. Also, Dottie had had some early coaching from Justin himself. He had never gotten over Tommy Lord—he considered the young man's demise a personal failure—so Paula could imagine the lectures he'd given the very young Dottie Crowe. Maybe men really were the singer's only "vice." Performing with Dottie's troupe the first time out was probably the best thing that could have happened to Dane. He would see firsthand that the kind of lifestyle the press reported on so frequently wasn't necessary to be a star.

"I'm glad," Paula told him. "I didn't want you tempted or disillusioned. And for sure I didn't want you doing anything dumb just to feel you belonged. I confess to worrying about it a lot."

Dane propped an elbow on the arm of the chair and rested his chin in his palm. "You worry too much. You should have had about six kids. All those young'uns to stew and fret over probably would have made you the happiest person on earth."

"I've been told that before," Paula said, smiling. "Verna used to accuse me of having an advanced degree in worry. I've often wondered what kind of mother I would have made. Probably overanxious and too protective. And if I'd had all those kids of my own, I doubt I would have had time to take a certain boy singer under my wing."

"Then said boy singer wants to thank you very much for not having all those kids."

"But Justin would have loved being a father," Paula said wistfully.

Dane did not especially want to hear anything about her late husband right now, which was ridiculous. If Paula hadn't been married to Justin Steele, by now she probably would have been married to a Birmingham man for twenty years and would be struggling to put two kids through college. Even if he had met her through Verna Gregg, she wouldn't have been in any position to help him. Being Mrs. Steele was what had brought her into his life. To call that a fortuitous circumstance was putting it mildly. So he listened.

"I think that's why he started giving all those unknowns a helping hand," she went on. "He referred to them as 'my kids,' and I'm sure that's the way he thought of them."

"Were they all young?"

"Yes. Very."

"Until me."

Paula laughed. "I don't consider you a man of advanced years."

"Do you consider me a kid?"

She wished she did. She would have preferred thinking of him the way she had in the beginning—as nothing but a man with an unusually good voice who deserved a break. Paula actually didn't like feeling close to him; it would make extricating herself from his life and career all the more difficult. She didn't like it that she had come to regard him as a very attractive man; and she certainly didn't like knowing how much she would miss him when his career took off.

"No," she said, "not as a kid. As a younger man."

Dane uttered an impatient sound. "I wish you'd cut that crap. Why do you even give age a thought? If I think of it at all, I think of us as being the same age."

"Well, we're not."

Never would he understand why the nine years that separated them were such a big deal to Paula, but apparently they were. And as long as they were, he wouldn't be able to get as close to her as he wanted, which was very close, indeed. Just how close he wanted to be to her had hit him like a thunderbolt only the night before.

Everyone else on the bus had been sound asleep, but sleep had proved elusive for Dane. Half lying in his seat, his face to the window, watching the black Arkansas night speeding past, he'd thought of Paula, and those thoughts had quickly turned yearning, aching. Another human being had reached inside him and touched him as no one ever had, and he'd wondered if, at long last, he had fallen in love.

In the bright light of day, however, realism had taken over. For a man like himself to fall in love with a woman like Paula required an abundance of gall. Compared to her, he had been little more than a street waif when he showed up on her doorstep.

Had been, Dane suddenly thought. No more. He was going to be somebody. It had occurred to him last night at the Little Rock concert, when two cute teenage girls had tried to climb up onstage while he was singing, that he could be a star. And when he was, he could tell Paula how he really felt. Then he would have something to offer her. Maybe then she would begin to see him in a different light.

Now he looked at her, seated only inches from him, so soft and beautiful, such a lady. From the beginning of their friendship, she had been the leader and he the follower; she the instructor, he the student. No wonder she thought so much of the years that separated them. The difference in their ages must seem like a yawning chasm to her. She had all but led him around by the hand, and women liked men they thought they could lean on occasionally, men who behaved like men, not schoolboys. How could he hope she would change the way she thought of him if he himself didn't change? Instead of playing the role of subservient student, he should act like a man who was attracted to a beautiful woman.

What did he say? Where were the words that would impress a woman like her? Sometimes she unwittingly made him feel so clumsy and inadequate, so oafish.

Dane reached for her hand. She had such wonderfully long, slender fingers, their tips covered by pale pink oval nails. "Paula, I . . ." Leaning forward, half rising, he bent his head, meaning only to kiss her tenderly, lovingly, to give her some idea of the emotion he felt for her.

But their lips were soft cushions pressing together. Dane got to his feet, pulling her with him, his mouth still on hers. He suddenly sensed Paula's willingness, and his mind reeled from the marvel of it. She actually was leaning into the kiss instead of merely accepting it. Her body seemed to have lost all its bones.

Then, wonder of wonders, she began kissing him back. Her lips parted; the tip of his tongue touched her teeth. He felt her palms splayed on his back, pressing him to her. It wasn't his imagination or wishful thinking. This was real. He scarcely could believe it was happening . . . but it was.

For one intense moment Paula felt herself slipping under his spell, giving in to a need that was thrilling and appalling at the same time. It had been a very long time since she'd been kissed, much longer still since she had been kissed like this—hungrily. And she was a woman who knew how to enjoy and appreciate what only a man could give her. Kissing Dane elicited some wonderful, long-forgotten sensations. For the moment it felt good to be held against him, absorbing his strength, feeling the very texture of her skin change wherever he touched her. Subconsciously, perhaps, she had been wanting this for weeks, and tonight it would be so easy. A man and a woman. Far from home. Plenty of time. So easy.

Then she came to her senses. Tomorrow was tomorrow, after all, and to elevate their friendship to the next higher plane would only create unwanted complications. With a great deal of effort, she pulled away from him. "Oh, Dane," she said with a gasp and a nervous little laugh, "stop it."

"Why?" he asked reasonably. "I got the distinct impression you were enjoying the hell out of it."

"Well, I...I'll admit it's been a long time, and, yes, I did enjoy it, but..."

"But what?"

"But we'll just ruin a very nice relationship."

He was incredulous. "How can a simple kiss ruin a nice relationship?"

Because it wasn't simple, she wanted to say. If it had been a simple kiss, there would be no problem, but there had been urgency and hunger in Dane's kiss. And in the split second before his mouth closed over hers, she had seen desire in his eyes. Worse, urgency, hunger and desire had been present in her own response, and that alarmed her. That kind of thing shouldn't be going on between them. They wouldn't be together much longer. He was on the threshold of a brand-new life, and she very well might be, too.

"It just complicates things," she said. "I think you and I have established a really remarkable relationship in a very short time, and physical affection has no place in it."

"Like hell!"

"No, really, Dane. You're probably thinking I'm making too big a deal of this, but, believe me, I know what I'm talking about. I want you to trust me and to like me, but I don't want you growing really fond of me." *And, dear God, I don't want to grow really fond of him!* "Do you understand?"

"Not even a little bit."

"I think you do," she said, rubbing nervously at the nape of her neck.

"I don't. What's wrong with becoming 'really fond' of you? You're the only person who's ever done a damned thing for me. You're the only person I've ever really trusted, the only one I never get tired of being with. How could I not become fond of you? And where I come from, people who are fond of each other sometimes kiss. And please don't tell me this isn't where I come from."

Dammit, he wished he knew what had happened. He had felt her response—he knew he had. So why was she all uptight now? Was it that she just didn't want to like him beyond the ordinary? He wasn't her type? He could well believe that. Paula's type wouldn't be a stranger to a tuxedo, and he'd attend charity balls and the like. Dane had never felt so frustrated in all his frustrating life.

Paula saw the frustration and was touched. She lifted a hand and placed her palm against his cheek. "I guess I say a lot of things that irritate you. I don't mean to. You simply interpret them differently than I do. You know, you really are a charming rascal."

Dane covered the hand with his own, held it a minute, then thrust it down. "You'd better be careful. That kind of thing might get you more of those kisses you don't like."

"I didn't say I don't like them. I said they have no place in our relationship, and they don't. Sit down and listen to me." With that she sank back into her chair.

Dane uttered an exaggerated groan. "I don't think I can stand another big sister lecture," he muttered. Still, he sat down.

"Dane, stop and think about where you are at this particular time in your life. On the brink of a new career. That's all you should be thinking of right now. Let's say, for the sake of conversation, that you did become...er, overly fond of me. We'd never see each other, so what would be the point?" Paula realized she was telling him this as much for her own benefit as for his.

Dane just stared at her a minute. "We might not be able to see each other a lot, but we could occasionally."

Paula sighed in exasperation. "Oh, Dane, is that really the kind of relationship you want with a woman—seeing her once in a blue moon? I don't think so. One of these days you'll meet the young woman you'll marry, the one who will give you a family. You're past due, you know. But for now, your career should be everything."

Again he simply stared at her a minute before saying, "You're afraid. You're afraid you might like me, too."

"Don't be ridiculous," Paula said, flustered. "I already like you."

"You know what I mean," he said impatiently.

"Yes, I know what you mean. It shouldn't happen, not between us. You'll always be someone special to me. I'll always be thinking of you and wishing you well, even if we go months or years without seeing each other."

"Years? Paula, I would never let that happen."

"You think that now, but the career takes over. It rules and dictates." Her chest heaved slightly. "Now, it's getting awfully late. Would you like to get something to eat?"

Dane sighed, giving up. "Yeah, I guess so."

"Will the restaurant still be open?"

"I doubt it, but the coffee shop stays open all night."

"Then shall we go?"

"Yeah. Sure, let's go," he said morosely, and stepped ahead of her to open the door.

Out in the hall, however, they encountered the members of Dottie's troupe, who had just arrived. They were ready to wind down after the performance and were far more interested in beer than food. There were the members of the band, the roadies, the bus driver and two young women who might have been wives but probably were groupies. Naturally they wanted Dane and his "lady friend" to join them. Dane quizzed Paula with his eyes; hers silently telegraphed a message: no, thanks.

He turned to the group. "Nah, Paula and I are going to get a bite to eat. I might see you a little later."

The others moved on. Dane and Paula continued on down the corridor. "Would you like to join them?"

she asked. "I can get something and take it back to the room."

"Is that what you want to do?"

"I don't care. I want you to do what you want to do."

"I wish you would tell me what you want," he snapped.

The tone of his voice startled her. "Why are we talking to each other this way?" she asked.

"I can't imagine," he said.

The coffee shop was almost deserted. Paula and Dane ordered sandwiches, then sat back and made awkward small talk, a first for them. *There's been a change,* Paula thought sadly, *a shift.* She didn't know where the relationship was now headed, but for sure it was in a new direction.

THE FOLLOWING MORNING, Paula woke determined to reestablish the easy camaraderie between them. Actually, it was simple since Dane was determined to do the same thing. Neither of them mentioned the previous night. They passed the time browsing in shops near the motel, then having lunch at a nearby restaurant. Dane didn't dare stray far from the motel since no one knew when Dottie would show up, so they said goodbye at the motel.

"When will you be home?" Paula asked.

"Maybe Tuesday."

"I'll see you then."

"Paula, I . . . ah, want to thank you for going to the trouble of coming up here. It was . . . well, it was great."

"I wouldn't have missed seeing you perform. I'm not in the least worried about Amarillo and Albuquerque. You're going to be wonderful. You'll just get better and better.''

The taxi Paula had called for pulled to a stop at the motel's entrance. Dane opened the back door, shoved her suitcase inside, then held the door for her. As she brushed past him, he detained her and placed a light kiss on her forehead. "Another kiss. So sue me," he said. "I'll see you Tuesday."

Paula couldn't help smiling. "You really are a charming rascal." She stepped into the cab and it drove away, leaving Dane to stare after the vehicle until it was swallowed up in traffic.

It was the "charming rascal" who occupied Paula's thoughts during the flight home and for days afterward. She seemed to ramble around the house purposelessly. The weekend lasted forever. Mitch and Rona spent it in Chattanooga with friends, so the big house was too empty. She couldn't concentrate on reading, television or anything else. She tried thinking about Vanessa and Hamilton House but couldn't even do that.

She was lonely, she decided, and if that was true, she was even more alarmed. Wasn't she the one who had always pitied people who depended on others for their emotional well-being? She wondered if she was too young to be going through menopause. Her entire body was out of whack, as if her hormones were shifting or something. Maybe she'd caught some kind of virus during her trip.

I miss Dane, she finally admitted, and was horrified.

To her private embarrassment she found herself wandering into Dane's room and simply touching his things, then going into the studio to listen to some recordings he had made. A few times she felt like crying when there really was nothing to cry about.

Something awful was happening to her. *This is ridiculous!* she thought, giving herself a mental shake. *Insane! I'm no impressionable youngster who can be rendered lovesick by something as simple as a man's kiss. I meant what I told Dane, and I still mean it. Anything but friendship between us isn't in the cards.*

Paula's mood brightened a little with Mitch and Rona's return Sunday night, and going to work Monday morning helped, too—at least, until Lou's phone call came. He wanted her to know he'd talked to Dottie before the troupe started home. "She said the Amarillo audience warmed to Dane so much she had to break her rule about no encores for opening acts. She was afraid they would lynch her if she didn't let him do another number."

Why hadn't Dane called to tell her that himself? So it had begun. His star was rising, just as she'd felt it would from the day she'd heard him on the riverbank. She didn't understand her sense of loss, the feeling that she was already slipping into the shadows. This was what she had wanted, wasn't it? This was what she had made happen, for heaven's sake. The gloominess descended again, and she snapped at her secretary for absolutely no reason.

Then it was Tuesday night, and Dane was walking through the door, suitcase in hand. Paula searched his face for the emotions she expected to see there—jubilation, triumph, elation. She had expected him to be percolating with excitement. Surprisingly, however, he only looked rather pensive. "All hail the conquering hero," she said. "I hear you're very big in Amarillo."

"Where did you hear that?" Dane asked.

"From Lou, who heard it from Dottie."

Dane scowled darkly. "Do you mean Dottie actually said something nice about me?"

"Is something wrong?" Paula asked, concerned.

"There must be. I just don't know what the hell it is."

"I don't understand."

"Can we talk about it in my room while I have a beer and change these clothes?"

Their cozy evening chats in his room had become part of their daily routine, but warning bells sounded in Paula's head. She had to rid herself of this absurd attraction to Dane. From now on her behavior toward him would be more in keeping with the true nature of their relationship. She would be friendly, interested, helpful and encouraging. But that was all. The evening chats in his bedroom would have to go. Before, their tête-à-têtes had not seemed intimate; now she feared they would.

Dane frowned at her hesitation. "Paula? Are you coming?"

"Of course," she said, giving up without a struggle.

While Dane changed in the bathroom, Paula made herself comfortable in the club chair, and they talked through the closed door. "So what's wrong?" she asked again after some initial small talk. "Obviously it has something to do with Dottie."

"Yeah, and it's got me stymied." The door opened and he came out. "The first day out, in Memphis, she was as friendly to me as a puppy. She even offered to let me travel on her bus. In Little Rock, she kept trying to get me alone. Then in Oklahoma City, boom! She did a complete 180. I can't figure it."

"How did you treat her?" Paula asked. "Were you . . . er, friendly, too?"

"I was nice to her, of course, but if you mean did I come on to her, no way." Dane sighed. "I really figured I'd be Dottie's opening act for a while, but I guess that's not going to happen. She's doing a major swing through the Midwest next month, and I certainly wasn't invited to come along."

So Dane had rebuffed her advances and had all but outshone the star in Amarillo. Neither was destined to endear him to Dottie. "Forget it," Paula advised him. "This tour was a good experience for you, and once your record is released, you won't need Dottie."

Dane frowned. "You know what I can't figure— why Oklahoma City? What happened there? It's always seemed to be that if a woman's interested, she doesn't give up after only two days. Most women would be more persistent."

"Dottie's not most women," Paula said. "Maybe it had something to do with my showing up."

"You?"

"For reasons I can't fathom, Dottie doesn't like me. We scarcely know each other, and yet she doesn't like me. It's as if she took one look at me years ago and came down with a bad case of instant aversion. I might add that I haven't lost any sleep over it."

Dane straddled the ottoman, putting himself squarely in front of her. "That is puzzling. Particularly since my initial reaction to you was exactly the opposite." His eyes twinkled mischievously.

Paula took a deep breath. "Don't start that."

"Start what?"

"Flirting."

"Why? I've thought and thought about all that stuff you said to me in the motel room, and I've come to the conclusion that it was a full ration of B.S. You once told me that Justin insisted you never deny your instincts, and I believe you advised me to do the same. All right. My instincts tell me that you and I could make beautiful music together."

"No, we couldn't. I can't carry a tune."

"I'll carry it for you."

Paula jumped to her feet as though she'd been on the receiving end of a jolt of electricity. "This is ridiculous. We shouldn't ever allow our conversations to stray along these lines."

"Why?" he demanded again.

"Because... because our lives are going to be heading in different directions. In six months you'll be far too busy to think of me, except perhaps as someone who helped you when you needed it."

"More B.S.! Paula, what in holy hell are you afraid of?"

Me, she could have truthfully said. *Of becoming utterly foolish over a younger man, then watching him soar off into the stratosphere while I have to remain with my feet solidly on the ground.* "N-nothing. This entire conversation is silly. I'm going to bed. Good night."

Dane watched her leave the room; she all but ran out of it. Surprisingly, he didn't feel rebuffed or discouraged. In fact, he was smiling. Paula was fighting the attraction hard, but there were more effective ways of discouraging him if she really wanted to.

He couldn't forget the way she'd kissed him in the motel room. Some things couldn't be faked. So he would wear down her resistance eventually, and then perhaps he would find out why the attraction bothered her so. Was it the age thing? She sure put a lot of store in that garbage. Maybe she thought of herself primarily as Mrs. Justin Steele and found it hard to let go of her husband.

One thing for sure, Dane thought with satisfaction. *It isn't me.* Paula cared for him. He couldn't forget that kiss.

THE NEXT THREE DAYS were difficult for Paula. Everything had changed between Dane and herself, and she hated that. Whenever she looked at him, the air palpitated, so she tried not to look at him—not easy when they lived under the same roof. And not looking at him did nothing to erase her awareness of him. She knew where he was even when she couldn't see him. She knew when his eyes were on her. Once, when their gazes happened to collide, he looked at her in a way that made her cheeks color and her insides grow warm.

Unaccustomed to having to fight her emotions, she was tense and as jumpy as hell. At work her secretary asked if she was coming down with something. At home Mitch and Rona shot quizzical looks in her direction, then between themselves. *What's going on here?* was the unspoken question. On Wednesday and Thursday nights, Paula brought unnecessary work home from the office. It gave her an excuse to hole up in her bedroom after dinner. By Friday she was exhausted. She also was dreading the weekend, when she would be around Dane virtually every minute. The worst part of it all was wanting to be with him and knowing she shouldn't be, not anymore.

Dane watched from the sidelines as she grappled with her desires, not really understanding but trying to be sympathetic. Unfortunately, she was stretching the limits of his sympathy. He'd always thought the man-woman thing was pretty straightforward. A simple matter of wanting, giving, taking. The only thing he'd ever demanded of romantic attraction was that it be mutual. Why wasn't it that uncomplicated for Paula? She was turning the attraction into a monumental crisis of the heart. He didn't find that rational, much less reasonable.

He guessed there was a lot about women he didn't understand, which wasn't surprising. Never before had he known a woman he wanted to learn much about. Now he did. And he was woefully unschooled in the art of getting inside a woman's head and heart and discovering what made her tick.

PAULA WOKE before dawn Saturday morning, mostly because she had gone to bed much too early the night before. Propping her hands behind her head, she thought of the long weekend ahead and wished she had something to do that would take her out of the house. She needed to think needed time to sort and analyze the unexpected complication in her life. Mainly she wanted to be sure it didn't get any more complicated. The crazy emotions Dane aroused in her would pass, she was sure. She just hoped they would pass before she did something foolish, like make a total idiot of herself over him.

Paula genuinely did not welcome the attraction. It wasn't wise. Dane should not—could not, really—devote himself to a woman at this stage of his life. Too much was happening to him, and he needed to be free to grab at any opportunity that came his way. And Paula wasn't even slightly interested in a short-term affair, no matter how exciting. She'd known so many women her age who'd indulged in them when they suddenly found themselves alone, and she couldn't think of even one that had ended happily ever after—especially one that had been conducted with a younger man. An affair was out.

She sighed. Last weekend she'd rambled around an empty house, feeling positively wretched. This weekend she would have given anything to be alone. She supposed she could spend the day shopping. Wasn't that the panacea that cured all female complaints? No. For her, shopping was a chore.

There were half a dozen acquaintances who were forever telling her to "call and we'll have lunch." But Saturday, she decided, wasn't a good day for that. Weekends were family times.

She could always go to the office; it was never difficult to find something to do there. She just didn't think she could stand to spend two days in this house with Dane. Now, for the first time, she understood Justin's periodic need to get away to his fishing cabin, simply to be alone.

Paula sat straight up in bed. The fishing cabin! What a wonderful place for a distraught mind—nothing but birds and squirrels, peace and quiet for company. Justin had always said there was nothing like a weekend at the cabin for whatever ailed you. He swore the place had mysterious rejuvenating powers.

Jumping out of bed, she went to the window and peered out. Daybreak was only beginning to pinken the horizon. If she hurried, she would be gone long before the household stirred. Then she wouldn't have to answer a lot of damned fool questions.

Quickly she showered and dressed in jeans and a short-sleeved polo shirt, then packed more jeans and knit tops. A nightgown and some underwear went in next. The makeup case she took on trips was always ready. Now so was she.

Paula moved soundlessly through the hushed house. She knew she couldn't leave without letting Rona know where she was, so she wrote a brief note—"I've gone to the cabin. See you Sunday night"—and laid it at the secretary's place at the dining table. Then she slipped out of the house.

She did not regard what she was doing as running away. Rather, she was confronting her problems head-on. She simply was going to do it far from Dane's disturbing presence.

CHAPTER ELEVEN

DANE WAS THE FIRST to find the note. He was up and about earlier than the others, filled with steely resolve. Paula was going to talk to him whether she wanted to or not. It was patently childish of her to avoid him as though he had a communicable disease, when all he wanted to do was kiss her, soothe her, treat her like a woman. If she came right out and told him to leave her alone, then he would. He didn't, however, think for a minute she was going to do that.

The house was very quiet since everyone usually slept in a little later on Saturday, but as he walked through the den toward the front of the house, he definitely smelled coffee. Martha rose with the chickens and made sure there was coffee for early risers. He crossed the foyer and entered the dining room.

That was when he saw the note. He might have ignored it since it obviously had been left for Rona, but when he noticed Paula's distinctive handwriting, he stopped and frowned. Why would Paula be leaving Rona a note when she would see her in a few minutes? Without considering the propriety of it, he picked up the note and read it.

She'd gone to a cabin? Where in the hell was the cabin and why in the hell had she gone there? To get away from him? It was the damnedest thing he'd ever heard of. She must have been struggling with something far more complicated than he'd suspected if she felt it necessary to get away from him.

He placed the note back on the table, poured himself a cup of coffee from the carafe on the sideboard and waited for Mitch or Rona to show up. Either one of them could tell him what he wanted to know.

The secretary put in an appearance first. Dane watched her pick up the note, read it, then frown and purse her lips. "How odd," she muttered.

"Does she do this very often?" Dane asked, getting Rona's attention. "Sorry, I read the note. Is this something she does periodically?"

"Never! That's why it's so strange."

"Where's the cabin, Rona?" Dane asked tersely.

She looked surprised. "I'm...not sure I should tell you that."

"Please. It's important."

Rona poured from the carafe, then carried her cup to the table and sat down. "Dane, I'm going to ask you a personal question, and I hope you'll answer it."

"Shoot."

"What in hell is going on between you and Paula? Nothing's been the same since you got back from the tour. My God, sometimes you could cut the tension in this house with a knife."

He snorted. "Tell me about it!"

"And bringing home work from the office? She hasn't done that in years. Her lackeys take home work from the office, not Paula. What's wrong?" Rona sounded genuinely puzzled and concerned.

"Oh...Paula has some hang-ups about...certain things."

"Paula? She's the most uncomplicated person I've ever known."

"Apparently not when it comes to matters of the heart."

Rona gasped. "You mean..."

"A strange thing has happened to me, Rona," Dane said. "I seem to have fallen in love with her."

The secretary leaned forward, titillated by the confidence. "And how does she feel about you?"

"Confused...and that's putting it mildly. She thinks physical affection has no place in our relationship. I say that's so much garbage. She thinks she's too old for me. Again, garbage. She says our lives are going to go off in different directions. I say why not worry about tomorrow tomorrow and just enjoy today?"

Rona shook her head. "I can see you don't know nearly as much about the woman you're lusting after as you should. Paula always thinks things through before she acts."

"I want to make her talk to me. Here, with other people around, she can hide from me, but at a cabin... Please, tell me how to find her. I think Mitch will let me borrow his car one more time."

"Oh, Dane, I don't know about this."

"Please."

Rona thought about it. A lot might hinge on what she told him. Was it right of her to send him to Paula when she obviously had gone to the cabin expressly to get away from him? Rona's loyalties lay squarely with Paula.

And yet, she liked Dane, really liked him. He somehow had become more important to her than any of the others before him had. Finally she capitulated with a sigh. "Okay, I'm going to do it. Why, I don't know. Maybe I'm a sucker for romance. Maybe I happen to think you'd be good for her. Maybe I don't want you moping around the house like a lovesick teenager all weekend. I'll get a map and show you how to find the place. But I'm warning you—the last couple of miles really should be made on horseback.''

"Does this cabin have a phone?"

"Yes."

"You won't call ahead and warn her I'm coming, will you?"

"Dane, if I were going to do that, I wouldn't tell you where she is in the first place."

HAVING DRIVEN the tortuous road leading to the cabin without incident or damage to her car, Paula pulled up to the structure with a sigh of relief. She had stopped in the nearest village to buy groceries to preclude the possibility that she would have to negotiate the winding lane more than twice—once in and once out.

Had she been foolish to come? In building the hideaway, Justin had opted for privacy above all; the word *remote* barely did justice to its location. However, there was a sophisticated security system that Justin had taught her to activate, and—she gulped at the thought—a loaded rifle that he had forced her to learn to shoot. When Paula had protested that she never would be able to shoot at a person, Justin had said, "You don't have to. Just point it. Nobody's dumb enough to walk toward a pointed gun."

It was a gorgeous day. Here in the woods, with a running stream nearby and tall trees blocking out much of the sun, it seemed many degrees cooler than in the city. Paula got out of the car, collected her makeup case and overnight bag and climbed the steps. The cabin looked rustic, but its appearance was deceiving. It was built as solidly as their home in Nashville and had been furnished with an eye toward easy living. Justin had not been one for doing without his creature comforts.

Paula unlocked the door and pushed it open. The cabin was an A-frame—one enormous room with a sleeping loft and a kitchen alcove. The interior had a musty, unlived-in smell. Leaving the front door open, she set down her luggage and returned to the car for the groceries. Then she opened windows to air out the place and began to poke around.

There was a layer of dust on everything, but otherwise the cabin was in perfect condition. Justin had kept it well stocked with canned goods, liquor, linens, cleaning supplies, toiletries and, of course, fishing gear. The little kitchen had all the usual appliances, and there was a wall phone. Justin hadn't wanted one, but she had insisted that it was far too dangerous to be in such a remote spot without some means of calling for help. Paula pulled open drawers and cabinets, refreshing her memory about what was there. Satisfied that if one wanted to be alone, there were worse places to be, she turned on the refrigerator, filled ice trays, put away the groceries, then set about seeing what she could do about the dust.

An hour later, the dust and cobwebs were gone, fresh linens were on the bed, and the bathroom had been scrubbed. The place was clean, which was more than Paula could say for herself. She felt as though an inch of grit clung to her damp skin. After closing the windows and turning on the air conditioner, she took a shower. Once she felt more human, she stepped out the back door to have a look around.

Though the woods in front of the cabin had been left in their pristine wild state, Justin had spent a mountain of money on the rear. First, a long, railed porch had been built, and the land had been cleared of all but the stateliest trees. The ground sloped down to the river, and he'd had a terrace and brick steps put in. Once it had been quite a beautiful spot, the perfect place to sit after dinner and commune with nature. With a little TLC, Paula thought, it easily could be that way again.

Paula slowly descended the steps, coming to a stop at the water's edge. Justin's fishing boat bobbed in the covered stall, where it was tied. She really needed to get serious about selling the cabin and the boat. She gladly would have given them to one of his cronies, but his fishing pals had been older than he and, sadly, were either gone or of such advanced age they weren't interested in the place. Neither was she, and if she got the nod to go to Dallas, she would have enough of a problem selling her house. She wouldn't want to have to worry about this hideaway, too. She had sworn she'd never sell any of Justin's possessions, only give them to people who would appreciate them, but she'd have to make an exception in this case. She simply didn't know anyone who would want either the cabin or the boat.

Stepping out onto the dock—a structure needing some repair, she noticed—she glanced up and down the stream. Here the world was unbelievably quiet, eerily so. Tiny, strange animal noises could be heard in the distance. Overhead, birds chirped. The water barely rippled. Paula shivered, even though the day was quite warm. She might have been the only soul on earth, and she thought about night, how very, very dark nights were in the country. Maybe she'd overdone the getting-away-from-it-all bit. Every time she'd been here before, Justin had been with her.

Shoving her hands into her jeans pockets, Paula retraced her way up the steps, her head down. She was halfway up when she lifted her head. A man stood at the top of the steps, watching her. She gave a start and uttered a cry of fright. Then the man moved, and she sank onto the step, going limp. "Oh, my God!" she cried.

"Sorry if I frightened you," Dane said.

"Frightened me? You scared me out of my wits!"

"When you want to get away from it all, you get serious about it, don't you? This place is the back of beyond."

Putting a hand to her forehead, Paula struggled to bring her breathing under control. "How in the hell did you find me?"

"What a warm welcome. I'm touched."

"How did you get here?"

"Mitch's car."

Shoving herself to her feet, she brushed at the seat of her pants and continued on up the steps, using an icy stare as a self-defense mechanism. But she was shaking inside. All of her grand plans about using the weekend to put her thoughts in order flew out the window. How could she think rationally with him here? "Didn't it occur to you that I came here to be alone?" she asked angrily, stomping across the porch and into the cabin.

Dane followed her, catching the screen door before it slammed in his face. "As a matter of fact, it occurred to me you were running away."

Caught completely off balance, Paula felt her face growing warm. "How did you find me?"

"I found the note you left Rona. After some arm-twisting, I managed to get her to tell me how to get here."

"She had no right. I'll kill her."

"No, you won't."

"Dane, please go."

"You gotta be kidding. It'll take at least twenty-four hours for me to get up the nerve to drive that last two miles again."

"You can't stay here."

"Why not?"

He had to be the most exasperating individual she had ever met, to say nothing of the most persistent and stubborn. "I want to be alone, that's why not. I have...some decisions to make, and...there are too many distractions at home."

"Me, for instance?"

She ignored that. "I...need to think."

"About us?"

She sighed. "There is no 'us.'"

Dane grinned. "There's you, and there's me, right? Doesn't that make 'us'?" He closed the space between them and, in a quick, fluid motion, took her into his arms. She made a halfhearted attempt to extricate herself, then gave up and stood rigidly in his embrace.

"I went to a lot of trouble to come here," he said, "because I have something to tell you."

"You...could have called." His nearness had her feeling completely disoriented. When he was close to her, she found herself wanting things she had no business wanting.

"No, this isn't the kind of thing you tell someone over the phone, at least not the first time."

Paula eyed him warily. "What is it?"

"I'm in love with you."

She slipped out of his embrace, and he did not try to hold her. "Oh, Dane, no you're not. You're grateful to me. I'm the first real friend you've ever had, the first person you've ever trusted, so you've got that confused with something else." Nervously she began twisting the ring on her right hand. "I guess that's not surprising when you're dealing with emotions you've never experienced before. But it's gratitude, that's all, and there's a world of difference between gratitude and love."

Dane listened patiently, knowing she was trying to convince herself, not him. When she finished speaking, he simply stood looking at her and smiling for a minute. Then he said, "Believe it or not, I know the difference. Maybe in the beginning, I was grateful to you, but you grew on me. Now I love you. You're all I can think about. You enchant me. I'm obsessed with you." Those were words he had never spoken to another human being, not even while in the throes of lust. He had wondered if he would feel foolish or embarrassed when he said them. Strangely, he didn't.

"Oh, for heaven's sake," Paula breathed. "Stop it. Please, stop it."

She was less than a foot from him, and suddenly nothing separated them. She was in his arms again, only this time he did more than just hold her. His hands stroked her back, then came to rest at the sides of her breasts. He buried his face in her hair, then dipped his head and began nibbling along her jawline and the underside of her chin. The strangest gurgling sound came out of her throat; she thought she was in heaven.

"I love you," he said huskily.

Paula could feel herself weakening. Her head was foggy, and her body seemed to have a mind of its own. "Dane...please...go pick on someone your own age."

"I can't. I love you." He placed a hand on each side of her face and studied it with the seriousness of an artist who was about to paint her. Then he began to kiss her, starting with her forehead, then moving down to the tip of her nose, both cheeks and finally her mouth. Paula went lax in his arms the moment she felt his lips part over hers. Her own parted. His tongue slipped between her teeth. Hers met it in welcome. Dane was ravenous; he tried to consume her with his kiss.

When they broke apart, gasping, her eyes were closed, her lips moist and puffy, and her hands were resting lightly on his chest. "I've...told you how I feel," she groaned. "You know...what I think about the difference in our ages, how I feel about...everything. And still you do this to me."

"Yes, you've told me how you feel—about two dozen times. But that won't do. You'll have to come up with something else. Tell me you feel nothing but friendship for me," Dane commanded her gently. "Tell me you don't want me. Tell me to go."

Paula's surrender was complete. Her hands crawled up the hard wall of his chest and locked behind his neck. "Heaven help me," she murmured. "I can't."

They kissed again and again and continued kissing and holding each other all the way up the steps to the loft. The bed, covered with clean white sheets, beckoned invitingly. Dane sent up a silent prayer that he would make this good for her. She had fought this like a champion, and he didn't want her to be disappointed or have regrets afterward.

He undressed her with as much tenderness as he could manage, flinging her clothes aside, murmuring hot, erotic words all the while. Then she returned the favor with trembling hands. When they were naked, they knelt together on the bed and faced each other.

Everything Dane knew about making love to a woman had been learned through trial and error, and he belonged to the limited group of men who found the art of arousing a woman almost as exciting as the coupling that followed. It was strange that this was so, for there hadn't been any careful and loving instruction at home. Most of what he knew about sex had come from the streets. Yet, he enjoyed the foreplay, the kisses, the hot, whispered words.

And through the years he had learned that lovemaking was far more complicated for women than it was for men. True, men experienced varying degrees of satisfaction, but not to the extent women did. How thrilling it was to learn just what buttons to push. Even more so now because of Paula. Every minute he had spent with other women had been a rehearsal for now. He had to bind her to him, make her want him again and again and again.

His capable hands were gentle, with underlying strength. He began learning her the way he would learn a new song. Her nipples rose to his touch; his mouth closed over one puckered point, then the other. His hands stroked her. All the while he waited for the obvious signs of complete arousal—rapid breathing, soft moans, pliancy, moistness.

After battling her desire so gallantly, Paula gave in to her eagerness for him. She blessed the genes that had kept her figure firm and supple—smooth thighs, high buttocks, small but erect breasts. She knew she didn't have to be ashamed of baring her body to him, which was good because he was the most beautiful man she had ever seen. It came to her with some surprise that she had never known the pleasures of such a young body. Justin, her first and only lover, had been older than Dane when she had met him.

Her hands roamed restlessly, searching, seeking, discovering. Never before had foreplay been this thrilling. How had a man with Dane's wretched background learned to be such a tender lover? It seemed she had barely begun her exploration when he rolled her over onto her back and covered her body with his.

Dane had hoped he could prolong the fondling and kissing, but having Paula touch him intimately proved more than he could bear. Her arching and writhing drove him out of his mind. Then he heard her desperate voice.

"Dane...please...love me," Paula gasped.

"Oh, babe, it's all I've thought about, all I've wanted...and I want you good and ready for me."

"I am ready. Please...."

He plunged into her. His head spun; his mind stumbled. "Oh, God, it's been a long time for me. I hope I don't botch this."

"It's been a long time for me, too. It doesn't matter...the first time. It's only the beginning."

Dane didn't see it that way. There was no doubt about the outcome of their lovemaking on his part; he would climax. But there was such a feeling of incompleteness when the woman didn't, too. Leaving Paula unsatisfied would make him feel wretched.

She wound her fingers through his hair and answered the tempo of his body thrust for thrust. Dane struggled for control. After wanting this so badly, he couldn't spoil it with a precipitous climax, but the pressure building inside him was torturous. Clenching his teeth, he stilled, swallowing thickly. Not yet. Not yet. It had to last until she could join him.

But the rotating motions of Paula's hips were frantic, frenzied. She had not known her body was so deprived until it was being satisfied. She wrapped her legs around him and lifted her hips. Turning her head on the pillow, she moaned his name. Dane was so masterful and she was so hungry that she reached the brink before she knew it. She hated for it to end, but the first tingling sensations had begun. There was no stopping it.

Mercifully, Dane felt the force of her contractions along the length of him. At last he could let go. A great wave of release exploded from him, and when it was over, he knew the most peaceful moments of his life.

He rolled his slick, limp body off her and pulled her against him. Paula lay weak and sated in the warm circle of his arm. Good or bad, right or wrong, wise or foolish, it was done, and she didn't regret it a bit. It had been wonderful and, perhaps, inevitable. Snuggling against him, her head on his chest, she felt utterly content, completely alive, and already she was anticipating the next time.

Dane lay as still as death; the only sound was his even breathing. Finally he stirred. "God, that was incredible! I was afraid I wouldn't be able to wait."

"I'm glad you did. It's always better when it happens together."

"It doesn't get any better than that."

"No, it doesn't," Paula agreed.

"How I love you!"

"Do you know something? I love you, too. I'm not sure this is the best thing that could happen to you at this point in your life, but—"

"Are you kidding? I feel like I could outsing the nightingales."

"I'm talking about your concentration, your focus."

"I'll work on them," he promised, "but right now, today, tomorrow, do you mind if I concentrate solely on you?"

They kissed, teased and touched until he had risen and hardened again. Paula marveled at how vital and virile he was. This time when they came together it was after protracted foreplay that had her pleading with him to enter her. Afterward they fell asleep in each other's arms, only to wake and find themselves ravenously hungry.

The day was idyllic. After lunch they set about exploring this new world, a world blessedly free of other people. It was wonderful to stroll through the woods and along the bank of the stream, making sure that some part of themselves touched at all times. Dane decided to try to catch their dinner, and miraculously the fish were biting. Paula thought it remarkable that she could so enjoy simply watching a man fish. She lay on the grassy slope, half dozing, smiling each time he uttered a yelp of triumph as another tasty morsel was plucked from the water. By the time the fish were cleaned and iced, the back porch was completely in the shade. They sat there and talked.

"You've never told me a thing about your childhood," he said. "Were you cute and precocious?"

Paula laughed. "No, I was gangling and as awkward as the devil. I almost killed myself trying to learn to ride a bike. My mom used to say I was hiding behind a door when coordination was handed out."

Dane smiled. An awkward Paula was not a picture that easily came to mind. "What did you dream about being when you grew up?"

"Lots of things. First, a teacher. Then a librarian. By the time I was a teenager, I'd gone through the usual stages of wanting to be a movie star, ballerina, opera singer—you name it. If it made you rich and famous, I dreamed of it at one time or another. I never particularly wanted to be a girl Friday, which I was when I met Justin, and I certainly never dreamed of the corporate life. That just happened." She cocked her head and looked at him. "What about you? How old were you when you discovered you had that incredible voice?"

"Early teens, I guess. After my voice changed. I'd always loved country music, so I saved enough to buy a guitar at a pawn shop. Taught myself to play out of a Chet Atkins songbook. Sometimes I'd sing along. People started telling me my voice was good, and I noticed that people treated me a little better when I was singing. I figured music might be a way to have girls notice me as something other than a troublemaker." Dane shrugged. "It wasn't anything very dramatic."

"Did you ever dream about being up on a stage, having people pay to listen to you sing?"

"If I did, I don't remember it." His eyes clouded. "Paula, my life was so damned miserable I didn't dare let myself dream about much of anything. Dreams were for others, people with hope.''

Her heart gave a lurch. Getting to her feet, she went to sit in his lap. ''But that's all over. Isn't that wonderful? So much lies ahead of you. From now on, the world will be your oyster. There's no limit to what you can dream. Your life will never be miserable again.''

He ran his hand over her thigh, up and down, up and down. ''It sure won't be as long as you're in it, babe.''

The sun was low on the horizon, obscured by the thick woods on the other side of the river. They went inside. Dane fried the fish and potatoes, while Paula made a salad. They ate leisurely and talked about nothing of importance. After dinner they curled together on the sofa and listened to music on the radio, wanting nothing but each other.

And when it was very late, they strolled down to the riverbank to stare mesmerized at the moonlight-dappled water. They kissed, but never again would one kiss be enough. They kissed twice, three times. They touched, and that became an embrace. Soon their kisses were hot and fevered.

''Have you ever made love standing up?'' he asked in a throaty voice.

She shook her head.

''Would you like to try it?''

She was trembling. ''Anything you want.''

Dane pressed her back against the trunk of an ancient tree and peeled her clothes off, then his. ''Like Adam and Eve,'' he whispered as the soft sounds of night in their own Eden enveloped them. They made slow, warm, ardent love, shatteringly explosive for both of them. It was a fitting finale to an exquisite day.

CHAPTER TWELVE

SOMETIME DURING THE NIGHT Paula woke to the sound of gentle rain on the roof. Snuggling deeper under the covers, she dovetailed her body into Dane's and smiled against the pillow. Deep in sleep, he stirred slightly and flung his arm across her hip in a possessive gesture. He was such an accomplished lover. Again she marveled that a man who had known so little tenderness was capable of dispensing so much of it. He had made her feel like a woman again. It was a feeling she savored.

She found it impossible to go back to sleep. For an hour or more she lay awake, her thoughts roaming back over the previous day's events, and a small sigh escaped her lips. Making love while standing against a tree trunk, of all things! She'd certainly never done that before. She still didn't know how they had managed the maneuver since they both had been trembling uncontrollably when it was over. Dane had unleashed a reckless, wanton side to her nature that she hadn't known existed. Now freed, it would have to be kept satisfied.

Every sensible cell in Paula's body told her that this involvement with him wasn't the smartest thing she'd ever done—for either of them. Trying to project ten years into the future, she simply couldn't see them still together. Everything would conspire to prevent a happily-ever-after ending for them. Maybe Dallas, for one thing. For another, she would be fifty-five in ten years, while he would still be a relatively young man...and in a business where young women were as easily obtained as a drink of water.

Yet, she, who had never been one for seizing the moment and damning tomorrow, didn't intend doing a thing to stop the relationship from developing further. Dane made her too happy.

He stirred again. Carefully Paula turned to face him. In repose his face looked so boyishly handsome that she had to restrain herself from dropping a kiss on his slack mouth. With a touch as light as the brush of a butterfly's wings, she ran her fingertips along his muscular arm. Dear God, she wanted him again! Her level of sensuality had risen dramatically. The temptation to wake him was strong. Instead, she put her arms around him and tucked his head into the curve of her shoulder. Burying her face in his rumpled hair, she at last fell asleep.

The rain was coming down harder when Dane woke several hours later. Finding himself nestled in Paula's arms, he thought how pleasant it was to wake beside the warm, soft body of someone who meant the world and all to him. She was a consummate lover, a woman who knew how to give and accept. He had wanted to tell her it had never been so good for him, but it sounded trite, and she probably suspected as much. The difference, of course, was love. Not long ago he wouldn't have believed that love like this existed, much less that it would happen to him. He wasn't sure he was worthy of it, but it seemed to be his, neverthe- less. How many times yesterday had Paula told him she loved him? A dozen? Love! The force of it staggered him. Sighing contentedly, he hugged her gently, causing her eyelids to flutter open.

"Good morning," he said.

"Good morning," she purred sleepily. "Oh, listen to that rain. Isn't this nice?"

"I'm in heaven, and there are a lot of folks back in Alabama who swore that's the last place I'd wind up."

Paula smiled and stretched luxuriously. Then she snuggled against him again. "I woke up once during the night, and I spent an hour watching you sleep."

"That sounds like an exciting way to spend an hour."

"It was. You're a very handsome man, you know. I just lay here, watching you and having lewd thoughts." With her foot she stroked his thigh, moving down his hard calf and back up. Suggestively, sensuously, up and down. She took one of his hands and placed it on a breast. Its nipple peaked instantly. "I feel I must tell you something. If you want me, I'm yours. I promise not to resist."

"Babe," he whispered, "you're going to kill me."

"Are you too tired?" Her fingers closed around him. "No," she said with a satisfied smile. "You're not too tired."

With an exaggerated growl, Dane lifted her up and over him, bringing her down to straddle his hips. Raising his head an inch, he took in the incredible sight of her. This time their lovemaking was a sustained, playful romp, culminating in wave after wave of ecstatic release.

Afterward they went downstairs to bathe together, then to have breakfast. Paula was no great shakes in the kitchen, but even she knew how to make omelets and put bread in a toaster. Dane made coffee, and they found some peach preserves in the pantry. And while they ate, Paula talked.

"We have to come down to earth long enough to discuss some things," she said.

"I can't handle anything heavy today," he said, concerned about the seriousness in her voice. "Can't we talk about the weather or some such thing? I'm off on cloud nine, and I don't want to land."

"We must. We seem to have started something here that we can't stop, and it's going to be difficult, if not impossible, for us to even see each other very often during the next few years. You're going to be on the road most of the time. You have no choice—the career demands it. And I—" she reached out to lovingly stroke the nape of his neck "—maybe I should have told you this before we made love, but I may be moving away from Nashville."

Dane choked on his coffee. "Moving?" he cried when he could speak.

Paula nodded solemnly. "The trip to Dallas was no ordinary business trip. Vanessa's on the prowl for her successor, and it seems I'm in the running. She's almost eighty and very concerned about Hamilton House's future. Of course, others are being considered, too, but I suppose I have as good a chance as anyone."

Dane was stunned. He, too, had given plenty of thought to the days, weeks he would have to be away. Long before now, back in the days when he'd only made love to Paula during fanciful flights of his imagination, he had regretted that the demands of the business would keep him away from her so much. He'd wondered if she would ever fly to wherever he was performing, just to be with him. He'd wondered if a schedule of a week on the road and a week at home could sustain both a career and their relationship. For a long time now, he'd known that keeping Paula in his life in some capacity was number one on his list of priorities. That she wouldn't always be in Nashville had never entered his mind.

"Do...you want that?" he asked.

She pursed her lips. "Oh, I have mixed emotions about it. I guess anybody would. I've worked hard for the company, and the promotion would be my reward, the gold star on my report card. In that sense I want it. But I would hate leaving home. Vanessa realizes that anyone who becomes president of Hamilton House is going to have to make some sacrifices."

A wave of panic hit Dane, and he tried a desperate measure. "Paula...darling...now that we have what we have, do you really need to continue working? You could travel with me..."

"I've thought about that, and the answer is...yes, I do. And if Vanessa offers me the presidency, I'll have to take it. That means moving to Dallas."

Dane set down his fork. "Then I guess that means I'll move to Dallas, too."

Her eyes grew warm. "Lou is in Nashville. Heron Records and Owen Brewster are in Nashville. In the beginning, at least, it'll be easier on you if you're there, too."

"I'm not looking for easy. I'm looking for happy. You told me that a lot of performers record in Nashville but are based somewhere else. Dallas might be a good place to settle." He took her hand in his, encasing it warmly. "I know we'll be apart a lot, but you can bet your life I'll arrange to spend every second with you I can. Please, babe, let's not think about what might happen next month or next year. Let's just think about right now."

"You're right, of course. And maybe nothing at all will happen."

Dane rubbed his chin and shot her a little smile. "President of a corporation."

"Isn't that something."

It's something, all right, Dane thought. He didn't know how he really felt about it. It was sort of scary, actually, thinking about the demands of her job coupled with the demands of his. When would they find time for each other? "Do Mitch and Rona know about all this?"

Paula shook her head.

"Lou?"

"Especially not Lou."

"Why especially not Lou?"

"It's hard to explain. Lou was absolutely devoted to Justin, and as far as he's concerned, I'm still Mrs. Steele and am supposed to behave that way. If he knew I was here in Justin's cabin with you, I'm convinced the man would have a fit of apoplexy. For me to move out of Nashville, to sell Justin's house—that would be the worst thing I could possibly do. Sacrilegious."

"That's pretty ridiculous."

"I agree. But I really should tell them, all three of them, and give poor Lou time to recover from the shock before it actually comes to pass—if it does."

"What do you think Mitch and Rona will do? Go with you to Dallas?"

"I have no idea, Dane. And I'm not in Dallas yet. May never be.... I thought we weren't going to mention next week or next month."

"So we weren't. And so we won't. Damn, I hate to leave this place."

Paula smiled wistfully. "So do I. It's been wonderful."

"Can we come back?"

"Anytime you want to," she promised.

"May I venture just one small question about the future?" Dane asked. "When we get home...what are we going to do about this new relationship we've established?"

Paula's eyes twinkled merrily. "Come to my room, of course."

"Will we shock anyone?"

"I don't know, and frankly, I don't care. Do you?"

"Hell, no!"

THE RAIN STOPPED by midmorning, and the sun came out. The day became unbearably steamy, so outside activities were vetoed. Paula and Dane spent the rest of the morning tidying the cabin; then they had lunch and packed up to reluctantly leave.

He followed her back to the city. As they pulled onto the sweeping driveway leading to the house, Paula noticed Lou's car parked at the foot of the steps. It was absurd, but she felt like a sixteen-year-old girl who was arriving home an hour after curfew. Lou naturally would have been curious about where she was. Paula wondered if Rona would have told him the truth.

The others were in the den when Paula and Dane entered. Mitch noticed them first and raised a forefinger in greeting, which got Rona's attention. The secretary shot Paula a fearful glance. She had agonized over her decision to send Dane to the cabin, but one look at Paula's face and she relaxed. The woman was radiant.

"Hi," Rona said quickly before Paula or Dane could speak. "Lou's been waiting quite a while, but I explained that you'd asked Dane to drive you to the cabin, just to check it out." Rona glanced at her watch. "Actually, you made it there and back in pretty good time."

Oh, this is so silly, Paula thought, but what could she do now? The truth would catch Rona in a bald-faced lie, and the secretary only had her best interests at heart. So, Lou thought she and Dane had only been gone a few hours. Well, maybe that was for the best for the time being.

"What kind of shape is the cabin in?" Lou asked.

"Perfect."

"I thought you were going to sell it."

"We'll see. There's no great rush." Wanting to get rid of the cabin had ended yesterday. Now Paula wanted it for herself and Dane. She would keep it until she went to Dallas, if she ever did.

"This is a switch," Lou said. "Last I heard you couldn't wait to unload it. It really is a useless expense."

"Money doesn't seem to be one of my problems, Lou."

She turned to face Dane's puzzled scowl. With her eyes she tried to convey a message to him. *I'll explain later.* He stared at her a minute, then muttered, "I'll be downstairs. See all of you later." With that he left the room.

Paula stuck around to make idle small talk for a few more minutes; then while everyone else was engrossed in something on TV, she nonchalantly left the room and went downstairs. Slipping into Dane's room, she closed the door behind her. "Dane, I—"

He whirled. "Let me get this straight. Is Lou never supposed to know anything about us?"

"I know it's dumb. I really wish Rona hadn't felt it necessary to lie to him, but... I've always known that if I ever became seriously involved with a man, I'd have Lou to contend with. I really don't care how miffed he gets at me, but right now you need him."

"You mean we'll have to sneak around?"

"Oh, of course we don't have to sneak around. Lou isn't here all that much. But when he is, I think a certain amount of decorum would be in order. He accepts our closeness, but no pats on the fanny or anything like that. I'm just not ready for him to know how familiar you are with my fanny."

"Paula, there's no way in hell anyone who watches me watching you wouldn't know I'm in love."

Paula smiled, rumpled his hair and pulled his head down for a kiss. "I've got some things to take care of right now, then dinner will be ready. We won't have a chance to be alone this evening, but ... I will see you later tonight, won't I?"

"You bet. I feel like a newlywed."

"With an insatiable appetite for sex?"

"Yeah."

"Good." Chuckling, she left the room.

IN SPITE OF THEIR best efforts, Paula and Dane couldn't hide their growing attachment to each other. No one who was around them for very long could fail to see they were in love. Rona thought it was wonderful; she absolutely wallowed in the romance of it. In manly fashion, Mitch didn't think about it one way or another. Fortunately, at that particular time, Lou was swamped with dozens of things that kept him away from the house. Paula had ceased caring whether or not her old friend knew she was in love with Dane, but for Dane's sake, she thought it best that Lou remain ignorant of their affair for a while.

So Paula and Dane had all the time in the world to be together, and as their closeness grew, he, for the first time, began to talk to her about his childhood.

"I don't know why Dad drank or when he started. Maybe it was when my mother left. It seems to have always been there, just part of my life. But the first time I really realized it was out of control was when I was twelve. We'd been somewhere—I don't remember where—and Dad stopped at a beer joint. He told me to wait in the car, that he had to go inside and talk to somebody about something. I waited and waited and finally fell asleep. Next thing I knew it was four hours later and some guys were dumping him in the back seat. I had to drive home. Twelve years old! Good thing some older kid had taught me the fundamentals of driving, but that was a far cry from really knowing how to drive. I was scared to death. I never went anywhere with Dad again, not until I got my license and could do the driving. Not long after that, Dad totaled the car, so we were without wheels until I scraped together enough money to buy a used truck." His voice broke slightly. "From that day on, the only things my old man owned were a patch of land and a ratty trailer. God, how I hated it!"

They were cuddled together in Paula's bed. If Rona and Mitch were aware of these late night trysts—and Paula couldn't believe they weren't—they never indicated as much. Not that it mattered. Not that she cared.

"Do you remember your mother?"

"No," he said sharply. "Nor do I want to. I don't think I would like her."

That Paula could understand. "Did you ever think about running away?" she asked.

"More times than I can remember," he told her truthfully.

"I wonder why you didn't."

"So do I."

"Dane, does it bother you to talk about these things?"

"Not to you. In fact, you're the first person I've ever mentioned them to."

"Was your father the reason you had such a reputation for trouble?"

"Yeah. Kids don't care what they say, and even though everything they said usually was the truth, I didn't want to hear it, and I was awfully free with my fists. Also, I had the smartest mouth south of the Mason-Dixon line. I never liked being in trouble all the time, but I never ran away from it, either."

Paula propped herself on one elbow so she could gaze down at him. "I think it's amazing that a man with that unpromising background could have turned out to be such a good person."

"Don't endow me with too much goodness, Paula. I still can be mean as hell when riled."

"I haven't seen any signs of that."

He grinned. "I haven't been riled lately." He pulled her closer to him. "Your appealing body soothes the savage in me." Then his eyes turned somber. "Can you begin to imagine how it stuns me to be here with you? It was incredible enough that you encouraged me, helped me, became my friend. To have you love me, too, knocks the breath out of me. A woman like you with a man like me...."

"Don't say it like that," she said, placing a fingertip over his mouth. "As if I'm somehow better than you are. That upsets me tremendously. I'm not any better. I grew up in the same place you did. My mother was a seamstress. We were as poor as church mice. You and I are more alike than we are different."

"You were decently poor. I was shabbily poor, straight from the wrong side of the tracks. Believe me, there's a world of difference between the two."

Paula thought about that. Of course he was right. There was a difference, especially in a small town, where economic barriers were more pronounced and harder to surmount. Actually, she'd had a great childhood. There hadn't been much in the way of money, but she'd been lucky in having a devoted mother who was an expert seamstress. While her friends went off to Birmingham or Montgomery to buy their clothes, her mother had copied hers from *Seventeen* and *Mademoiselle*. She had been the poorest best-dressed girl in high school. And she and her mother had become experts at having fun doing things that didn't cost money. Dane hadn't had any of that. He didn't remember his mother, and he actually hadn't had a father, either.

"Maybe I just had better chances," she told him. "So, hush. No more talk about the differences between us."

She loved the way her breasts felt when they were crushed into the forest on his chest. In fact, there was a perfect place for her all along the length of him. Her hands stroked his broad back, then moved down to his bare buttocks. She could feel his arousal begin. "Do you suppose we do this too often?"

"I'm not sure that's possible, like being too thin or too rich," he said, nibbling at the seam of her lips.

"Sometimes I feel horribly guilty about keeping you out of circulation. You should be finding a younger woman, someone who can give you a family, and—"

"Now, you hush." He kissed her deeply. "I don't want a family. I just want you...only you...."

He kissed her into senselessness, until he was Paula's only reality. He stroked her until she ached inside, and he told her how much he loved her, wanted her, needed her. He aroused her to the point when his mere breath fanning across her breasts caused her to tremble.

It was easy to believe they would be together forever when their bodies were fused like this. In a haze of passion anything seemed possible. Only in the languid aftermath did Paula admit it probably wasn't to be. The time was coming when he no longer would need her help with his career. Not only that, but he would have to work like the devil even to find time for her. They both would go off to do interesting, exciting new things, but they wouldn't do them together. The rift that neither of them wanted would begin.

The world was beckoning to him, and he would change. Dane himself did not think so. He insisted he would never change where she was concerned, but Paula knew better. Sadly, he would change. He might feel the same inside, but other people and other circumstances would change him.

He had only to wait until life became an endless round of adoring, upturned faces, until he started receiving royalty checks that allowed him to buy anything he wanted or thought he wanted. Until hordes of young women tried to storm his bus after a concert. Until he was bombarded on all sides with requests for autographs, photographs, interviews, personal appearances. Everyone would want something from him, especially the fans. And in the midst of it all, he would have to keep the records coming.

Paula sighed and buried her face against his chest. He would be a rare man indeed if he could avoid all the temptations that awaited him.

CHAPTER THIRTEEN

FOR THE FIRST TIME, Dane had someone to share life with, and life, he decided, was wonderful, even if he did seem to be living it in a daze. The days followed, one after another, and all he was really aware of was Paula. She had become everything to him. Had he been forced to make a choice between his lady love and the spectacular career everyone was so sure he would have, Paula would have won hands down.

But the career was important because, above all, he wanted her to be proud of him. He wanted to do things for her, give her things; up until now she had been the one doing all the giving. He knew she already owned everything she wanted that money could buy, but that wasn't the point. He wanted to give her things that reminded her solely of him.

With some of the money he'd been paid from the Crowe tour, he had bought her a gold charm bracelet with a tiny gold record hanging from it. She wore it every day, which pleased him no end. Dane's plan was to present her with a new charm every time he made a record, something he hadn't mentioned to Paula for fear it would sound impossibly ambitious and vain.

With so much time to himself, time in which he had little to do but think, he began analyzing his life until now—a depressing pastime since so much of it seemed useless. He had wandered through the days, never thinking about much, never caring about anything. Dane supposed the adjective *unmotivated* would have described him pretty well. What a waste!

But no more. Now that he sought Paula's approval above all else, even fame and fortune, he had begun to read in earnest, not just for entertainment but for knowledge, as well. He devoured every publication that came into the house, everything from *Billboard* to the *Wall Street Journal*. He asked Rona to teach him the rudiments of the financial side of the music business. When the time came, he wanted to be able to keep a knowledgeable eye on his own affairs. A woman like Paula couldn't have an uneducated country bumpkin at her side.

At her side. The jolt of knowing that was where he wanted to spend the rest of his life had hit him with the force of a runaway locomotive. He could count on the fingers of one hand the times he had seriously contemplated the idea of finding one person to spend his life with. Now that he had, she had turned out to be as perfect as a goddess. Now he had to prove to her that he actually belonged at her side.

Paula would have been distressed to know Dane still had her placed on a pedestal. She thought they were perfectly suited to each other, and nothing interfered with their growing attachment. True, when they were around others, they kept a discreet distance, but the best times were when they were alone. She couldn't remember ever feeling so attuned to, so comfortable with another person's presence. Still, were Dane not to come to her with his periodic permeations of love, she was sure she would wither as quickly as a morning glory in the afternoon sun.

Yet, even fairy tales had their ogres and wicked stepmothers. For Paula and Dane their thorn was the demands and conflicts inherent in their respective careers. This came to Dane with startling clarity one afternoon as he was reading the latest issue of *Music City News*. The cover story was an interview with a singer who had burst on the scene with a runaway hit record the previous year. In the article the singer was quoted as saying, "I've been home exactly five weeks this past year." Five weeks? The thought was revolting. And what, he wondered, if his five weeks at home coincided with Paula's periodic trips to Atlanta or Charlotte or Jackson? If Paula became president of Hamilton House, she would probably have fifteen minutes a day to call her own.

Yet, this was something they never talked about, nor did they mention Dallas again. They lived for today and each other.

But if Dane and Paula stumbled through the days in a haze of happiness, others in the household were less starry-eyed and more observant. One night as they were preparing for bed, Rona suddenly turned to Mitch and asked, "Have you noticed something peculiar lately?"

He frowned. "Do you mean the lovebirds? Hell, they're not peculiar. They're besotted."

"No, I don't mean Paula and Dane. I mean our dear, close friend, Lou Howard."

Mitch's frown deepened. "What about Lou?"

"Where in hell's he been?"

"I don't know. Busy."

"He's always been busy, but he's never stayed away from this house so long. Never."

"What are you getting at, Rona?"

"I don't know," she said thoughtfully.

"Then why did you bring it up?"

"I wondered if you'd noticed his absence from our lives, that's all. I'm surprised Paula hasn't mentioned it, but lately she hasn't noticed much of anything but Dane." Rona crawled into bed. "Do you think Lou could possibly have learned about Paula and Dane? You know how he'd feel about that."

"How could he have learned about it?" Mitch asked sensibly. "You and I are the only ones who know, and I damned sure haven't told anybody. You're borrowing worry, hon. Lou's busy, that's all. He'll show up any day now. Everything here—Justin's house, Paula, everything—means too much to him."

"It's still peculiar," Rona said, getting the last word.

"TEARS I'VE SHED IN VAIN" was released the following week, and suddenly *Billboard* and *Cash Box* and *Music City News*—publications that had been coming into the house for years, which Paula had mostly ignored—became her favorite reading. When she'd married Justin he had already been a certified superstar with a string of hits a mile long, so she had no idea how long it took for a record by an unknown singer to receive recognition. Owen assured her that Heron was saturating the country with Dane's record, along with the publicity package he and Lou had put together months ago. They weren't looking for a gigantic boffo success, the producer kept reminding her; what they wanted was a steady chart climber. If it broke into the top twenty, he would be satisfied.

So, what Paula had worked so hard to obtain for Dane was about to become reality. She ignored the small twinge of fear that was trying to remind her that his success could signal the beginning of the end for them. To celebrate, she bought champagne, and she, Dane, Rona and Mitch spent a glorious but slightly tipsy evening at home. Paula tried all day to reach Lou to ask him to join them, but he was tied up. She was a little disappointed, but she reminded herself that he had a lot of clients who were a constant drain on his time. Still, she thought it odd that Lou, who was Dane's manager, the architect and mastermind of his career, didn't at least call to congratulate his newest client.

For the next few weeks Paula concentrated on keeping Dane's confidence at its zenith. When stardom came she wanted him ready for it—not cocky, just confident. She also drilled and redrilled him on the way to conduct his life. She didn't want the fans thinking of him only as a good singer; she wanted them to adore him. And she didn't think spreading it around that he was deeply involved with an older woman would be the greatest public relations move they could make in the beginning.

"Until you're established," she told him, "I think you and I should be very discreet."

"Hide the relationship, you mean. Dammit, Paula—"

"Trust me. Everything I do and say is aimed at helping you, darling." She bit her lip. "I'd better stop calling you that so much. I might slip up in public."

"I can't believe that people who buy records honestly give a hoot who the person who made the record sees or doesn't see, eats or doesn't eat, likes or doesn't like, wears or doesn't wear.''

"Oh, Dane, you have a lot to learn. They do. They'll want to know everything about you, or at least they'll think they do. And they'll want to approve. The problem is, what they approve of can get pretty complicated. For instance, they'll forgive you five divorces as long as you love God, Mom, the flag and baseball. You can be an ax murderer but not an atheist. That kind of thing.''

"Then how come so many bubbleheads who booze it up and shoot up hotel rooms make several million a year?''

"Even more bubbleheads vanish as quickly as they appear, so you concentrate on being a nice guy.''

Dammit, Paula thought irritably, *why isn't Lou here telling him all this?* There probably were two dozen things Dane needed to know that she either hadn't thought of or didn't know herself. That was why performers hired agent-managers. Yet, her calls to Lou's office went unreturned, and he never seemed to be at home anymore. It had been weeks since Lou had stopped by the house. She wondered if her old friend was acquiring a dollar sign for a heart, concentrating his efforts on the clients who were making him money instead of an unknown like Dane, who needed him. Paula couldn't recall a time when she had been really irritated at Lou, but now she was. And she intended telling him just that the next time she saw him.

PAULA WASN'T SURE at what point she began to suspect that something was amiss. Both she and Dane had remained tense, waiting for all hell to break loose. Instead, during the following days, nothing seemed to happen. Abruptly, time began to plod. They tried reassuring each other. "Our trouble," she told him, "is that we're novices. We don't know how long these things take. But I'm sure you can't release a record one day and have it on the charts the next."

"Yeah," he agreed halfheartedly, refraining from mentioning that it had been considerably longer than one day since the release date. "I thought Lou would be around, holding my hand and dispensing wisdom."

Paula didn't even want to talk about Lou. She was too furious at him. She, too, had expected Lou to be guiding Dane every step of the way at this crucial point. But she learned from his secretary that Lou was in Europe, playing advance man for Dottie Crowe's upcoming overseas tour. Didn't he have people who did that sort of thing for him? It was doubly strange that he had left without saying goodbye. Maybe turning Dane over to him hadn't been the smartest move she could have made. True, Lou had gotten him a recording date right away, but now was when they really needed him, yet he was busy with his "important" clients. She'd often wondered in the past if Lou had overextended himself, taken on more than he could handle, but never once had she doubted that he would be here now, rooting for Dane like a hyped-up cheerleader.

More days passed, and uneasiness slowly built inside Paula. Dane's record had yet to show up on the charts. Of course she knew that plenty of recordings were released and never heard from again, but she also knew that shouldn't have been happening to Dane's. Not as good as he was. Not with so many heavyweights behind him. Something was wrong. She just wished she knew what it was.

Dane's thoughts paralleled Paula's. Something just didn't feel right, and when one had grown up the way he had—making do, doing without, distrusting everything and everybody—one learned to rely heavily on sixth sense, second sight and pure instinct. He definitely smelled a rat. Right now he needed a guiding hand, so where was Lou? In Europe, that was where. The man was his agent-manager, for Pete's sake! What was he managing? The phone wasn't exactly ringing off the wall. In fact, not a damned thing was happening. As far as he could tell, the record wasn't even getting played, and Lou supposedly was on palsy-walsy terms with three-fourths of the DJs in the country.

As Dane's bubble began to burst right before his eyes, he experienced a sense of acute frustration unlike anything he'd ever known. After expecting so much, the letdown was awesome. He could barely handle it. He was disappointed in himself and was sure the others were disappointed in him, too. Paula, especially. If he had learned to expect a lot, she had expected even more. His diminishment in her eyes had him feeling sick.

Paula saw his despair and felt terrible for him. She also felt a little guilty. She had all but promised him a fantastic career, so dammit, it was up to her to see that he got it. She wasn't exactly sure how she could accomplish it, but she had to do something.

With Lou out of pocket, her biggest contact in the music business was Owen Brewster. The following day, Paula, after brooding away most of the day, left the office early and drove to Music Row and the Heron

Building. Owen's office featured a wall-to-wall record collection and photo display; a golf bag was propped in one corner. Since today was perhaps the third time ever that Paula had been in the office, Owen couldn't have been more surprised by the visit.

"Paula!" the cheerful, portly man exclaimed. "How good to see you. Is this business or pleasure?"

"Business. Definitely not a pleasure."

"Problems?"

Paula got right to the point. "Owen, what's going on with Dane's record? Why isn't it being played?"

"I don't know. Sometimes these things can't be explained. A pretty good record comes along and nothing happens. It just lies there."

" 'Pretty good,' Owen?"

"All right, damned good. I thought we had a winner on our hands."

"How often have you been wrong?"

"Immodestly, not often."

"You know this business inside and out. Why don't we have a winner?"

"I told you, I don't know. It's a good record. It should have been a hit. It doesn't wash." Owen regarded her seriously. "This is important to you, isn't it?"

"Very. We all—you, me, Lou—promised, almost guaranteed Dane a glittering career. He's very discouraged, and I don't blame him. I know there's a world of things I don't know about the music business, but I lived with Justin a long time, and I absorbed a lot. I've been giving this some thought, and last night something occurred to me. All those protégés—so many of them got recording contracts and made records. Some of those records didn't do very well, but they all got played! At least for a few weeks. As far as we can tell, Dane's *isn't* being played. Why?''

Owen tugged on his chin. ''What are you getting at, Paula?''

Her chest heaved. ''I think somebody important doesn't want the record played, for some reason I can't imagine. Maybe several somebodies. Since when do all the DJs at every country music station in North America single out one record for oblivion? Here we have an unknown singer with a fantastic voice singing an old standard on a respected label. Tell me, Owen. Please, tell me.''

Owen wondered just how important Dane Markham himself had become to Paula. She was very impassioned about this. ''Tell you what—I'm going to ask some questions. When I get some answers, I'll get in touch with you.''

Paula had no choice but to go with that. *It doesn't wash.* Those words echoed over and over in her mind for the remainder of the afternoon, and she was still thinking about them when she returned home and went on the prowl, looking for Dane.

The big house was very quiet. Mitch and Rona had gone away for the weekend, something they were doing more and more often these days. Their absences gave her a chance to be alone with Dane for two whole days and had always been so welcome. Paula wondered about this weekend, however. These new developments had cast such a gloomy pall over their relationship. They still loved each other, but Dane was miserable, and she was heartsick over the way things had worked out. That made loving a bit difficult.

She expected to find him in the studio, but he was in his room with his back to the door. She walked in and forced some cheerfulness into her voice. "Hi."

He turned. "Hi. I didn't realize it was so late."

Paula went to him and placed a sound kiss on his mouth. "What did you do all day?"

"Not a whole helluva lot of anything, which is the way I seem to spend most of my days. Sit down, babe, I want to talk to you."

A tremor of trepidation swept through her. She didn't like the way he sounded. "Sure." Sinking into the easy chair, she crossed her legs and watched him as he paced around the room.

"Paula, I've done a lot of thinking, and I can't in all conscience continue to live here and sponge off you."

Alarmed, she jumped to her feet and went to put her arms around him. "Of course you can stay here. You will stay here. You're my lover."

He looked down at her earnest face and gave her a sad smile. "Do you have any idea how that sounds? Like I'm a gigolo."

"Oh, that's patently ridiculous! It bothers me to hear you talk like that."

"Face it, those great plans of ours were a wonderful dream for a while, but they're not going to happen, Paula. I think we all know that by now, so let's be honest. I need to get a job, start doing something useful."

"A job? What kind of job?"

Dane shrugged. "Anything I can find. I told you, I'm a pretty fair mechanic."

Paula was horrified. "Oh, Dane, you can't be a mechanic!"

"Why not? It's a perfectly respectable trade. And it's something I'm good at. Obviously I'm not good at making records. Or is it that you don't want a mechanic for a lover?"

She was so stunned by the callous remark, which was totally unlike the Dane she loved, that she took a backward step, widened her eyes and covered her mouth with her hands. The hand came down and made a fist at her side. "I can't believe you said that."

Dane's shoulders slumped, and he reached for her. "I can't, either. You know I didn't mean it. I don't know what's wrong with me. I told myself I could handle the disappointment. I remind myself daily of how little I had when I came here, how much I have now. You, especially. And I've been introduced to things I didn't know existed. But nothing helps. I feel like hell."

"I know you do," Paula said, instantly forgiving him. Taking him by the hand, she led him to the chair, pushed him onto it, then sat on the ottoman facing him. "Now, I want to talk to you. I went to see Owen today. He says you made a good record, one he expected to be a hit, and it's not getting played. And he says that doesn't wash. That doesn't wash! When he said that, something went off inside my head."

Dane shook his head in bewilderment. "Sorry, babe, I'm not following you."

"Dane, this didn't just happen. Somebody made it happen. Someone's messing with you, darling, and I want to find out who and why. Especially why."

He took her hand and turned it over and over between both of his. "Your loyalty and faith in me are commendable, but didn't it occur to you that maybe the record isn't getting played because the DJs don't like it? Or maybe they did play it a couple of times and nobody bought it.''

"No!'' she said decisively. "That doesn't wash, either. Owen's going to ask some questions and get back to me with the answers. We'll find out what's going on. I promise, we'll find out.''

That said, she left the ottoman to crawl onto his lap and put her head on his shoulder. "This is all going to work out, Dane, and you're going to have that career. Tell me you believe that.''

In spite of himself, Dane smiled. "When you wind this appealing body around me, I can believe anything.''

"Good. Now let's please concentrate on spending two lovely days together.''

She kicked off her shoes; they fell soundlessly onto the thick carpet. Dane's hand slipped down to the hem of her skirt, then up to run sensuously along her stockinged thigh. Between kisses Paula said, "You know, we've never made love in your bed, always in mine.''

"An oversight that needs to be taken care of immediately. Let me close the door.''

She kept him so preoccupied and enchanted with her that weekend that he couldn't think about anything else. For two glorious days everything troublesome was put on hold. She loved him until they both were exhausted.

But Paula's mind never stopped. She needed some help. During all the years she had been married to Justin, she had scrupulously avoided using his name, his contacts and especially his influence, which was considerable and widespread. Now, if necessary, she would. She'd stop at nothing. Whoever was trying to destroy Dane's career had just acquired himself a powerful adversary.

IT WAS TUESDAY AFTERNOON when her secretary informed Paula that a Mr. Brewster was on the phone. Her heart knocked against her ribs as she reached for the instrument. "Owen?"

"May I invite myself over for a drink tonight? I have something to tell you that I think you'll find interesting. I don't know if it'll help, but it's damned sure interesting."

"Of course. Five-thirty? Will you stay for dinner?"

"I have a dinner date tonight, but give me a rain check. Will Dane be there?"

"Yes."

"Good. He might find it interesting, too. See you then."

Paula phoned the house to tell Martha to serve dinner a bit later that night. Then she spent two largely unproductive hours at her desk, her thoughts all on this evening's meeting with Owen. She ended up leaving early so she would have time to change before the producer arrived. When they heard that Owen was coming to talk to Paula and Dane, Mitch and Rona tactfully made themselves scarce.

"Did he give you any idea what it was he found out?" Dane asked.

"No," Paula said. "Only that it is interesting. Lord, I hope we're getting to the bottom of it all."

Owen was prompt. Since this visit wasn't a social one, as soon as he had his bourbon highball in hand he got down to business, looking squarely at Dane.

"How long have you been in town, young man? Long enough to make some powerful enemies?"

Dane looked startled. "Not powerful or otherwise."

"Sure?"

"Positive."

"Damned if I can figure it," Owen said with a puzzled shake of his head. "I got in touch with a DJ I know in Knoxville. I asked him what in hell happened to the record by a new singer named Dane Markham. He said the word he got was that Heron didn't want it played."

Paula and Dane exchanged glances, then turned back to Owen.

"I asked him who gave him 'the word,' and he said he couldn't tell me, that he was sworn to secrecy. He also said he thought it was a shame because the record's a good one, but his was not to reason why, et cetera. I pumped him for a minute or two, but I didn't get another peep out of him. In fact, he sounded nervous about talking to me at all. Made me madder'n hell, but I had to be nice to the guy. When you produce records for a living, you need those DJs like babies need milk."

Paula leaned forward. Owen had been right; this was very interesting. "Owen, have you ever heard of anything like this happening before?"

"Nope, can't say I have. I've heard of records not getting played because DJs thought they were in bad taste—there's some raunchy stuff produced in this town—but for someone to go to the trouble of calling around and keeping one off the air... It doesn't make any sense to me. But let me tell you something else, and this was pure coincidence. I was sitting at my desk, mulling over what the guy in Knoxville had said, when I got a call from a fellow I know in Memphis. He owns a pretty fancy supper club there, and on weekends they have live entertainment. Get some pretty big names. Maybe not the current superstars, but the ones who've had their day in the spotlight and now belong in the durable category. And the up-and-comers. The guy just called to touch base with me, but during the course of the conversation—and this is where the coincidence comes in—he asked when Dane would be available. 'Available?' I asked. Seems the club owner had been at the Dottie Crowe concert in Memphis and was kinda taken with Dane. Wanted to book him for a weekend or two. The agency he deals with reported that Dane was unavailable for personal appearances at this time.''

"Unavailable?'' Dane exclaimed. "Man, I'm the most available singer in Nashville.''

"Which agency was it?'' Paula asked.

"Not one you'd have heard of, but never fear, I called. The lady who owns the place said she vaguely recalled getting in touch with someone here in Nashville about a singer named Dane Markham, but she can't remember who it was. She was lying, but what could I do? Now, I figured that anybody wanting to book Dane would get in touch with our agency, so I went over there and asked around. Seems a memo was circulated around the office a while back saying Dane Markham wasn't available for personal appearances. No one can remember who signed it, or if it was signed, or who was the first to see it or anything.''

Owen paused for emphasis. "I swear if I didn't feel like goddam Columbo by that time. I don't guess I did you too much good, but this cloak-and-dagger stuff is kinda out of my line. Sure is puzzling. You were right, Paula. Somebody's going to an awful lot of trouble to keep that record off the air and Dane off a stage." Owen looked at Dane again. "Are you sure some big shot hasn't caught you making a move on his wife or something like that?"

"Honest, Owen," Dane said, "I only know a handful of people in this town."

"Well, somewhere, somehow you've made somebody awful mad. Just wish I could have found out who it was."

"Owen, you've done more than you think you have," Paula said. "You told me what I needed to know. I appreciate it. Both of us do."

"If you're determined to get to the bottom of this, why don't you hire a pro, a private detective?" Owen wanted to know.

"If these people won't talk to someone in the business, someone whose name carries weight, what are they going to say to a complete stranger?" Paula said.

"The pros have their methods. You might want to think about it."

Owen finished his drink and left soon afterward. Dane noticed Paula's suddenly buoyed spirits and was curious about them. "Maybe I missed something somewhere, but it doesn't seem to me we've learned much to be happy about."

"I'm encouraged," she told him. "We know you're good, that the record's good, and now we know that you're a victim of a conspiracy. Somebody doesn't want you to be successful, for whatever reason I can't imagine, and I'm going to find out who it is if it's the last thing I do. If there's one thing I am, darling, it's tenacious."

Who could it be? They both asked that over and over. Paula made Dane recount every minute of every day he'd been in Nashville, at least to the point he could, but that was frustrating. He had punched out an unknown drummer in an unknown band, but Lonny What's-his-name hardly was someone with connections. The recording session had gone smoothly, as had the tour.... Dane's thoughts stopped as he recalled Dottie Crowe's peculiar attitude toward him after Oklahoma City. Then he dismissed that as feminine whim and didn't remind Paula of it. Except for those few outings, he had spent his time in the company of Mitch or Rona or Paula. It was perplexing, a real mystery.

Paula could have killed Lou for not being there when she needed him, but he wasn't, so it was up to her. And she was smart enough to know she couldn't do it alone. Her credentials in the music business did not go beyond being Justin Steele's widow. But that name could get her in to see some powerful people.

Owen had done all he could; she decided against asking him to pursue the matter further. He was a record producer, nothing else. She needed someone who was more.

For the rest of the evening she thought and thought about the people she knew in the business. There were plenty who owed everything to Justin and would help her because of that. But she needed someone whose name got attention, someone who could walk through doors nobody else could, someone who had access to just about anyone he wanted access to. Above all, she needed someone she could trust implicitly. Suddenly it came to her.

Marty Oliver, of course!

CHAPTER FOURTEEN

THE RESTAURANT WAS Nashville's last word in elegance, the sort of place where small pots of fresh flowers adorned the tables and huge, lush tropical plants stood in specially lighted niches. As Paula walked up to the front desk, she was approached by a tall, suave maître d'.

"*Pardon,* ma'am. May I help you?"

"I'm joining Mr. Oliver for lunch," she informed him. "Has he arrived?"

"Yes, a few minutes ago." He bowed and invited her into the elegant dining room with a sweep of his hand. "This way, please."

Marty got to his feet when he saw her, his face breaking into a wide smile of welcome. He was very nattily attired in a dark blue business suit, pale blue shirt and subdued silk tie. Paula was sure that if the music business had a best-dressed list, Marty and Lou would be placed near the top. "Hello, Paula. You look beautiful, as always."

"Thanks, Marty." The maître d' held out her chair as she sat down. "And thanks, too, for seeing me."

"I'd drop everything to see you, anytime, anywhere, for any reason. Alicia sends her love. Would you like a drink before ordering?"

"I don't think so." The maître d' scurried away.

Paula and Marty perused the extensive menu. Finally Marty looked up. "My mama always told me never to eat in a place that put tassels on the menus."

Paula smiled. Marty was so debonair that it was easy to forget that he had come to Nashville from a place called Pickens Corner, Georgia. It was he more than anyone who had taught her that charm, manners, suavity—all those things normally lumped together as the social graces—could be learned. "They're certainly proud of their food," she commented. The prices were astronomical.

"It's my nickel, so eat hearty."

"Then I'll fall asleep at my desk this afternoon. A salad and the angel hair pasta will be all I can handle."

Once they'd ordered, Paula folded her arms on the table and looked at Marty solemnly. "I'll tell you right off that I have a problem, and I'm hoping you'll be able to help me solve it."

"It's about time I got a chance to help a Steele. Justin wouldn't let me do a damned thing for him. But then, what could anybody do for Justin Steele?"

"I know how busy you are, and I wouldn't ask if this weren't awfully important to me. It concerns the new singer I told you about."

"Your protégé?"

"Y-yes." How strange it seemed to still refer to Dane as her protégé. He was so much more. He was everything. As succinctly as possible, she explained the situation to Marty. "Dane's record isn't getting any play. When I realized that, I went to see Owen, and he did some checking for me. The record isn't being played because someone has sent out word that Heron doesn't want it played. Not only that, but it's also gotten around that Dane isn't available for personal appearances. No one would say where the word came from. Owen's completely baffled, and so am I. Dane simply hasn't been around long enough to ruffle any feathers or step on any toes. Yet someone has this...this vendetta against him. What possible explanation can there be for what's happened?''

Marty frowned, tapping his mouth with a forefinger. "Why would someone want to sabotage an unknown singer's first record? That's a poser. Like you said, he hasn't been around long enough to make enemies. Not that that's so hard to do anymore. I'd sure hate to be an unknown trying to break into the business these days. It always was hard work, but it used to be kinda fun, too...back when we were dismissed as hillbillies and were left alone to do our own thing. Now, it's an industry, and like most industries, it's run with the head instead of the heart. There are some slimy handshakes out there, Paula. We've got con artists and cutthroats in this town who would make their counterparts in Hollywood and New York look like rank amateurs.''

"Apparently. Justin used to grouse about the same thing," Paula said. "I'm wondering who in the business has enough pull to call a DJ in a fairly large market, tell him not to play a certain record and get what he asked for?''

"I can think of a lot of people," Marty said frankly. "I just can't think of anyone who would want to do it.''

"I know. It's so puzzling.''

"I take it you want me to find out who's behind it.''

"If you can. I know it's asking a lot, and I know you're busy, but—''

"Never too busy for you, darlin'. Cheer up. If someone's messing with your boy, Paula, I'll find out who it is. I've done some nice things for a lot of folks over the years, so—'' he winked at her ''—it's paying back favors time at the old corral. But tell me something—why isn't Lou on top of this?''

Paula's chin lifted. "I've asked myself that very thing many times. Unfortunately, Lou is in Europe right now."

Marty said nothing, but the expression on his face clearly told her he found that a bit odd. Then the waiter brought their salads, and the business with Dane was put on hold while they ate and indulged in a lot of "remember when." Paula supposed the food was excellent, but she didn't pay much attention to it. She was too busy congratulating herself on seeking out Marty. He probably could get through doors that even Lou couldn't. Now she had an ally with clout.

THE FOLLOWING AFTERNOON, Marty Oliver could be found in the office of Johnny Larsen, the program director of Nashville's largest—and arguably the country's most prestigious—country music station. It was Marty whom Johnny had to thank for his job and other favors too numerous to mention. The two men spent a few minutes reminiscing before Johnny asked, as he always did whenever he saw Marty, "What say, pal? A ten-minute on-air interview. Give our listeners a thrill. Ten minutes, tops."

"Well, I might," Marty said, which wasn't his customary answer to such requests. If he did all the interviews he was asked to do, he wouldn't have time for anything else. "But first, I want to ask you a question. Heron just released a record by a new singer named Dane Markham. It's an old Justin Steele classic—'Tears I've Shed in Vain.' I thought it was damned good, but it's not being played. How come?''

Johnny looked puzzled. "How come? The word we got was that Heron doesn't want it played."

"Oh?"

"Yeah. Seems this Markham guy has turned out to be too unmanageable, a real maverick. Heron's fixing to unload him."

"Who told you that?"

Johnny looked away. "I...don't remember."

"Come on, Johnny. This is ol' Marty. Don't give me the idiot treatment."

"Honest, Marty, I'd tell you if I could, but I'm sworn to secrecy."

"Let me get this straight. Whoever told you Heron doesn't want the record played also made you promise not to reveal the source of your information?"

"That's about the size of it."

"Must have been a pretty big big shot."

Johnny said nothing.

Marty sat back in his chair and glanced idly around the cluttered office, hating himself for what he was about to do. "How's your little girl?" he asked. "Karen, isn't it?"

A pained expression crossed Johnny's face. "Aw, come on, Marty. That's hitting below the belt. Karen's fine, and if you hadn't paid for that operation, she'd be dead now. But I can't tell you. Ask for something else—a quart of my blood, maybe."

Marty sat up straight, all business. "Do you think I'd resort to such tactics if this wasn't damned important? And at the risk of sounding like a pompous ass, I can do more for you than anyone else in this whole crazy town. No one, but no one, can touch you if I'm in your corner. I don't think I have to tell you the reverse of that."

Johnny stared at him in openmouthed astonishment. Marty Oliver was the nicest guy in the world. This must be damned important for him to use threats. And Johnny knew how much he owed him. "What is this Markham guy to you?"

"He means a lot to someone who means a lot to me. Who told you that Heron doesn't want his record played?"

Johnny expelled a labored breath, hesitated, then turned to Marty. The pained expression had intensified. "Listen, pal, you gotta promise you'll never tell a living soul where you heard this. . . ."

Twenty minutes later Marty left the station, after granting a surprised and delighted disc jockey a ten-minute on-air interview. He instructed his driver to take him home. Thirty minutes later he walked into his wife's sitting room and told her to pack some glad rags, a nightgown and her toothbrush. They were having dinner at a supper club. . . in Memphis.

PAULA WAS READY to jump out of her skin by the time Marty contacted her six days after their initial meeting over lunch. "Where do you want to talk, Paula?" he asked. "My office, your office, your house, where?"

"At the house. Five-thirty. Have you got something for me?"

"Plenty. I would have made a hell of an investigative reporter."

Hopefully, whatever Marty had found out would clear up the matter once and for all. Something had to be done. Dane's spirits had reached their nadir. She was sure of that when he had asked her to stop wearing the charm bracelet. Despite her protests, he had filed at the state employment office. He'd said he was embarrassed to continue living with her while contributing nothing. Although she had begged him not to be hasty, to wait and see what they found out, she knew how desperately he needed to do something, anything. The idleness was getting to him, and his darkening mood was getting to her. Nothing was wrong between them, but nothing was exactly right, either. She blamed herself for getting his hopes up too high, and she definitely blamed Lou for not following through on his promises. Dane, on the other hand, didn't place the blame on either of them, only on himself.

"Dane!" Paula called when she entered the house.

It was Rona who answered. "He's not here, Paula."

"Well, where is he?"

"I don't know. He borrowed Mitch's car and said he was going out for a while and not to wait dinner on him."

"Damn! Of all times."

"Something wrong?" Rona asked.

"Marty Oliver's on his way over here, and I wanted Dane to be here." As she hurried upstairs to change, Paula frowned worriedly. Where could he have gone? People in the kind of mood Dane had been in lately sometimes did stupid things. By the time she had changed into slacks and a polo shirt and had brushed her hair, her stomach was churning like a blender whipping up a batch of daiquiris.

Marty rang the doorbell promptly at five-thirty and was ushered into the den, where Paula waited. "How about a drink?" she offered.

"Love one. Scotch on the rocks." While she poured it, he wandered idly around the room. "It's been a long time since I was here. You've made some changes, haven't you? This room doesn't look the same."

"We rearranged the furniture and bought a new sofa. That's about it." Paula came out from behind the bar, handed him his drink and indicated the sofa. When he was seated, she took a nearby chair and fastened her rapt attention on her visitor.

"I have been one busy man," Marty began. "First I talked to a radio station program director. Then I went to Memphis and had an interesting discussion with the owner of that club Owen told you about. And I talked to a woman at the booking agency, then a piano player who got pretty chummy with Dane when they were traveling on the band bus during the Crowe tour. I went to see Tony Grant, and—" Marty noticed Paula's impatience. "Well, I don't suppose you care so much how I got my information as what I learned, so here it is. Dane's been blacklisted."

"I suspected as much," she said grimly, "but why?"

"Now that I don't know. But the word is—and I got this from both Tony Grant and that club owner—that anyone who books Dane will never get Dottie Crowe. That's some pretty heavy stuff, Paula. She's *the* act in country music right now. That pretty well leaves your boy with beer joints, dance halls and shopping malls."

Paula's eyes widened. "Dottie?" she asked incredulously. "What on earth does she have to do with this?"

"I don't know that, either, not for sure. But my gut instinct tells me she's behind it, somehow. The piano player told me she had the hots for Dane real bad, but she didn't get anywhere with him, and apparently Dottie can't handle that kind of rejection. He also said the band had been told before the tour started that Dane would be their opening act for a while. Then he went sailing off with some good-looking chick in Oklahoma City, and Dottie dropped him like a shot. When he described the 'good-looking chick,' I had the funniest feeling he was describing you. Right?"

Paula nodded distractedly. "Oh, Marty, a woman scorned wouldn't stoop to such drastic measures. I mean, she wouldn't go so far as to try to ruin a man...would she?"

"Tell me something—are you and Dottie friends?"

"Hardly. As a matter of fact, I've always had the impression that she can't stand me. I don't know why. We barely know each other."

"Hmm. So not only did Dane resist her charms, he took up with a woman Dottie doesn't like. Let me tell you something, Paula. I've worked with Dottie on a couple of forgettable occasions, and she is first and foremost focused on Dottie. I'm not saying she doesn't have her good points. I understand she's generous to a fault with the people who work for her...provided they don't cross her. Then she's as mean as a snake. If, as you say, she really can't stand you, she might get to you through Dane. I've heard of crazier things."

"Thin, very thin," Paula said. "But let's assume she really is that mean and vindictive. She couldn't do what's being done to Dane. Be realistic. Dottie's making a bundle of money for RCA these days, but she doesn't have any real clout in this town, certainly not enough clout to break a career.''

"You're right. She couldn't do it alone. She'd have to have somebody powerful in her corner."

"Who, for instance?"

Marty looked down at his hands. Paula saw his Adam's apple bobble up and down, as though he were swallowing with some difficulty.

"Marty?"

"This is the hard part, the part I found hardest to believe, the part I dreaded telling you most. Dottie has that kind of clout when she has Lou Howard backing her up."

Paula sat back. She felt as though she'd been slapped. "L-Lou?"

"Yes. He's the one who's keeping the record off the air."

"I...don't believe it."

"Neither did I, but too many people mentioned his name too many times. You'd be surprised how many faulty memories have been jogged by the sight of this familiar kisser of mine. Lou's told the stations that Heron doesn't want the record played. Do you have any idea how powerful your friend is? When Lou Howard says don't play a record, it doesn't get played. Anyone who owes him anything, especially a career, will do whatever he asks. He doesn't have to do anything more strenuous than pick up a telephone."

"It can't be, it just can't be. Lou has everything to gain by Dane's success. Why, Marty, why?"

"I was hoping you could tell me. I'm as puzzled by it as you are. I've asked myself why Lou would want to ruin Dane. Could it be because Dane's close to you?''

"No, no, Lou doesn't know about—'' She stopped as something occurred to her. "Dottie! She could have told him about Dane and me and Oklahoma City.'' Then she shook her head. "No, Lou would never be that mean. He might disapprove of Dane and me. If he knows about us, I'm sure he does, but that wouldn't cause him to keep the record off the air.'' She looked at Marty. "And you think Dottie and Lou are in cahoots?''

"I just get this feeling, but I can't prove any of it.''

"It doesn't make sense. I know Lou's her manager. I know he's masterminded her career, and I know he thinks the world of her. But ... we're like his family.'' Paula raised anguished eyes to the man seated across from her. "If any of this is true, Dottie must have an incredible hold on him. What could it possibly be? Some deep, dark secret in his past?''

"I don't know, Paula. I can't imagine. I've told you everything I was able to find out.''

Silence fell over the room. Finally Marty squirmed restlessly. "I sure hate to drop bombshells and run, but I really do have to go. Alicia will be waiting for me.''

"Oh...'' Paula shook herself out of her dismal thoughts. "Of course.'' Getting to her feet, she saw him to the door. "I can't tell you how much I appreciate all the trouble you've gone to, Marty. If there's ever anything I can do for you—''

"If I started in tomorrow and did nothing but favors for you the rest of my life, I couldn't begin to repay you for all Justin did for me. You let me know how all this comes out. I'll bet I can get that man's record played. Hell, I'll put together a tour of my own and let him open for me. Might be fun to see if I can still draw a crowd. There are a lot of people out there who would consider me a bigger attraction than dear Dottie.''

Paula hugged him gratefully. ''We just might take you up on that. Good night . . . and thanks.''

Such loyalty, she thought as she closed the door behind Marty. Immediately her eyes clouded and her mouth set in a grim line. Lou! Now Paula knew how Vanessa had felt when she'd discovered Dolph Wade's duplicity.

Well, she had no intention of keeping her discovery under wraps the way Vanessa had. Paula had learned from Lou's secretary that he was due back from Europe on Wednesday. Wait until she got through with him! When it came to Lou, Paula had an ace up her sleeve, and she intended playing it, even if it was dirty pool.

Oh, it was all so clear now. The sudden lengthy absences. The extended European jaunt just when Dane needed a manager the most. Lou hadn't been able to face any of them. Small wonder. They had been harboring a Benedict Arnold in their midst.

But why? Paula couldn't believe Lou would do that to her and to Dane.

And that reminded her—just where in hell was Dane?

AT THAT MOMENT Dane was sitting in a darkened movie house watching what possibly would go down in history as the worst film ever made. The theater showed five films simultaneously, each in a separate concrete room. He hadn't paid any attention to what was showing in any of them; he'd just walked through the first door he'd come to. His bad luck was holding. Any one of the others probably would have been at least a little enjoyable, but this one was god-awful. Watching it made him long for great old films like *Godzilla Versus the Smog Monster.* He endured it as long as he could, then left the theater.

The night air was sultry. It seemed to have the consistency of something you could scoop up with a spoon. He got in Mitch's car, turned on the engine and cranked up the air conditioner. Then he began driving aimlessly, going nowhere in particular, listening to music on the radio and negotiating the traffic. He knew he probably should go back to the house; Paula would be wondering where he was. But he hadn't been very good company lately, and she exhausted herself every evening trying to lift his spirits. She might enjoy a breather.

Ever since Owen had talked to them, Dane had thought and thought, trying to come up with someone who might want to destroy his dream, but it was useless. There was no one. So why was it being done? And what would he do if the damage couldn't be undone?

That scared him. If he wasn't a singer, if he didn't have a career, he would go back to being a nobody. And a nobody couldn't have Paula. Every time that thought crossed his mind, he felt himself turn cold. Already he detected subtle changes in their relationship. She was trying too hard to be cheerful. During their lovemaking he sensed her trying to reassure him. It was time for something to change. Unfortunately, the only change he could foresee would be one for the worse.

The aimless driving did little to ease his troubled mind. Dane finally pulled into a service station and filled up the tank. He was giving serious thought to stopping somewhere for a couple of beers and some music when he spotted the brightly lighted coffee shop across the street. Given his lousy mood, that was a better place for him.

The minute he stepped into the place he realized how hungry he was. At home dinner would have been served long ago. *At home,* he thought disdainfully. *Listen to me. It isn't my home, no matter what Paula says.* He didn't belong there. He was beginning to think he didn't belong in Nashville, either, and he'd never go back to Alabama, so where did that leave him?

Sliding onto a stool at the counter, he picked up a menu that was stuck between the sugar dispenser and the salt and pepper shakers. A silver-haired waitress placed a glass of water in front of him. She was anything but young, but there was a delightful sparkle in her eyes that belied her obvious age.

"Hi, honey, what'll it be?"

"Are the burgers any good?" Dane asked.

"They haven't killed anybody yet. Least, not that I know of."

"Marvelous recommendation. Let me have one. With cheese. Hold the onions."

"Fries?"

"Yeah, I guess so."

"What'll you have to drink?"

"A cola."

As she walked off scribbling on her pad, Dane propped his elbows on the counter and rubbed his eyes tiredly. He had to get busy and find something to do.

The idleness was killing him. Mitch and Rona came up with dozens of meaningless chores for him every day—at Paula's request, he was sure—but that was just staying occupied. He wanted to do something that had merit. He was pretty good at a lot of things but an expert at nothing. He was giving serious thought to going to trade school. Maybe he was a little old for that, but it would be a start.

"Bad day at the office, honey?"

Dane opened his eyes and saw the waitress smiling at him sympathetically. "Just a bad day, period."

"You in the music business?"

Dane chuckled mirthlessly. "I was for about a day and a half."

"Lots of folks in the business come in here. Some real stars, too. Let's see now.... You're too cute to be stuck in the background on rhythm guitar. Bet you're a singer, right?"

"I thought I was."

"What's your name, honey?"

"Dane."

"I'm Gracie. The town's getting you down, right?"

"Right."

Gracie's silver curls danced as she shook her head. "Can't let it do that to you. How long you been in Nashville?"

"Only a few months."

"And you're already discouraged? You'll never make it if you get discouraged that easily. You gotta just keep on trying. Me, I tried once, and I got close, real close. Got me a contract with a record company. Even cut a record. So you see, I got closer than a lot of folks." The pride in her voice was unmistakable.

"What happened?" Dane asked.

"The company went bankrupt before the record was released."

"Gracie, you and I must have been born under the same star. How come you didn't go back home? I assume you're from somewhere else. Everyone is."

"Back to Kentucky?" Gracie asked, her tone implying she had never heard anything so ridiculous. "I'd never be anyone in Kentucky. At least in Nashville I had a chance of getting someone to listen to me. I even bought the dress I planned to wear when I debuted at the Opry. 'Course, I never got to wear it, but just looking at that dress kept me going plenty of times when I wanted to fold my tent. I didn't give up, that's for sure. I carried that record around to every company in this town. A few people said they liked it, but by then most of the labels had filled their quota of girl singers. Finally I got married, had some kids and came to work here, but I never stopped hoping. Who knows? It might still happen someday. I got a contract once, so who's to say I won't again? You just stay and keep trying, honey. If you got a voice and some gumption, it might happen to you, too."

Hope springs eternal, Dane thought, and smiled his first genuine smile of the day. "When did you first come to Nashville, Gracie?"

"In 1949. I was twenty. Oops, there's your food. Be right back."

Good grief, the woman was sixty-one and had the enthusiasm of a teenager, while he'd been walking around with his chin on his chest for weeks. He rubbed his eyes again, and when he removed his hands, Gracie was placing his food before him. She was also greeting a sixtyish man in faded jeans who was sitting down on the next stool. "Hi ya, honey. Where ya been?" she asked the new arrival.

"Around."

"This is Dane, Larry. He's a singer." To Dane she said, "Larry's a songwriter. Good one, too. He's gonna write a big hit someday. You guys might get together. What'll it be, honey?"

"Just coffee to go, Gracie," Larry said.

As the waitress scurried away, Larry turned to Dane. "You working?"

"Nope."

"Join the club. Ever make a record?"

"One."

"Did it do anything?"

"I'm afraid not."

"You gotta keep trying. There are a dozen ways not to make it in this business. Makin' bad music is only one of 'em."

Dane smiled. "Would I have heard any of your songs, Larry?"

The writer mentioned a couple of titles. Dane frowned and shook his head as he reached for the catsup bottle. "No, I guess I don't know either of them."

"Neither does anybody else. Ever hear of Homer McCall?"

"Sure." McCall was a genuine success, having written a dozen or more hits for some really big names.

"Homer and me kinda collaborated once. For one night. We both used to booze it up a bit, and one night after we'd had a few, we wrote six guaranteed number one hits. Unfortunately, we didn't think to write 'em down, and the next morning neither one of us could remember even one of 'em. End of collaboration."

Gracie brought Larry's coffee in a foam cup. He paid her and stood up. "Nice meeting you, Dane. Hang in there, son. It'll happen one of these days...to me and to you. See you around, Gracie."

Dane lifted the top bun of his burger. He didn't know why he always did that, as though he expected to find something unusual there. Replacing the bun, he took a bite. Gracie was right; he had to keep trying. If the Gracies and the Larrys of Nashville hadn't given up, he shouldn't, either.

His problem was he'd thought it would come easy, and nothing worthwhile ever did. He had been trying to join an exclusive club without paying his dues; he'd just been riding on Paula's coattails, sitting around and waiting for wonderful things to happen to him. Where was the pride of accomplishment in that? He needed to depend on himself, not someone else's contacts. So now he would try it the conventional way.

Suddenly feeling more confident than he had in a long time, Dane wolfed down his burger and fries, which were excellent. Then he left Gracie a two-dollar tip. "You come back and let me know when the good stuff starts happening, honey," the waitress called after him as he made his way to the cashier's stand.

"Count on it," he called back. And when he left the diner he drove home as fast as the law would allow. Paula was waiting for him, her face a portrait of worry.

"Where have you been?" she cried, half in anger, half in relief that he was home safely.

"Having a hamburger and listening to one of this town's great thinkers. Her name is Gracie."

"Huh?"

"Never mind." Dane slid his arms around her and kissed the tip of her nose. "How are you, love?"

"I guess I'm all right now, but I've been sick with worry. I was afraid you'd gone out to drown your sorrows or something."

"The only thing I've had to drink tonight is a cola."

Paula pulled back to study him. "You look in a better mood than you have in quite a while."

"I am. I want to talk to you. I've decided what I'm going to do."

Paula listened patiently while he explained his plans. He would make a demo, audition, make the rounds, hound producers and record company execs. Haunt the places where anyone who wanted to could get up and perform. Play roadhouses and clubs in small towns where the Dottie Crowes of the business wouldn't appear, anyway. Slowly build a hard-core base of fans. He was through depending on Paula and who she knew. He knew the road ahead was going to be rough—maybe it was supposed to be—and he knew he might not make it. But he had to try. He couldn't tuck tail and run.

Since he was so up, Paula hated to deflate his spirits yet another time. But he had to know. "Save it, darling," she said with a sigh. "I want to talk to you, too. I hate to tell you this, but you're up against more than you know."

CHAPTER FIFTEEN

"MY GOODNESS, Paula, you're up and about town early this morning!" exclaimed Marilee Townsend, Lou's secretary.

"Yes, I am, but I have something very important to discuss with Lou, and I wanted to get it over with before the workday begins in earnest. I don't want to be too late getting to my own office." The Lord knew, Paula thought, that she'd given far more time and attention to Dane and his problems than she had to her own job lately. But perhaps today would put an end to that.

When Paula set her mind to accomplishing something, it usually got done. Now all her energies were focused on her confrontation with Lou. When she left this office, she would know something. She might not like what she learned, but she would have some answers.

She had not called ahead for obvious reasons. It would be too easy for Lou to beg off seeing her, citing the workload that had accumulated during his absence. She was counting on Marilee to send her right in without being announced, since in the past Paula had always had full access to Lou at all times. "Is Lou in yet?" Paula asked.

"Yes, he got in about ten minutes ago. Why don't you just go on in before he gets tied up with something?"

"Thanks." Paula squared her shoulders. At some point last night, while she had been helping Dane cope with the shock of learning it was his agent-manager who had been instrumental in keeping his record off the air, she had decided she couldn't barge in and begin accusing Lou of vile deeds. She wanted him to admit what he had done before he realized he was doing it. And above all, she wanted him to tell her why. Perhaps the damage was irreversible. In the back of too many minds would lie a caution: Isn't this the record we aren't supposed to play? So "Tears" might never be a hit, and Dane would have to start all over. But Paula had to know why. What had been done infuriated her, but why it had been done mystified her.

She soundlessly opened the door and stepped into the office. Lou was seated at his desk, his head down in concentration. Paula stared at him a minute, overcome with some powerful emotions, all of them unpleasant: anger, of course; bewilderment; a sense of loss—Lou had been a big part of her life for a long time; a curious kind of sadness that any of it had happened; and uncertainty about any sort of friendship between them in the future. If anyone had tried to tell her the day would come when she dreaded facing Lou, she wouldn't have believed it, but dread this she did.

Lou apparently sensed the presence of someone else in the room. Glancing up, he did a double take. "Paula!"

"Good morning, Lou. Marilee said I could come right in. Welcome back."

"I . . . er, thanks. What brings you here so early in the morning?"

"I have a few things I want to discuss with you, and I wanted to get them out of the way before I got tied up at my office."

Lou collected his wits and got to his feet. "Please, have a seat."

Paula crossed the room and sat in a leather chair facing his desk. "How was Europe?"

"Busy. I didn't see much of it but airports."

"We were surprised to hear you had gone. Even more surprised that you didn't call before you left."

"The trip came up suddenly, and I had a million things to take care of. How are Mitch and Rona?"

"Very well. Surprisingly, so is Dane, although he's naturally been at something of a loss without his manager to guide him at this critical juncture in his career."

Lou did not look at her. "I can't be everywhere at once."

"No, I suppose not, and I'm sure Dottie's European tour is considerably more important than an unknown singer's lone record. You know it's been released."

"Well, of course . . . it would have been . . . by now."

"Have you had time to check on how it's doing?"

"Ah . . . no, I haven't. I'm swamped here, as you can see." Lou spread his hands to indicate the formidable amount of paperwork before him.

"Then I'll spare you having to take the time. It's not doing well. It's not doing anything. It's not even being played. You must know how disappointed he is after the buildup you gave him. Halley's Comet, wasn't that what you told him? I believe you also said that if he stuck with you, he might wind up in the Hall of Fame. You're the expert at this. What could have happened?''

Lou shrugged. "Well...I'm not sure. You know how these things go.''

"No, I really don't, Lou. After all, I'm not in the business. I can't imagine how a record that Owen produced and you touted to the heavens could fail so miserably. With your contacts, you could make a star out of me. Even Owen said it didn't wash.''

"Owen?'' Lou looked uncomfortable and began unnecessarily shuffling papers.

Paula felt sick. Somewhere in the dim recesses of her mind she had hoped there would turn out to be a logical explanation for Lou's shenanigans, but such a hope had evaporated. She was making him too nervous. "Yes, Owen. When weeks went by and Dane's record didn't show up on the charts, I naturally had to do something. You weren't here, so I talked to Owen. He agreed that something wasn't right, so he asked around. It seems someone has sent out the word that Heron doesn't want the record played. Of course, that's not true. It cost money to produce a record, and Heron isn't a charitable organization. We've all— Owen, Marty Oliver and I—scratched our heads over this one.''

Lou paled slightly. "Marty?''

"Yes, I talked to him, too. I've been so upset over all this. We finally decided that if anyone could help us solve this mystery, you could. Who could have done such a thing, Lou?''

"Paula, dear, I'm sorry, but I'm too busy to think this morning. I thought you had something important to discuss—''

"This is important!" she exclaimed.

"I can't believe you would trouble Owen and Marty with this nonsense."

"Nonsense? If this happened to Dottie Crowe, would you consider it nonsense?"

"I don't think Dottie and Dane Markham are in quite the same league. Now, can we discuss this global crisis some other time?"

"No!" Her resolve to remain perfectly calm no matter what crumbled. *"Judas!"* she cried.

Lou looked at her, startled. "What?"

"You heard me." Paula got to her feet and began pacing the room. "Did you honestly think I wouldn't at least ask some questions? Did you think I would just shrug and say, 'Ah, well, it's just one of those things?'"

"What are you talking about?"

"Drop it, Lou. You know what I'm talking about. You deliberately sabotaged that record. But you messed with the wrong person. I have some pretty important friends in this town, people who owe everything to Justin. One of them very kindly consented to do some snooping for me. You—not just a spokesperson but you personally—have called DJs all over the country and asked them not to play Dane's record. You informed a club owner in Memphis that Dane wasn't available for personal appearances. You told Tony Grant not to put him on his show again. How could you? Mitch and Rona and I have been your family, and you knew how very much we wanted Dane to be successful. What you've done is traitorous and, given your lofty position in the industry, probably unethical. Justin would have been horrified."

She had thrown that in for emphasis, and it got results. Lou jumped to his feet. "Don't lay that on me, Paula! It was for Justin that I—" He stopped, horrified over saying too much.

Paula stared at him in astonishment. "It was for Justin that you did it. Is that what you were going to say? How could that possibly be?"

"I . . . Forget it." Lou sank back into his chair.

"No, I won't forget it. I'll never forget it, but I want to know why. I won't leave this office until I learn the truth. Why?"

Lou truly was agitated. Paula knew him well and could tell. "Paula," he said in a shaken voice, "drop it. This involves things you're better off knowing nothing about. Forget Dane Markham and his future or lack of it, and get on with your life as it was."

Paula regarded him defiantly. "Forget Dane? Hardly. I'm in love with him."

Lou's lips pinched together. "How could you make a fool of yourself over that man?"

"Make a fool of myself? I fell in love with him. It happens to all sorts of people every day. Is that what was behind this? My relationship with Dane?"

"He doesn't have your class. He's a peasant courting a princess."

"Oh, come off it. It's not Dane—it's any man. You wouldn't want me involved with anyone. You want me to make a career out of being Justin's widow. I can't do that, and Justin wouldn't want me to."

"I cannot believe that a woman in your position would chase all over the country to rendezvous with . . ." Lou hesitated.

An unpleasant smile curled Paula's lips. "Ah, Oklahoma City. Now, I wonder how you found out about that? Which brings me to another very important question. What does Dottie Crowe have to do with all this?''

''Dottie? What makes you think—'' Again he checked himself.

''What makes me think Dottie has anything to do with this? Several things. First of all, word has gotten around that anyone who books Dane can't have Dottie. Odd, wouldn't you say? Second of all, Dottie apparently took a shine to Dane while they were on tour, and he was less than interested. Dottie doesn't strike me as a woman who's accustomed to rejection. But to be fair, she also doesn't strike me as someone vindictive enough to ruin a man's career just because he preferred someone else. There has to be more to it than that. What?''

Lou scowled darkly and studied his hands.

''You might as well tell me, Lou. My friend is very influential in the business. People who wouldn't talk to Owen readily talked to him. I'm sure if I ask him to, he'll keep digging. Or, if necessary, I'll hire a private detective. I understand those people can find out anything.'' Paula resumed her pacing. ''There are just so many puzzling things about all this,'' she went on. ''You had everything to gain by Dane's success. What did you have to lose? I've asked myself that over and over. Dottie? Did she threaten to hire a new manager? She's making you a bundle of money, true, but... No, that doesn't fit. You have a lot of clients making you money. It has to be something else.''

Paula paused for dramatic effect, then very quietly asked, ''Did Dottie ask you to get Dane blacklisted?''

A long minute passed. Paula waited. Outwardly she knew she looked calm and very sure of herself, but her insides were churning with agitation. She wasn't nearly as confident, didn't have nearly as many answers as she wanted Lou to think. "Did she?"

"Yes," Lou finally said with a sigh.

Paula's shoulders sagged. "And you did it? She simply asked and you ruined a promising career without hesitation?"

"Believe me, it wasn't without hesitation."

"You betrayed your closest friends for a woman who, as far as I know, is nothing but a client. One of many. But if she could get you to do something so despicable, she must be more. What, Lou? Just what is Dottie Crowe to you?"

"I...can't...tell you!"

"Why?"

"I...promised."

"Promised who?"

Lou said nothing, merely bowed his head and resumed studying his hands. Paula surveyed him, seeing not her dear old friend but a complete stranger. And some strange sixth sense told her she was on the verge of uncovering more than she had bargained for. "If you won't tell me, I guess I'll have to figure it out myself. You're an important man in this town. You tell people what to do—they don't tell you. Who could extract a promise from you that was so binding you would turn on a promising new singer and your dearest friends—"

Suddenly Paula stopped, whirled and snapped her fingers. "Justin! It would have to be. You promised Justin something, didn't you? What was it?"

"Drop it, Paula," Lou said, his voice pleading and desperate. "Just drop it."

"Not a chance. You know, I've always thought it peculiar that you and Justin were so taken with dear Dottie. I mean, she only had a so-so voice, and until the two of you got through with her, she wasn't even much to look at. Yet you and Justin treated her like the find of the century. What's her hold on you?"

Paula didn't expect an answer and got none. "Well, I'll find out. I won't rest until I do. Something tells me this is much more complicated and goes back much further than I originally thought. I think I just might have to dig into Dottie's past. Her real past, not that fiction she feeds to the papers. She's lived here all her life, hasn't she? Her mother's here. Maybe I'll talk to her mother. Any number of people should be able to tell me how to find her."

Lou jumped to his feet. "No! Listen to me—"

Paula shook a fist at him. "No, you listen to me! I have never been so furious in my life as I am over what's been done to Dane, and I won't stop until I find out everything. Everything. I meant it when I said I'd hire a detective. A team of detectives! I don't care what it costs or how long it takes. I just want to get to the bottom of this, and I have a lot of questions. For instance, why did Dottie take one look at me years ago and loathe me on sight? I thought it was peculiar then, and I'm doubly curious about it now." Paula tucked her handbag under her arm and made a move toward the door. "I guess I'm going to be one very busy woman for the next few weeks. Don't underestimate me, Lou. I will find out what I want to know." Keeping up her facade of bravado, she reached for the doorknob.

"No, wait!" Lou cried.

Paula turned. Thank God, she thought. If he had let her leave, she wasn't sure what her next move would have been.

Lou's face was flushed, as though from physical exertion. "You're right, I did underestimate your reaction to all this. Good God, I can't have detectives questioning people all over town!"

In a strange way, Paula felt sorry for him. He looked weak and defeated. What kind of Pandora's box had she opened?

"Sit down, Paula," Lou said wearily. "I'll tell you what you want to know."

Suddenly feeling exhausted herself, Paula crossed the room and once again sat facing the desk. Lou arranged and rearranged papers, picked up a pencil, put it down, then poured a glass of water from the carafe sitting on his desk. She braced herself for whatever was coming.

"It was a long time ago," Lou said dully, keeping his eyes focused on a spot across the room. "After Marjorie died, before Justin met you. He took up with a woman named Alma, a nice, respectable young woman who was a secretary at Heron Records. They were together several years. I don't think Alma was ever actually in love with Justin, and I know he wasn't in love with her, but they liked each other a lot, got along well, and Alma certainly enjoyed all the nice things Justin bought for her. Justin was a man who had to have one woman in his life. He couldn't function without one. He couldn't play the field—always had to get involved. I used to warn him that . . ." Lou paused as he realized he was digressing. "Naturally, the thing with Alma wasn't a platonic affair. No great love match, but it was mutually satisfying."

Paula couldn't imagine what an affair Justin had had between marriages had to do with Dane's problems, but she was alive with curiosity, mostly because relating the story seemed so hard on Lou. He looked as though he were being put through a wringer.

"Well, as often happens," Lou went on, "Alma got pregnant. I don't now if they ever considered terminating the pregnancy. I do know they discussed marriage and decided against it. They both knew that such an alliance had practically no chance of succeeding, and Justin's image was such that he didn't want to be another divorced country singer. Alma decided that passing herself off as a widow appealed to her. It was 'respectable.' This may sound terribly like a business arrangement, and it was, because that's the kind of relationship they had. Eyes wide open, and all that. So, Justin sent Alma to a place he owned in Florida, and their child was born. A daughter. When the child was three months old, he bought them a fine home here."

Paula was astonished. Not shocked, just astonished. So Justin had had a child, after all. She leaned forward. "The little girl, Lou...well, she wouldn't be little anymore. Did Justin stay in touch with her? Is she well?"

"Oh, yes, quite well. Justin took care of her handsomely. Alma, too. They both receive a percentage of his royalties for life."

"Then Rona must know about this," Paula said. "She took care of all Justin's business and financial affairs."

Lou shook his head. "No, this part of his life was handled very discreetly by yours truly. Rona and Mitch know nothing of it."

"Well, tell me something about the daughter. Does she live close by? Is she married? Did Alma ever marry? What did they do about the child's name?"

"The little girl always used Alma's name." Lou cleared his throat. "Crowe."

Paula's eyes widened. "Dottie?" she gasped.

"Yes."

"Dottie Crowe is Justin's daughter?"

Lou nodded.

"Oh, my God!" Paula had to sit back while her poor, stunned brain tried to assimilate it. Certain things began to fit. "Well, that certainly explains Dottie's meteoric rise to stardom."

"When Justin came to me with the news that Dottie wanted a singing career, I told him to to forget it, that she'd never make it. He swore she would, and he was right. Everyone gives me the lion's share of the credit for Dottie's success, but that was far more Justin's doing than mine."

"It's all so incredible. He must have spent hundreds of hours with her, and I never knew a thing about it."

"Justin doted on her. When she was very young, Dottie only knew Justin as a nice, generous man who was her mother's 'friend.' She and Alma had a wonderful life. They had a nice home, car, beautiful clothes—everything. The fly in the ointment came later, when Dottie, quite by accident, learned Justin was her natural father. He had written a statement admitting paternity—I witnessed it—and had given it to Alma. Just in case something happened to him and someone wanted to halt Alma's and Dottie's royalty payments. An insurance measure, he called it. Unfortunately, Alma kept it in a lockbox at home instead of in her safety deposit box at the bank. And one day

Dottie was going through things she had no business going through. From that day on, she badgered Justin to marry her mother.''

"Ah," Paula said with a nod. "Another mystery cleared up. The reason Dottie hates me so much. Justin married me instead of Alma."

"That's a lot of it, yes."

"So when Dane preferred me to Dottie... Well, in some twisted way, I guess I can understand that." Then Paula's eyes narrowed. "What I don't understand is, when Dottie came to you and asked you to get Dane blacklisted, why didn't you laugh in her face?"

Lou's face contorted. "I couldn't. She...threatened me."

"With what?"

"With going to the media with all this."

Paula simply stared at him a minute. "So? Who cares? Let her call ten press conferences. It might make page sixteen on a slow news day."

"You don't understand."

"You've certainly got that right."

"I promised Justin it would never get out. I gave him my solemn word. So did Alma. Hell, she liked things the way they were. She was a rich 'widow.' She certainly didn't want anyone to know she'd had a child out of wedlock. Sounds quaint, doesn't it? But you have to remember the moral climate of the time. Justin and Alma told Dottie she must never tell anyone because it would hurt Justin badly, but it always bothered me that Dottie knew. When she's steamed, there's no telling what can happen. She might have been bluffing when she threatened to go to the press. I couldn't take a chance."

Paula threw up her hands, hardly believing what she was hearing. "And a talented man's career is being ruined over this nonsense! It's ludicrous. Dane is being punished for something people he never met did thirty-odd years ago. Do you see how ridiculous that is, Lou? So Justin had an affair between his marriages and fathered a child. Who would care?"

"Justin cared!" Lou roared. His face turned so red Paula feared he might have a stroke. It was his turn to get up and pace.

"Lou, Justin...is...dead."

"The legend lives on!"

"Oh, God! This is too much for me."

"You don't understand what Justin's image meant to him. Coming along on the heels of Hank Williams's life of self-destruction, Justin was like a breath of fresh air. Gentleman Justin Steele, the Mr. Clean of country music. The fans adored him. He was more than just a good singer. He was their idol, someone they could look up to. And he loved it, relished it, reveled in it. He wouldn't drink or smoke in public for fear it would offend a fan somewhere. That image meant everything to him. And make no mistake about it—thirty-two years ago plenty of his fans would have been shocked to learn he'd had an affair, fathered a child and hadn't bothered to marry the child's mother."

Lou stopped for breath. "You might think that's ridiculous. I might think he carried the image thing too far. It doesn't matter what we think. What matters is what Justin thought. I promised no one would ever know. I'd ruin a dozen talented singers in order to keep a promise to Justin."

If anything had been carried too far, Paula thought, it was Lou's devotion to Justin. It bordered on being sick. She watched Lou sink back into his chair, prop his elbows on the desk and put his head in his hands. "But I have broken it, haven't I?" he said miserably. "I told you."

Paula's voice was impassive. "You didn't have much choice, did you? I was deadly serious about hiring a detective. If I had, there's no telling how many people would have found out about Justin and Alma." She folded her hands in her lap and spoke crisply. "All right, Lou, I'm glad you cleared this up for me. Now, let me tell you what you're going to do."

"Now, just a damned minute!"

"I'm not finished. You're going to call all those DJs you got in touch with and tell them to start playing that record and to play it every hour until you tell them to stop, which might be sometime after Christmas. Then you are going to get busy and do all those wonderful things you promised Dane you would do. You know the drill. An album. Opening all across the country for some really big name. You are going to turn Dane Markham into the busiest new performer in Nashville."

Lou's fist hit the desk. "I can't do that! Dottie—"

"Tell Dottie to call the press. I'm betting she won't, but tell her to, anyway."

"And if I don't?" he asked defiantly.

Paula took a deep breath. She had so hoped she wouldn't have to play her ace. It seemed as low as Dottie's actions, but she had to do it. She was doing all this for Dane. "If you don't turn Dane into the star you promised him he'd be, you'll never be welcome in Justin's house again."

The color drained from Lou's face. "You can't do that! I deserve to be there more than the rest of you, because I loved him more than all of you put together."

"No, you didn't," Paula said quietly, sadly. "You just *thought* you did. You wanted to believe you did, but it would have been impossible to love Justin any more than I did. Friendship is a wonderful thing, but you've allowed yourself to become obsessed with Justin. I'm wondering if you shouldn't get some help with that. Professional help. As wonderful as Justin was, as much as I loved him, he wasn't a god."

Lou looked as though she'd thrown ice water in his face. "He almost was to me. No one's ever understood. Do you think I'd have what I have, be what I am, if it weren't for Justin? Hell, no! I'd be Joe Oblivion. When I came to this town, I thought I could sing. Then I heard Justin and knew I couldn't. When he made that first record and it took off like a rocket, half a dozen people wanted to handle him, but he insisted on me. I owe him everything!"

Paula tried to feel some compassion, but she couldn't. The man she loved had been through some hellish times lately, and the man responsible for that was seated directly across from her. "Then you of all people should despise a blacklisting. So, tell me, Lou, does Dane get his career?"

"I can't believe you've let him come to mean so much to you."

"Believe it."

"I honestly thought..."

Paula waited for him to finish the sentence. When he didn't, she prodded. "What? You honestly thought what?"

"I thought...if Dane's career stayed in limbo, he'd get discouraged and move on."

Paula shook her head in disbelief. "I'm trying, but I simply don't understand your attitude."

While they sat staring at each other, assessing the situation, the door to the office opened quietly and Marilee stepped inside. The secretary spoke in a hushed, almost furtive tone.

"Lou, Paula...I'm sorry to interrupt you, but... Lou, you have a very unhappy and impatient caller in the waiting room. Dottie Crowe."

"Oh, God," Lou muttered under his breath.

"Perfect," Paula said. Slowly she turned to face Marilee. "Send her in," she said. Behind her she heard Lou gasp.

Marilee looked uncertain and glanced questioningly at her boss. "Is...it all right?"

"Paula, what do you think this will accomplish?" Lou asked. The emotional confrontation with Paula had drained him. He didn't think he was up to another one with Dottie.

"Don't you think it's time to clear this up once and for all?" Paula asked. "Send her in, Marilee."

By now Marilee realized she had stumbled into something that was private and none of her business, but Dottie was outside seething over being kept waiting so long. Again she looked at her boss, quizzing him with her eyes.

Lou sighed. "All right, Marilee. Send Dottie in."

CHAPTER SIXTEEN

DOTTIE SWEPT into the office, saw Paula and froze in her tracks. "I expected Lou to be alone," she said icily.

"As you can see, he isn't," Paula replied. "Come in, Dottie. You're just the person I want to see."

Suspicion, doubt and confusion were etched on Dottie's face. "I can come back later."

"No need for that," Paula said quickly. "You're already here, and I'd like to talk to you. Have a seat."

Dottie glanced at Lou. "Is it all right?"

"Yes, it's all right," he said. Lou's insides were churning. He couldn't tear his gaze away from Paula, who had such a strange look in her eyes. He couldn't begin to imagine what she was going to do, and he wondered if Paula herself knew. In some curious way, he was glad it was out in the open. Maybe Paula wouldn't believe it, but he had suffered many pangs of conscience lately. After a lifetime of being scrupulously honest with his clients, he hadn't engaged in deception without qualms.

Paula watched Dottie move into the room, hesitantly, uncertainly, with none of the self-confidence she radiated onstage. She wore jeans, a T-shirt, little makeup, and her wild mane of blond hair had been tamed with a large gold clasp. She probably could have mingled among a dozen of her fans without being recognized.

For the first time, Paula really studied the woman. She searched for something of Justin in his daughter and found what she was looking for—the eyes, the shape of the nose, the way the corners of her mouth curved upward slightly even when she wasn't smiling. Dottie was not beautiful in the accepted sense of the word, but Justin and Lou had instilled flash and flair in her, so one soon forgot her lack of classic beauty. Justin's daughter! Incredible!

Unless Dottie wanted to sit on the far side of the room, she had no choice but to take the chair next to Paula's. The air all around them was charged with tension. The young woman would have had to be dense indeed not to notice that. "What's going on here?" she demanded bluntly.

Paula decided not to hedge, either. She addressed Dottie directly. "I came to see Lou about Dane."

"What about him?"

"Naturally I was curious about why a career that seemed so promising wasn't going anywhere."

"Sometimes those things happen."

"Maybe so," Paula said, "but in this case someone made it happen. While Lou was in Europe, I had some friends ask around, visit people, make a few phone calls. What we learned was very interesting. One, disc jockeys all over the country had been told not to play his record. Two, the word was out that anyone who booked Dane couldn't have Dottie Crowe. None of that made much sense to me. Why would the two of them go together? What was the connection? I decided that if anyone could solve the mystery for me, Lou could. And he did."

"What . . . did he tell you?"

"Everything."

Dottie's face turned crimson, and she faced Lou with blazing eyes. "You didn't! I told you what I would do."

"Yes, you told him what you would do," Paula said, her voice as calm as if she were ordering lunch. "But, Dottie, if you think about it, what would going to the press accomplish? You can't hurt Justin anymore. If you think you can hurt me, you couldn't be more wrong. It doesn't distress me in the least to discover you're his daughter."

Dottie gasped. She looked at Lou murderously. "You told her? You actually told her?"

"I had to," he said contritely. "She already knew too much and threatened to hire detectives."

"Dottie, the only person you would hurt by revealing your father's identity is your mother," Paula reminded her. "She has her reasons for not wanting it known, and she's kept her secret a long time. I don't think she'd appreciate having it all come out now."

Dottie rubbed the bridge of her nose and uttered an unintelligible sound deep in her throat. "I . . . wouldn't have gone to the press," she confessed. "I told Lou that because I knew it'd get a rise out of him and he'd do what I asked."

Paula cast a sideways glance in Lou's direction to gauge his reaction to that statement. His expression told her that nothing Dottie did really surprised him. She returned her attention to the younger woman. "That's another thing. Lou has admitted that you're the one who asked him to have Dane blacklisted. Do you really think it's fair to ruin the career of a man who had absolutely nothing to do with any of this?"

Dottie's chin lifted slightly. "I wasn't trying to be fair."

"It wasn't really Dane you wanted to hurt, was it?"

"No."

Paula had to give her credit for being honest.

"It was me, wasn't it? And it was because I married Justin."

"Yes," Dottie hissed. Jumping to her feet, she walked to the window and stared out, her back to both Paula and Lou. "All I ever wanted was to be able to call him Daddy. Once I honestly thought he might marry Mom. I was about eleven, and by that time I realized there wasn't much he could deny me, so I began pressuring both of them. They had to get married for my sake, I told them, and I thought they were weakening. Then—I remember it was a Saturday afternoon. Justin had come to the house with some gifts he'd bought us on his last trip. I took him off to one side and started in on him again. Finally he said, 'Tell you what, sweetheart—you let me think about this a bit. I'm not real sure this is what your mom wants to do.' I told him not to worry about Mom, to leave her to me. And he said he had to go to Birmingham to do a benefit, and while he was gone he'd make up his mind. I knew I'd won."

Dottie turned and looked squarely at Paula. "He came back from Birmingham four days later, and I don't think he ever mentioned marrying Mom again. I asked him why, and he said he'd met someone he was really interested in. Mom didn't care, but I was devastated. When he married you, he said it wouldn't make any difference, that things wouldn't change, but that was a lie. Of course they changed. I wasn't his 'best girl' anymore. You were. I hated you—I couldn't help it. After a while, I felt like I had to compete with you for him, for his time and attention. If he spent an hour with you, I wanted equal time. If I heard he'd bought you an outlandish gift, I expected him to buy me something, too. I looked for him in every man I ever had anything to do with. For sure I looked for him in both my husbands. Naturally, he wasn't there. And too often after he married you, the real Justin wasn't there for me, either.''

Paula rubbed her temples. Poor Justin, she thought. How he must have felt pulled apart by the idiotic rivalry that she hadn't even known existed. Instead of anger, she just felt an emptying kind of sadness. After harboring so much hate and competitiveness for so long, Dottie must have been furious when she learned that Dane had been with her that night in Oklahoma City. But such a misguided channeling of energies.... That something as petty as feminine jealousy had forced Dane to endure all that he had was senseless.

''I wish Justin hadn't felt it necessary to keep you a secret, Dottie, I really do,'' Paula said quietly. ''He needn't have shouted it to the world, of course. Your mother didn't want that, and his fans probably wouldn't have liked it. But he could have told me. We could have had you over to the house, taken you on some of our private trips. Later, as one of his protégés, you could have spent a lot of time with us. You and I might have become friends—who knows? I always wanted a daughter to buy things for.''

Dottie stared at Paula as though she were a creature from another planet. Having expected almost any reaction but that one, she was speechless.

''I know it must have been hard on you,'' Paula went on. ''My father died when I was very young, so

I know what it's like to grow up without one. But at least you knew your father and had some great times with him. I don't even remember mine."

Thoroughly distracted and disarmed, Dottie looked at Lou, then returned to the chair beside Paula. "I just adored Justin," she said simply. "I would have done anything for him."

Paula sighed. "He seemed to have that effect on legions of women." Her eyes met Lou's. "Men, too."

"I guess it was easy to hate you and blame you when he stopped seeing so much of me. My mom was the practical one. She'd say, 'Oh, for heaven's sake, stop moping. Of course Justin's busy. He has his career and a new wife,' and that would make me furious. I guess that's one reason I wanted to sing. I knew he'd help me, and that would mean he would have to spend a lot of time with me. I was right. And then when I met Dane, I thought I saw a little of Justin in him. It just didn't seem right that you, of all people, had him, too."

"Perhaps if he had met you first . . ." Paula meant that to sound kind; unfortunately, it came out sounding rather patronizing. "But he didn't, and I'm not going to lie to you. Dane and I are extremely close, and it's terribly unfair that he has to suffer because of it. I'm asking both of you—" her eyes drifted to Lou, then back to Dottie "—to drop this ridiculous vendetta against him. He's done nothing but try for a career in music. You know there are enough obstacles in the path to success without deliberately strewing it with more."

Paula stopped and chewed her bottom lip. Dottie was expressionless, and she wondered if her pleas were falling on deaf ears. Of course, Dottie knew nothing about obstacles and stumbling blocks. Her career had been handed to her on a silver platter, thanks to Justin and Lou. What did she know about struggling? "The secrets are all out in the open, so there's no more leverage there," she reminded them on a practical note. "Just get the record played and let Dane accept whatever dates he can get. He's perfectly willing to build slowly, to start out at smaller clubs in small towns that couldn't get Dottie Crowe to begin with. Give us a break. We'll take it from there. That's all I ask."

That "us" grated on Lou's nerves, something else he had to fight. When Dottie had first told him about Paula's trip to Oklahoma City, he had fervently hoped she was simply keeping tabs on her protégé. He might even have accepted an infatuation of brief duration. But the involvement went much deeper than that, and he wasn't sure he could ever resign himself to that. "And if I don't?" he asked.

"I might have to call a press conference of my own," Paula said quietly, amazed that she would even think of such a thing. "In a town like this, filled with unknowns trying for a break and veterans who've been through the struggle, I think *blacklisted* might be a dirty word. The mere idea that an influential man could destroy a career with a few phone calls wouldn't, I don't think, sit very well with a majority of those in the business."

Silence fell over the room. There didn't seem to be anything left to say, so Paula got to her feet and left the office, leaving two very stunned people behind. Neither Lou nor Dottie said a word for several long minutes after the door had closed behind her. Finally Dottie lifted her eyes and looked at her mentor. "I've

hated her for such a long time—twenty years or more.
But do you know what's really bugging the hell out of
me?''

''What's that?'' Lou asked.

''I hate it that she turned out to be so nice.''

Lou silently drummed a pencil on the desktop. He
wondered how ''nice'' Paula would prove to be. Nice
enough to forgive him his treachery? He had betrayed
her, betrayed Justin's memory while seeking to pre-
serve it. He had also betrayed a client of his, which
could cost him credibility in the business if the word
got out. Yes, Paula could destroy him with a press
conference, and she knew it. Would she do it? It
wouldn't be characteristic of her, but she might after
what he had done.

He looked at Dottie, who'd had such a strangle-
hold on him all these years because she was Justin's
daughter. She wasn't a bad kid, just misguided at
times, spoiled rotten and self-serving above all.
Through the years she hadn't hesitated to milk his devotion to Justin for all it was worth, and that had been
plenty. Perhaps Paula had been right—perhaps he had
carried that devotion to extremes. Now, how did he
atone?

Get Dane's record played, for starters. It was a good
record, and he'd do all right. *But,* Lou conceded, *now
he'll probably do all right without me.*

''Are you going to do what she asked you to?''
Dottie asked.

''Wouldn't you?''

''Why? What can Paula Steele do to a man like
you?''

Lou glowered at her. ''Call a press conference, for
one thing. She was absolutely right about how this

town would feel about a blacklisting. Give it up, Dottie. I'm sorry it ever got started in the first place."

Dottie slumped dejectedly in her chair. "Why does she always win?"

"Maybe because she never realized she was in a fight."

PAULA THOUGHT about the confrontation all day. She couldn't get it out of her mind, and she wondered if she ever would be able to forgive Lou. The death of a friendship was a sad thing, but right now she felt harsh and unforgiving toward him. Perhaps time would change that. Perhaps she would forget. She would have to wait and see.

She had reached one decision, however: Dane would get a new manager. She feared the feelings between the two men would never allow for the close artist-manager relationship that was almost mandatory for a successful career. She also feared Lou would never accept Dane's role in her life.

It wasn't until the spate of morning phone calls had been fielded and quiet settled over her office that Paula recalled something she had said to Lou: *You are going to turn Dane Markham into the busiest new performer in Nashville.* Had she said that without thinking? Did she want that? When would they ever see each other?

But, yes, she wanted it. She had to want it for Dane's sake. It was the only way he would have his career. And if the career proved to be the wedge that drove them apart...well, perhaps she'd never really had Dane to begin with.

They'd only ever discussed the future in terms of his career, never in terms of the two of them together, forever and ever, amen. She had thought of marriage plenty of times and usually had come to the conclusion that it wouldn't be fair to him. She had no idea if Dane ever thought about it or not. They loved each other, were friends and were extraordinarily compatible in and out of bed, but were they marriage material?

Maybe not. Maybe theirs was destined to be a bittersweet love affair that would give her memories to dwell on in old age. God, that made her feel empty and sad, but it shouldn't, she realized. With Dane she'd known more joy than most women ever did. And wasn't she the pragmatic woman who'd said from the beginning that she couldn't see them growing old together?

Still, she gave in and admitted she wanted him to be her husband. In spite of the age difference, in spite of being apart more often than they'd be together, she wanted the whole death-do-us-part thing. That couldn't give them more time together, but there was such permanence, such a sense of belonging in marriage that could be obtained through no other relationship. How did one convey that need to a man without coming right out and asking, "Will you marry me?"

Would that be so shocking? her inner voice asked.

Were such things done?

Everything's done these days, the voice replied.

Paula didn't think she could do it. What if he said no? That would break her heart.

If he says no, he might pack his bags.

Not surprisingly, Paula had a difficult time concentrating on the fortunes of Hamilton House that day. Mercifully, things were slow, so she felt no guilt about being out of the building and on her way home by four-thirty. Today, for the first time since talking to Vanessa in Dallas, she wished she would get the nod to be C.E.O. Even though it would mean a gigantic upheaval and leaving wonderful friends like Marty and Owen, she felt the need for a change. This whole Dane-Lou-Dottie business had left a bad taste in her mouth.

Also, during her preoccupation with it she had neglected to tell Mitch and Rona about Dallas. She had to do that soon. Tonight. But first, she wanted to talk to Dane.

As always, the minute she had checked the stack of mail and sniffed the flowers on the foyer table, Paula went in search of Dane. He was in his room. "Stop the presses, hold the phone!" she exclaimed as she walked through the door.

"What's up?" he asked.

"I locked horns with Lou today. And with Dottie. The record's going to get played."

"If it does, great."

The nonchalance in his voice astonished Paula. "That's it? No hoorays or anything?"

"Let's say that this time around I'm going to be cautiously optimistic." Dane looked at her with a strange little smile. "Don't I get a kiss?"

"Sorry. Of course you do," she said, and gave him what he wanted. "I don't understand this lack of enthusiasm. I got Lou and Dottie to admit their skulduggery, and while they didn't exactly get down on their knees and apologize for it, I do expect atonement. Thus, the record gets played. You know what that means."

"No, I don't . . . and neither do you. We only know what we hope it means . . . but we've been down that road before, haven't we?"

"Dane, didn't you hear me?" Paula asked in exasperation. "Your career is about to take off."

"I heard you. Come here, love. I want to talk to you." He backed into the easy chair and pulled her down onto his lap. "I hope the record does get played. I think I hope it more for you than for me at this point, because, God knows, you've worked your pretty little butt off to get it for me. And if it does, if things start happening for me, it'll be wonderful. But I'm through sitting around waiting for that to happen. And please don't fight any more of my battles for me."

"Oh, that's ridiculous! I haven't fought anything."

"Of course you have. From the beginning, you called so-and-so, you got in touch with so-and-so. And when the bottom fell out of the dream, you fought like a caged lioness."

She shook her head. "I merely enlisted the aid of a few friends. That's what friends are for, to be there for you when you need them." That statement immediately made her think of Lou, and her eyes clouded. "At least, that's what they're supposed to do. I can't believe Lou would do what he did. I want to forgive him because he was so close to Justin, because he's been part of the scene so long, but I'm not sure I ever will."

Dane ran a fingertip along her jawline, then pressed it against her lips. She kissed it. "Want to talk about it?" he asked.

"He did it, Dane. Every bit of it. Called the disc jockeys, sent out word that you weren't available. Every bit of it."

"Did you find out why?"

Paula uttered a bitter little laugh. "Yes. Dottie asked him to."

Dane pursed his lips. "Hmm. I knew I wasn't her favorite person, but that's a shade drastic."

Paula smiled. "That's the trouble—you were her favorite person at one time, but you preferred me. That's when it hit the fan."

"There must be more to it than you've told me."

"There is. Much more." She settled comfortably on his lap, kicked off her shoes and began relating to Dane the encounter in Lou's office. The story seemed to take forever to tell. When she was finished, Paula said, "You know, it's odd how I feel about all of it. Oh, I'm furious at Lou, of course. But since I don't know Dottie very well, my feelings toward her are less sharply defined. She had a hang-up about her daddy. People have worse ones, I suppose. The person I'm having the biggest problem with is Justin. That image thing was ridiculous. And since I'm a woman, maybe a part of me thinks he should have married Alma and given Dottie his name. I suppose that sounds positively medieval in this day and age, but Dottie wasn't conceived in this day and age."

That was the first time Dane had heard Paula say a word about Justin that wasn't completely laudatory. "It doesn't sound to me like Alma would have cooperated," he said quietly, at a loss to know why he thought it necessary to justify her late husband's actions.

"I wonder," Paula mused. "She might have known Justin's true feelings and decided not to risk losing what she had. Maybe she only pretended not to want marriage. In those days, people had a far different sense of propriety than they do now. I just wonder..."

"'Might,' 'maybe....' You'll never know, so why waste time even thinking about it?"

"You're right, of course. This has just been such an emotional day for me."

"I can imagine. You know, you said something that bothers me a little bit. Dottie told you she thought she saw something of Justin in me. Do you?"

Paula pulled back to look at him. "No, nothing. Dottie admitted to looking for Justin in every man she met. I never did. You are your own person, unique." She thought Dane looked relieved and knew he would have hated thinking she might have been attracted to him because he reminded her of Justin, but he could rest his mind on that score. She quite simply had never known anyone like Dane, and though it sounded trite, she didn't think she could live without him in her life. "Darling, we're going to have to find you a new manager. You realize that, don't you? You and Lou simply won't be able to work together, not now."

Dane thought about that. "Whatever you say, Paula. I've never gone wrong listening to you."

She settled her head on his shoulder, and a pensive quality crept into her voice. "So all those wonderful things are going to happen to you. Before long, you'll be busier than you want to be, and I'll be moping around this house, waiting for you to come home, feeling like a sailor's wife half the time."

"Our reunions ought to be...er, memorable."
Suddenly Dane sobered. "Paula, sweetheart, in spite
of your efforts, I've never felt like I belonged in this
house. I still don't. An itinerant country singer in this
mansion? It doesn't fit."

"An itinerant country singer bought this house."

"After he'd become a superstar," he reminded her.
"Not before."

"But you belong here because this is home. Home
is where the heart is, remember? And isn't your heart
with me?"

"You know it is."

"And you also belong here because you're going to
be my husband." Paula honestly hadn't known she
was going to say that until the words were out.

"I am?" he asked with remarkable coolness considering his wildly racing heart, considering the bar-
rage of emotions that made him ache inside.

"Aren't you?"

"Are you proposing to me?"

"I guess I am. I...got tired of waiting for you to do
it." Paula swallowed thickly. "Do you mind?"

"Do I mind what? Your proposing or your getting
tired?"

"Dane, don't tease," she protested. "I'm serious."

She was serious; he could see it. That alone filled
him with wonder. He was having a damnably hard
time coming to grips with this. He had thought about
marriage on the average of half a dozen times a day
ever since that weekend at the cabin, and he'd wondered if he'd ever get up the courage to actually ask
Paula to be his wife. Now she was doing the asking?
She wanted it, too! His stunned mind found that dif-

ficult to accept. "Would you really do that?" he asked.

"Do what?"

"Marry me?"

"Eureka!" she cried with a laugh. "Excelsior! You said it! Yes, yes, yes. In time I'll probably even forget that I coerced it out of you." Flinging her arms around him, she covered his face with kisses, crying and laughing at the same time.

Finally, gasping, Dane pulled away slightly. "I can't give you anything, sweetheart. Someday maybe, but not yet. Just my love."

"Just your love? That's everything. Look around. I own things, lots of them. But what you do for me, what you give me—" kissing him tenderly and deeply, she took one of his hands and laid it lightly on her breast "—is priceless."

She could arouse him with a look; when she set out in earnest to arouse him, it didn't take long. In no time at all, his eyes were smoldering, and the familiar heaviness had settled in his loins. "Go close the door," he said in a thick, hoarse voice. "And lock it."

Paula complied, and when she returned to him, he was on his feet and holding out his arms. Wordlessly she went into them, where she felt safe, wanted and needed.

AFTER DINNER that night, Paula, Dane and Mitch and Rona sat in the den and talked. Paula tersely recounted her confrontation with Lou, which naturally had Mitch and Rona reeling with surprise. She would have preferred sparing them the details of their old friend's actions, but they were completely baffled by

Lou's absence from their lives, so an explanation was called for.

"It's the hardest thing in the world to accept," Rona murmured. "Lou! I wonder... what will this mean? That he won't be around anymore?"

"I'm sure there'll be a marked change in my relationship with him," Paula confessed, "but you and Mitch are welcome to have him over anytime you want. I'll be courteous. Now, for the next item on the agenda." Her eyes met Dane's, and they exchanged a smile. "Dane and I are getting married."

Rona's eyes didn't even widen. "That's a news bulletin? I would have been surprised if you weren't getting married." Getting to her feet, she hugged both of them warmly, and Mitch leaned across to shake Dane's hand.

When the minor stir that news had created settled down, Paula folded her hands in her lap and regarded Mitch and Rona solemnly. "This next might be more difficult for the two of you to deal with. Vanessa Hamilton is in the process of choosing the next president of Hamilton House. I'm being considered along with several others. If I'm chosen, I'll have to move to Dallas. You need to know that so you'll have time to decide what you want to do."

"How do you feel about that, Dane?" was Rona's first question.

He shrugged. "I don't feel anything about it. For me it's pretty cut-and-dried. If Paula goes to Dallas, I'll go to Dallas."

"And you, Paula?"

"Let's put it this way. If I'm not selected, I won't be disappointed. If I am selected, I'll accept. I owe it to the company, and I owe it to myself. You two are the ones I'm concerned about. You've always lived in Nashville. If you don't want to leave, I'll understand. I'll feel as though someone cut off my right arm, but I'll understand. I wanted to give you some time to think about it, talk between yourselves and decide what you want to do.''

Mitch and Rona exchanged a glance. In that mysterious way that longtime married couples have of silently communicating, they telegraphed a message back and forth. Paula saw Mitch nod. Rona turned to her. ''We don't have to think about it, Paula. There's nothing to decide. Of course we'll go with you. What else would we do? It's never been Nashville per se or this house. It was always Justin and you and, now, Dane. You're the ones we want to stay with, not a place.''

Paula felt her eyes sting, and a lump lodged in her throat. Overcome with emotion, she didn't know what to say. But then, she really didn't have to say anything. Both Mitch and Rona had always been able to read her like a book, which was one of the reasons she felt so comfortable with them. She'd be damned if she was going to get all maudlin and embarrass everyone.

Her eyes met Dane's, and they shared a smile. Then she got to her feet and walked to the bar. Taking an open bottle of wine out of the refrigerator, she placed four glasses on the bar and filled each three-quarters full. As if on cue, the others stood and crossed the room. The glasses all clinked together. ''To whatever lies around the corner,'' Rona said.

''To us,'' Paula countered. ''The four of us.''

EPILOGUE

A FEW STRATEGICALLY PLACED phone calls from Lou Howard's office was all it took. "Tears" came on the charts at number forty and began its steady climb to break into the top twenty. It was selling, in Owen Brewster's words, "like peanuts at the circus."

With the success of the record—and no interference from high places—came Tony Grant's invitation to Dane to appear on *Today in Nashville* again. That appearance coinciding as it did with the appearance of the record on the charts, launched his career with a bang. He had signed with Heron to turn out three new singles in the next two years, but now that "Tears" had taken off, he had been called back to the studio to make his first album. Owen would produce them all.

And he had acquired a new manager, Vic Cole, who was as enthusiastic as Lou had been in the beginning. Together he and Dane were in the process of putting together a band, and that fall there would be three weeks of one-nighters throughout the South—at auditoriums and fairgrounds in small cities and some smaller clubs in big cities like Birmingham and Jacksonville. It had begun, and though Paula didn't particularly welcome all of it—the three weeks away from home, for instance—she knew it was necessary.

In the middle of all this activity, Paula and Dane had managed to work in a wedding—a small ceremony at home with Mitch and Rona, Marty and Alicia Oliver and Owen Brewster in attendance. The first person Paula had called after the ceremony was Verna Gregg, who was, to put it mildly, flabbergasted. After gasping her surprise and finally getting around to offering congratulations, she had begun to laugh. She laughed until she choked. And once she could speak, she said, "Oh, this is too good, too good! Wait until I spread the word. Dane Markham has a hit record and is married to Justin Steele's widow. There aren't two people in the entire county who'll believe it. Paula...I'm just...so happy for you." Which, of course, had prompted a small ocean of tears.

Sadly, Lou no longer was part of the scene, although Mitch and Rona tried to have lunch with him occasionally. They never volunteered any information about their old friend, and Paula asked for none. But with all the good things happening to Dane, and in her newfound state of utter bliss, Paula found it difficult to harbor grudges or ill will toward anyone. Lou had made a mistake, but wasn't she the one who believed in a second chance for everyone? She could feel herself weakening.

It was a lazy Saturday morning. Canada had sent them a gift in the form of a cold front, so instead of sweltering under ninety-plus temperatures, they were enjoying days of unseasonably cool weather. Paula and Dane were having coffee on the patio and relishing the fresh morning air. Suddenly she said, "I think we should give a party."

"Party? What kind of party?"

"Oh, a cocktail party, something like that. Say, fifty or sixty people."

"If you want to give a party, give one."

Paula sipped at her coffee and idly drummed on the table with her fingers. "I...thought it might be a good time to invite Lou. You know, he might not feel so uncomfortable in a crowd."

Dane had been staring across the broad expanse of lawn toward the driveway, where his new car was parked. It was the first new car he'd ever owned, and he could look at it all day. Paula's remark, however, brought his head around with a jerk. A knowing smile touched his lips. "Sure."

"You wouldn't mind?" she asked.

"Why would I mind, with all I have going for me?"

"I just thought...it's time."

"You're probably right." Getting to his feet, Dane walked around the table, bent and dropped a kiss on her mouth. "You've missed him, haven't you?"

Her eyes dropped for a second, then came back up. "He was just around so long. And time does heal. I guess everyone does regretful things once in a while. And as long as I'm full of all this goodwill, I might...even invite Dottie."

At that, Dane's eyes widened, and he looked at her doubtfully.

"I just said I might," she quickly amended. "She's Justin's daughter. I think it's terrible that she's never been to this house."

Dane smiled at her adoringly. "Whatever you want, sweetheart. It might be a nice gesture. Now, I've got some errands to run, and the car needs gas. Come with me. It's not often we have a whole day to spend together. I hate to have you away from me for even an hour."

"You're on. I'll tell Rona we're leaving."

They made half a dozen stops that morning before pulling into a service station for gas. Dane had filled the tank, paid the attendant and slid behind the wheel again when a blonde head suddenly appeared in the window on the driver's side. *"It's you!"* the young blonde woman cried. "I told myself I was imagining things, but it really is you!"

Paula and Dane exchanged a startled glance before he turned his attention to the woman. "Who?" he asked reasonably.

"Isn't your name Dane? Didn't I see you on Tony Grant's show the other night?"

Paula smiled. His first face-to-face encounter with a zealous fan. It would be interesting to see how he handled it.

"Yes," Dane said.

"Don't you remember me?"

He frowned and studied her more closely. "Well, I must admit you do look a little familiar."

"Trudy! You know, that night at Miller's. Jeez, I really am sorry about what happened that night. Crummy luck."

"Oh, yeah." Dane wouldn't have thought of that night for a million tax-free dollars. "How're you doing, Trudy? How's that...er, charming boyfriend of yours?"

"Lonny? I unloaded that jerk a month ago. Look up 'loser' in the dictionary, and Lonny's picture will be there. Say, you were really good on the Grant show. I've been hearing your record, too. It's great. To think I once sat on a bar stool next to a star."

"I'm hardly a star."

"You're gonna be."

Dane sat back. "Oh, by the way, Trudy, this is my wife, Paula."

"Hello, Trudy," Paula said politely.

"Hi, Paula." But Trudy was totally intent on Dane. "Say, Dane, would you wait here just a sec? I'll be right back."

She hadn't given him time to beg off, and he hated to drive away and leave her standing there. "Who is she?" Paula asked sotto voce.

"She is the young lady who was indirectly responsible for my short stay in the Nashville jail," he told her with a grin.

"Oh." Paula craned her neck and took in Trudy's curvaceous rump and shapely legs as she bent over the seat of her car, reaching for something. "Pretty cute," was her verdict. "Awfully nice tush. I wouldn't mind having one just like it. Guess if I were a man on the prowl, Trudy might get my attention."

"Yeah, but a little young. I like older women."

"It's a good thing," Paula said wryly. "You seem to have acquired one."

Trudy was back, thrusting her arm through the window and handing something to Dane. "It's my demo. I wrote the song, too. Would you listen to it? Please, just listen to it? My address and phone number are right there, see? If you'd just listen to it, I'd be ever so grateful. A couple of people have said it's pretty good."

Dane looked at the pleading eagerness on her face and felt instant sympathy. Thanks to Paula, he'd never had to do this—waylay anyone he could and beg for listening time. But most did. Now it was paying-back time. How long did it take to listen to a song? "Sure,

Trudy, I'll be glad to listen to it. I'll be in touch right away."

Trudy looked as though she might faint. "Gee, thanks. Thanks ever so much. My luck's gone from lousy to rotten lately. I can't believe I pulled in for gas at this particular station at this particular time. Maybe things are changing for me at last."

Dane wished she wouldn't let her spirits soar out of sight simply because he had agreed to listen to her demo. But maybe that was what it was all about—just getting heard. A matter of chance encounters. What if Paula hadn't decided to take a walk in the Alabama woods one morning in June? Or what if she had happened upon him and he hadn't been singing? Chance. "By the way, what's your last name?"

"Ashton."

"Trudy Ashton. Has a nice ring to it." Dane turned on the engine and flashed her a smile. "Be talking to you."

The car pulled out of the station and headed for home. "That was nice," Paula said, "really nice. I'm glad you did it. You'll be asked to do the same thing a thousand times, you know."

"Maybe. I feel sorry for anyone trying to do what Trudy's trying to do without someone like you in the background."

A few minutes later, they were pulling into the driveway of the house. Several minutes after that, Paula and Dane were seated in the studio, listening to Trudy's demo. He switched off the machine when the number was finished and turned to her. "Well, what did you think?"

Paula looked thoughtful. "Her voice has a quality to it that I like. I guess the word is *appealing*. And it's very strong. Anyway, I think she's pretty good. Promising, especially since she can write her own stuff."

"Yeah, I thought the same thing. I might ask Vic and Owen to listen to it."

"Why don't you tell her that?"

"Huh?"

"Call Trudy. There's her phone number. Tell her you want your manager and your producer to hear her demo. She'll have the best weekend of her life."

Dane looked doubtful. "Ah, I don't know, sweetheart. I hate to get her hopes up."

"Darling, haven't you been here long enough to have learned that survival in this town is a matter of keeping one's hopes up?"

That sounded reasonable. "Yeah, I guess you're right."

Paula listened as he placed the call. From the pleased grin on his face, she could imagine the delighted squeals on the other end of the line. The circle hadn't been broken. There would always be someone else needing a leg up. Dane replaced the receiver and turned to her. "That is one happy woman."

Paula stood and walked to him, slipping her arms around his waist. "Feels good, doesn't it?"

"It does. You know, when I first came here, I kept wondering why you were doing all those great things for me. I asked myself over and over what could possibly be in it for you. Now I know. The sheer kick of it. God, I hope something comes of it for Trudy."

"At least you've given her a first chance."

"You might have to help me with this. I'm new to this mentor business."

Dane picked up Trudy's demo and followed Paula out of the studio, switching off the light and closing the door behind them. Arm in arm they went upstairs. "We've done our good deed for the day," Dane commented. "Now let's have some fun, just you and me."

"What do you have in mind?" Paula asked.

"How about the cabin?"

She stopped. "You romantic rascal!"

"We've talked about going back to the place where it began, but first one thing and then another has kept us from it." Dane kissed her lingeringly. "I'm in the mood for a reprise."

"A rerun, as it were?"

"Gesture for gesture."

"Whew. That was a pretty frisky weekend, as I recall. Are you sure you're up to it?"

"Wait and see."

"Up to and including . . . the tree?"

Laughter bubbled up from his chest. "Even the tree," he seconded.

"You're on. Let's go throw some things in a bag."

Like young children, they raced up the stairs, hand in hand. They had not entered into a conventional marriage, but the years ahead would be busy, productive and fulfilling for both of them. It didn't matter whether they lived in Nashville or Dallas. What mattered were times like this; they had to seize every moment, grasp every chance they had to be together and make the most of it.

But first there was the weekend ahead. From experience, Paula knew it would be glorious, indeed.

You'll flip . . . your pages won't!
Read paperbacks *hands-free* with

Book Mate · I

The perfect "mate" for all your romance paperbacks

Traveling • Vacationing • At Work • In Bed • Studying • Cooking • Eating

Perfect size for all standard paperbacks, this wonderful invention makes reading a pure pleasure! Ingenious design holds paperback books OPEN and FLAT so even wind can't ruffle pages – leaves your hands free to do other things. Reinforced, wipe-clean vinyl-covered holder flexes to let you turn pages without undoing the strap . . . supports paperbacks so well, they have the strength of hardcovers!

Pages turn WITHOUT opening the strap

SEE-THROUGH STRAP

Reinforced back stays flat.

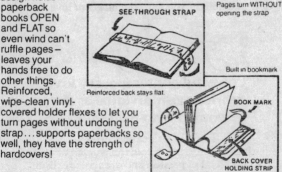

Built in bookmark

BOOK MARK

BACK COVER HOLDING STRIP

10" x 7¼", opened.
Snaps closed for easy carrying, too.

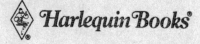

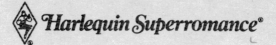

Harlequin Superromance®

**Here are the longer, more involving stories you
have been waiting for . . . Superromance.**

Modern, believable novels of love, full of the complex
joys and heartaches of real people.

Intriguing conflicts based on today's constantly
changing life-styles.

Four new titles every month.
